YOU NEVER KNOW

Also by Connie Briscoe

CONNIE BRISCOE

YOU NEVER KNOW

A Novel of Domestic Suspense

AMISTAD

An Imprint of HarperCollinsPublishers

HarperCollins books may be purchased for educational, business, or sales promotional use. For information, please email the Special Markets Department at SPsales@harpercollins.com.

FIRST HARPERCOLLINS PAPERBACK PUBLISHED IN 2024

Art by S. Borisov/Shutterstock, Inc.

Library of Congress Cataloging-in-Publication Data is available upon request.

ISBN 978-0-06-324659-1

24 25 26 27 28 LBC 5 4 3 2 1

For Daddy,
in sweet memory of all the mystery novels
we swapped and read together.

Prologue

"So, tell me, Mrs. Roberts," Officer Sands said, "exactly what happened to you here tonight?" The officer spoke slowly and clearly, having learned that the victim was nearly deaf and wore a cochlear implant. EMT workers had just treated her badly battered and bloody feet and legs, and wrapped her shivering, wet body in a dark, heavy towel. She cradled a bruised elbow in an ice pack on her lap. Her damp curly hair clung to her cheeks as she rocked back and forth on the living room couch.

The EMT workers packed up their medical gear and let themselves out the front door of the townhouse. The white stucco contemporary end unit sat on a hillside overlooking one of several manmade lakes in the planned community of Columbia, Maryland. Wilde Lake was not the deepest of the lakes, ranging from eight to thirteen feet, but its deceptively beautiful shimmering waters were dangerous enough to end a life. And had nearly ended hers. The assault had started in the upstairs primary bedroom and ended with her struggling to stay afloat in the pitch-black depths of the lake. Crime scene investigators were still gathering evidence from blood spattered on the floors and furniture tossed about. Others were down at the water's edge, searching in the dark with flashlights.

Alexis lifted her eyes and gazed sharply at the officer, a petite round-faced woman with short blond hair and piercing dark eyes who appeared to be about the same age she was, late thirties. Alexis's hearing was a lot better since she'd upped her hearing aid to a cochlear implant several months earlier, but she still depended a little on her lipreading skills. "Have you contacted my husband?" Alexis explained that she had texted him herself numerous times with no luck.

"We're working on that," Officer Sands said.

Alexis nodded and tightened her grip on the ice pack. She mentioned that she dreaded the prospect of reliving the painful events of the past few hours.

"Just take your time," the officer said soothingly.

Alexis took a deep breath. "Well, I was asleep upstairs. My husband . . . Marcus had to work late again. So, it was just me, and I heard this thumping. I mean, I couldn't really hear anything, since I take my implant off at night. But Marcus is tall and solid, and I can feel his footsteps when he walks across the room.

"I thought he had come in but didn't want to disturb me. Or maybe he was still upset 'cause we argued a bit before he left for work. I wanted to talk so I sat up, called his name. When he didn't respond, I thought it was odd. I was about to turn on the lamp and that's . . . that's when I saw him."

She paused and squeezed her eyes tight. Her hands trembled even now, more than an hour after the vicious attack. "Sorry. This is hard."

"You're doing fine," the officer said as she glanced up from her notepad. "Just describe what you saw."

Alexis bit her bottom lip. "It . . . it was this figure, a strange man, standing on the other side of the room. Over by the dresser in front of my jewelry boxes. It looked like he was wearing all black with something, something dark, draped over his head. I thought he was stealing my jewelry. But now he knew I was awake since I had called out. I had to get out of there. I wanted to grab my cochlear implant. I always store it in a case before I go to bed. But there wasn't enough time.

"I jumped up and ran to the door." She pulled the towel more snugly around her shoulders. "And . . . and that's . . ." She paused, her voice cracking. "That's when he grabbed me."

She said it in almost a whisper. The officer leaned forward. "Grabbed you where?"

"From . . . from behind. He wrapped his arms around me. It felt like he was choking the life out of me. I could hardly breathe. He yanked me up, clear up off the floor. Started dragging me back toward the bed." She paused and rocked jerkily back and forth.

"At first, I was too freaked out to fight. But it came to me that he was going to do something horrible to me. I knew. I kicked as hard as I could, but he just would not let me go; he kept dragging me.

"Then I remembered using my metal nail file while waiting for Marcus to come home. I had left it on the nightstand and managed to grab it. He had long sleeves, but I kept stabbing as hard as I could. When he loosened his grip, I reached up and jabbed the pointed end at his face. I couldn't believe it when he finally let me go.

"I ran out and down the stairs. I was scared to death; I had no idea where he was or if he was following me since I can't hear much without my implant. Not even my own screams. But I kept screaming and running. When I got down toward the bottom of the stairs, I noticed that all three locks on the front door were still locked. That startled the crap out of me; I had assumed he came in that way. It would take time to undo all of them, and I didn't want to stop. For all I knew, he was right behind me. So, I ran down the back hallway into the sitting room."

Alexis paused to catch her breath, her heart pounding. The officer sat and waited, patiently tapping her pen on the notepad. Alexis was tempted to say that it was too much, too difficult to go on. But she knew she had to get through it if she wanted them to get him.

"The door in that room leads to the patio and straight down to a walkway by the lake," she continued as the officer nodded with encouragement. "I almost never go out there by myself at night. It's too close to the water. I was very athletic as a child—baseball, basketball, track—but I never learned to swim all that well. I worry that I'll walk too far and fall in. But I recently started swimming lessons; my husband insisted after we got married and I moved in. And so, I decided to take a chance. I didn't think I had much of a choice.

"Before I could reach the door, I felt something really sharp cut my feet. The big pane had been completely smashed. Broken glass was all over the floor in front of the door. That was where he broke in. I reached down to brush the glass off my foot. It was all wet and sticky with blood. I gasped. I wasn't sure how loudly and thought maybe he heard me. So, I decided to hide.

"As soon as I turned around, I slipped and almost fell because of all the blood. I ran and ducked behind the couch, tried to figure out where he was. Maybe he was gone. I just didn't know. I worried that he would sneak up from behind any second and I wouldn't even know he was coming. I've never been so freaking scared in my life, except the time I nearly drowned in the Chesapeake Bay."

Her mind raced back to memories of her six-year-old self, how frightened she had felt thrashing wildly about and gasping for air as murky water filled her lungs. A sunny day at the beach had suddenly morphed into a terrible nightmare. Her father, a police officer in the Prince George's County Police Department, had finally reached her side and pulled her from the bay.

"I kept hoping that Marcus would come home, you know, but I knew I couldn't count on that. I was completely on my own. Alone. I finally worked up the nerve to peek around the edge of the couch just as the door opened. I saw his boots turn in my direction and I almost screamed. I crouched down and hugged the floor, trying to feel the vibration of his feet.

"When it felt like his steps were getting close, I stood and tried to run. Out of nowhere, he dove and snatched my feet. I tripped and smashed my elbow on the floor. Hard. I couldn't believe the pain. It was excruciating; felt like it had cracked open. I honestly thought it was broken. I screamed and screamed. I remember thinking it was hopeless. I was tempted to give up. But I couldn't.

"He groped at my thighs, and I could feel his fingernails digging into my flesh. I flipped onto my back and kicked like hell at that mask on his face. He had trouble holding on to my legs, probably because they were all bloody. Finally, he let go. I jumped up and grabbed the floor lamp and flung it down behind me to block his path.

"The glass tore up my feet, but I didn't care at this point. I reached the door and, thank God, it opened right up. My feet were throbbing, the pain was so bad; I was limping but got down the stairs and out to the yard.

"All the houses on our block were pitch-black. I was about to go bang on one of the doors when I saw something move over by the house. I ran and hid behind the bushes down near the lake and just prayed that I wouldn't make a wrong move and fall in.

"And then, before I knew what was happening, he grabbed me from behind. Yanked me clear off the ground. I kicked and screamed. Next thing I knew, I was falling . . . in midair. Then I hit the water. Everything went black. I barely had time to catch my breath. I was flailing all around like crazy, trying to get back to the top. But I just kept spinning and spinning. I really needed a breath of air, but I couldn't tell which way was up. It felt like I was going sideways. Or further down. And the harder I fought, the deeper I sank."

She paused to rest her voice.

"I remembered my father telling me that the one thing *not* to do was fight. So, I closed my eyes and tried to relax. When my head popped up, I could finally breathe again. It was dark, but I could see flashing lights up near the front of the house. I swam until I reached a post on the walkway and yelled until one of your officers leaned over the side and pulled me out."

Alexis leaned back, attempting to relax. Only then did she realize she had been sitting stiffly on the edge of her seat the entire time. Officer Sands glanced up from her notes and nodded; she stood as another officer approached and whispered something in her ear, then looked down at Alexis.

"Mrs. Roberts," Officer Sands said, "we reached Mr. Roberts. He's on his way."

Alexis nodded appreciatively, a shiver crawling up her spine. It was so darn cold, she thought as she pulled the towels tightly around her nightgown.

PART 1

1

The background noise was deafening. A cacophony of music, speech, and laughter that merged into a blaring roar and drowned out the lone voice of Alexis's friend and co-worker speaking from only inches away.

"There's . . . guy behind . . . keeps staring or . . ."

She leaned in as Michelle spoke with one arm wrapped around her waist, the other twisting the ends of her giant auburn Afro. Alexis struggled to hear as they stood in the middle of the banquet hall at Oakland Manor in Maryland, just south of Baltimore. It had the slick, glittery look of banquet halls everywhere. With fluted columns, lush wallpaper, crystal chandeliers, and tables adorned with colorful gold and teal tablecloths.

Alexis prided herself on her lipreading skills, honed over decades as she gradually lost more and more hearing. Combined with a hearing aid, lipreading was her lifeline and played a huge part in helping her navigate day-to-day life. But that and hearing aids were not miracle workers, as some people seemed to think. They helped in quiet settings with one or two other people. In noisy environments like this, they were not much help at all.

Which was why these big, boisterous events made her uneasy, why she avoided them for the most part.

This fundraiser was one of the few for which she regularly made an exception. It was an annual silent auction organized by AASNC, or Arts and Athletics for Special Needs Children, a non-profit organization in downtown Columbia where both she and Michelle worked—Alexis as a program administrator, Michelle as a department manager. Alexis had attended every year since she had started working there four years earlier. Michelle had been coming even longer.

Alexis never bid on any of the fancy items up for auction; she couldn't afford to. She left that up to the room full of bigwig doctors, lawyers, and businesspeople mingling amid the gleaming decor in their designer suits and little black dresses. They'd happily hand over thousands of dollars for goodies like ski trips to Colorado and expensive bottles of wine. Or lunch at a fancy DC or Baltimore restaurant with a famous local celebrity. Items that often sold for far more than they were worth. Although she couldn't afford to contribute personally, the cause was near and dear to her heart. So, the event was worth a few hours of frustration.

A small group of people standing behind Michelle burst into loud, raucous laughter. Alexis frowned with annoyance and leaned in closer as Michelle spoke. She shook her head and pointed to her ears. "I can't hear you with all the noise."

Michelle placed her wineglass on a table already filled with used napkins and half-empty dessert plates. Her tall, slender frame was dressed in a black women's tuxedo and four-inch heels. Several big, bold silver cocktail rings flashed prominently on her fingers as she signed and spoke. Although hearing, Michelle moonlighted several times a month as a sign language interpreter. Her signing skills were fast and fluid. Alexis had taken a couple of sign language classes at Howard Community College in Columbia, Maryland, when her hearing had really begun to decline. She was passable but no way near as proficient as Michelle, and she struggled to keep up. She shook her head now and signed the words "Repeat slow."

"This guy behind you," Michelle repeated, signing and speaking slowly at the same time. "He's been staring at you like crazy all night." Michelle's eyes wandered somewhere in the distance over Alexis's right shoulder. She shoved her hands into the pockets of her tuxedo jacket and fixed Alexis with a teasing smile.

This time, Alexis got it. She started to turn and check things out for herself. She was curious, as she and Michelle knew most of the people at the affair. They either worked for AASNC or did business with the organization and attended every year. This man was obviously unfamiliar to Michelle.

Before she could turn enough to get a good look, Michelle grabbed her arm. "Girl, don't you dare," her friend said, her eyes growing wide. She stared intently at Alexis. "He'll know we're talking about him."

Alexis shifted her stance and resisted the urge to turn, even though she was dying to check the guy out. "Then you're going to have to tell me what he looks like after getting me all curious. How old does he look?"

"Mmm. Probably mid-forties. Tall, nice physique. Kind of dashing. Or debonair."

"Dashing? Debonair?" Alexis said, struggling to hold back a fit of giggles at her forty-five-year-old friend's choice of words. "Now you're starting to sound your age."

"You're not all that far behind, you know."

"Excuse me? I'm like eight whole years behind."

Michelle rolled her eyes upward. "Anyway. He's got this . . ." Michelle paused. "Well, damn. Never mind. I think you're about to find out. Told you that you were going to start something wearing that tight dress." She smiled stiffly and pointedly stared at her rings.

The gesture was clearly a signal of some kind, but exactly what it meant Alexis had no idea. "It's not *that* tight. What am I about to find out?" And then she got it as the man approached and stopped beside them. He smiled and looked directly at her, a twinkle in his soulful brown eyes. He wore a sharp navy-blue suit with an elegant silk tie; his thin mustache and goatee were trimmed just so.

"Hello, ladies," he said. "I'm Marcus. And you are?" He signed a little as he spoke and then extended a hand toward Alexis. She took note as she shook it, pleasantly surprised that he was able to sign. Although there were a few deaf people at the event, most were hearing. And almost no one was signing. Marcus's signing abilities seemed to be about as good as her own. Passable. But he got an A+ in her book for trying.

"Hey. I'm Alexis," she said, shifting in her heels to a more erect posture.

"Alexis," he repeated. "I like it," he added, gazing at her intently. It made her feel awkward but also brought on a tinge of excitement.

"Thank you." He was obviously a charmer. She'd have to watch this one.

"What brings you . . ." Marcus paused as Michelle stuck her well-manicured hand between the two of them.

"Hello," she said pointedly. "I'm Michelle."

He glanced at Michelle. Then he smiled, and they shook hands.

"Sorry, didn't mean to interrupt," Michelle said. "You were saying, Marcus?"

"I was about to ask what brings you . . . the two of you here?"

"We work for AASNC," Michelle said.

He nodded. "I see. I attended last year. Don't remember either of you. I definitely would have noticed." He looked at Alexis.

"I got here really late last year." For a moment she thought back to the nasty argument she'd had with her boyfriend that night a year ago but quickly pushed that aside.

"And I left early to meet a client for dinner," he said. "That explains it."

A client, Alexis thought, tempted to ask what kind. But she held back. She had just met the man and didn't want to come off as nosy.

Not so Michelle. "Client?" Michelle pressed. "You must be a lawyer. You look like a lawyer."

Alexis suppressed a smile. That was just like her girlfriend. Blunt and to the point. Sometimes Alexis loved it; other times, it could be downright embarrassing. This time, she felt a little of both.

Marcus merely laughed and nodded. "You got me. Our firm represents one of the annual presenters. Hence, the invitation."

They both nodded. So, he was an attorney, Alexis thought. She didn't meet many Black lawyers who also signed. In fact, she had never met a single one, ever. She was impressed.

"Are either of you deaf?" he asked. "I ask because I see you signing, but you both also speak."

"I'm hearing," Michelle said.

"Hearing impaired," Alexis said. Although technically considered deaf, she had some hearing and preferred that label. When she labeled herself deaf, people often started shouting, unintentionally distorting their voices. That made it even harder to understand them. Or they used awkward, distracting hand gestures. She knew they meant well and always tried to be patient, but it could get frustrating. "Hearing impaired" seemed the best way to avoid some of that. "You're obviously hearing," she said. "Where'd you learn to sign?"

"My mother," he said, turning to face Alexis. "She was deaf."

"Really?" He was becoming more interesting by the minute. "Born deaf?"

He nodded. "She passed away last year. I haven't used sign much lately. I'm afraid my skills are getting rusty."

"They're good enough," Alexis said. "I'm sorry to hear about your mother."

"Yes, sorry to hear that," Michelle said. "Look, I think I'll go check out the auction items again and grab another drink. Nice to meet you, Marcus."

He nodded. "Same here."

Michelle stepped behind Marcus and gave Alexis an enthusiastic two thumbs up. Alexis averted her eyes and had to strain to keep from breaking into a big grin. She was sure she'd hear more from Michelle once they caught up later in the evening.

"Were you born deaf?" Marcus asked, still signing as he spoke.

She shook her head. "I was born with a mild hearing loss inherited on my mother's side of the family that got progressively worse over time."

"I thought as much; your speech is good."

"Excuse me?" she asked.

"Sorry," he signed when he seemed to realize he hadn't signed his last comment. He repeated himself using voice and signs.

"Let's step out to the patio," he added. "It'll be quieter out there."

"Good idea," she said.

"What are you drinking?"

"Just rum and Coke." She smiled. "But I'm not sure I need another one."

"I'll drive you home if you're worried about that."

Unh-unh, she thought. She wasn't about to hop into a car with a man she had just met, no matter how tempting. "I'm riding with Michelle, but thanks." She shrugged. "Yeah, why not? Another rum and Coke sounds nice."

"I'll grab the drinks and meet you out on the patio."

Alexis opened the glass door and stepped outside to a balmy late-spring evening. In all the years she had attended this event, she'd never been out here on the patio. She looked across the expansive grounds and took in the scent of colorful lavender flowers dotting the lawn. It felt like the perfect evening for a little romance, something sorely missing in her life of late.

She had no trouble meeting men. She'd always been trim and fit, dipping in and out of just about every sport available in school, at least until she discovered boys. These days, she kept herself in good shape with regular jogs around Lake Kittamaqundi near her apartment in Columbia. And hiking and biking with Paul— the athletic boyfriend who wasn't here with her tonight because they'd recently had yet another big disagreement. The same one who hadn't been here with her last year because they'd just broken up after she discovered he was cheating on her. With his supposed ex-girlfriend.

Somehow, some way, she and Paul had gotten past all that early ugliness—after the requisite breakups, I'm sorrys, and nasty yelling spats—and moved on to have a good relationship. For nearly a year now, Paul had gone out of his way to be open and honest, giving her all his logins—cell phone, email, laptop. He had endeared himself to her, and she'd finally let up and begun to fall in love with him. They had become a good fit.

And then he'd brought up marriage, and all her old fears and doubts about him resurfaced. Did she want to marry a man who had once lied and cheated on her? Could she ever *really* trust him?

They were extremely compatible, had actually started out as

good friends before moving on to become lovers. They were the same age, their birthdays two days apart. Paul was a workout fanatic, and he had the physique to prove it—lean and muscular. He didn't sign much. If anything, his signing skills were weaker than Marcus's, and she often teased him about them. But he had a deep voice and sexy lips she never tired of staring at. Or kissing. She had always found him easier to understand than most and extremely easy to lip-read.

Yet there was another major issue between them besides the cheating. As a high school teacher and girls' basketball coach, Paul was especially good with children. He often talked about wanting someday to have a bunch of his own. She wasn't sure she ever wanted to be a mom since her deafness was hereditary. She had real qualms about bringing a Black child who might possibly be deaf and female into a harsh world filled with racism, sexism, and bias against people with disabilities.

Even the police department in Prince George's County, Maryland, where she'd grown up—the majority of its residents Black—had a dark history of racism and excessive use of force. Michelle often spoke about the mixed bag of emotions she'd had when her twenty-year-old son turned seventeen and got his driver's license. She'd been filled with pride at this milestone in his life but was also consumed with worry that he would be pulled over by the police. That she would get the phone call that so many Black moms feared. Now that her son was older and wiser about the risk of "driving while Black," Michelle's anxiety had subsided somewhat. But not by much.

Alexis had mentioned this to Paul during one of their conversations about having children. "What if our son—or a daughter, for that matter—were also deaf and had trouble understanding some racist or badly trained cop?" she'd asked. "Imagine the confusion and misunderstandings that could lead to." She'd shuddered at the thought.

Paul had nodded. "I get it," he said. "That could make it a lot riskier. But we'll figure it out."

They had long, deep discussions trying to bridge their differences, but if she was honest about it, they never had. Now that he was talking marriage and kids, she realized her gut was having a hell of a time really getting past the cheating. She wanted to. She could envision a good life with Paul.

So, she had suggested they cool it for a few weeks. Think things over. He wasn't at all happy with that idea. Claimed he didn't need time to think things over.

"I don't get the point. We've been together for more than a year. We do everything together. I'm ready to take the next step."

They had just left a small gathering with friends and were sitting in his ten-year-old Lexus SUV outside her apartment when he brought up the topic of marriage again. She shook her head in frustration. "I need more time. I'm not ready. I . . ."

"Fine, Alexis. Take more time. But I won't wait around forever."

She didn't like his tone or his words. Paul was impatient when he really wanted something. But she wasn't going to be pushed on a matter that would be life-altering. "I'm not asking you to wait forever."

"How long then?"

She shrugged. "I don't know. Maybe a few weeks."

He tapped his fingers on the leather-wrapped steering wheel. He sighed. "Okay. Take whatever time you need."

"I appreciate that, Paul."

He smiled, squeezed her hand. "And I'm not going anywhere any time soon. You know that."

They kissed goodnight—not the hot, wet kisses they usually

shared. This one was brief, cool. Dry. She opened her door and went up to her apartment. Alone.

She had spent the next few evenings going over and over their time together as a couple—the good, the bad, the ugly. She would come home from work and grab a bite to eat, then climb into bed and rack her brain trying to figure it all out. She hated cheating. She didn't want to lose Paul, but she also didn't want to risk being hurt again.

Days later, she decided she needed a break from torturing herself—to take her mind off it all for a while and come back to it later. She pulled out her laptop and finally started writing the mystery novel she'd been carrying around in her thoughts for months about a deaf, Black woman who was an amateur sleuth, obsessed with forensics. She went about solving crimes in the picturesque coastal town where she lived, a fictional place similar to Oak Bluffs, Massachusetts. Then she found herself personally caught up in a murderous case.

She'd placed a couple of articles on living with hearing loss in magazines, but getting a book published had been a dream since childhood, when her father had held the family captive at the dinner table with tales of his adventures as a police officer. Even as she got older and realized that he hadn't shared the worst of his experiences—the deadly weapons, bloody crime scenes, and lives lost—she could easily recall the constant fear she'd held for him in her gut. But there was also a sense of admiration and curiosity about his work. She got a huge thrill from the whole cat-and-mouse, back-and-forth game involved in finding and capturing bad guys—and gals—until finally they were nabbed in the end.

She hadn't told a soul she was thinking of writing a novel, fearing that talking about it would jinx her chances. Or that she was beginning to have mixed feelings about her nine to five. She loved helping children, but all the back-office politics and infighting about budget constraints and who should get increasingly limited funds were starting to get to her. Michelle enjoyed getting in the thick of all that, but not her. She just wanted to help the children. And write.

She could easily remember the minute she had first sat down at the little desk in the corner of her bedroom. She'd felt liberated. The words tumbled onto the page. Through online research and books about writing, she had learned that she needed several chapters and an outline to try and land an agent. She'd been spending nearly all her free time working on it, digging into every bit of information she could find on crime scene investigations.

Just then, Marcus walked up from behind, bearing two drinks. She jumped a mile, clutched her chest. "Oh. I didn't hear you." She had been so deep in thought that she forgot to keep an eye on the patio doors as she normally would have just to avoid this kind of thing.

"I'm sorry," he said. "Didn't mean to startle you."

"No problem," she said, smiling as her heart settled down. He looked so darn handsome standing there in the twilight, his sparkling eyes smiling down at her. She got the feeling he was the epitome of cool. Unlike Paul, who was quite intense at times. Marcus was refreshing.

He handed her a glass and lifted his. "Here's to meeting new, fascinating people."

"I like the sound of that," she said as she raised her glass.

"Your hair is beautiful." The comment caught her completely off-guard. He gently swept a lock of her jet-black hair off her shoulder. "It actually feels like I've known you longer than only an hour or so." She blinked. She was thankful to have a head full of long, curly hair. Made it easy to hide her hearing aid. But normally, a man putting his hands on her so soon—on her hair or elsewhere—was irritating. She was mildly surprised that she didn't mind Marcus touching her at all, or even his over-the-top come-on line.

She smiled. "Really?"

He nodded. "You're one of the most lovely, poised women I've ever met. And you know what's most charming?"

She arched her eyebrows, curious to hear more.

"You're unaware of just how beautiful you are."

She smiled shyly. Here she was getting flushed and feeling like a schoolgirl. She was torn between wanting him to keep the compliments coming and feeling painfully self-conscious.

With his one free hand, he deftly removed his cell phone from the inside pocket of his suit. "Let me get your number, so I can contact you."

Whoa, she thought. Getting a bit bold, are we? Then she looked up into his soulful eyes and the numbers tumbled from her lips.

He leaned in closer, dropped his phone back into his pocket. "I'll text you later tonight."

She smiled. "I'm looking forward . . ." Alexis paused as an insanely gorgeous brunette with dark almond-shaped eyes and a smooth sandy-colored complexion stepped out onto the patio. She was elegantly clad in a slinky red dress and six-inch heels that she walked in with ease. She carried herself like a model. Alexis had never seen the woman before, but something about her facial expression made her uneasy.

The woman stepped straight up to Marcus, and Alexis couldn't help but notice that he stiffened. She braced herself for what was to come.

"Aren't you going to introduce me to your new friend?" the woman said. Her voice dripped with sarcasm as she slipped her arm into his.

"Yes, of course." Marcus seemed to have recovered and was composed once again. "Claudia, this is Alexis."

Claudia nodded, not so warmly. Alexis returned the not-so-warm gesture, then took a generous gulp of her cocktail.

Claudia moved closer to Marcus and whispered into his ear, something Alexis could not hear. Given the look on Claudia's face, she expected pouting lips and rolling of the eyes next. It didn't happen, but that was the kind of vibe coming off the woman. She noticed something new flash across Marcus's eyes. Annoyance? Impatience? Embarrassment? It had come and disappeared so quickly that Alexis couldn't be sure. Perhaps she had even imagined it. This whole episode was so bizarre.

Marcus reached out and touched Alexis's hand gently. "It was nice meeting you, Alexis."

She instinctively pulled her hand back as she nodded. Out of the corner of her eye, she saw Claudia tug at his arm, and they sauntered off.

Alexis downed her drink. "Crap," she muttered under her breath. These men were going to drive her nuts.

2

"So, tell me," Michelle said. "Did Mr. Debonair ever call?"

It was the following Monday afternoon, and Alexis and Michelle were making their way to lunch at Sushi Sono, a popular spot on the waterfront of Lake Kittamaqundi in downtown Columbia. It was a short stroll from the offices of AASNC, located in a mid-rise office building near the mall. The vibrant community of Columbia was situated about midway between Baltimore and Washington, DC, and had opened to much fanfare in 1967. It was now the second most populous community in Maryland, after Baltimore.

The city of 100,000 made up for its modest size with a dazzling array of activities and amenities. There was extensive shopping, wide-ranging dining styles, wooded pathways, biking trails, and theaters. Live music, arts and wine festivals, kayaking, and canoeing were plentiful. And each summer, the Merriweather Post Pavilion held the Capital Jazz Fest, featuring major musical talent from India Arie to Smokey Robinson and Kenny "Baby-face" Edmonds.

Summer was beginning to settle in, with noontime temperatures reaching the mid-eighties. In a few short weeks, the blazing sun and mushy humidity would make the short stroll from office to restaurant a lot less pleasant. Alexis and Michelle hadn't had much of an opportunity to talk during the workday. Michelle had been in meetings all morning, and Alexis was deep into a new sports project that she was developing for deaf children with one of her co-workers. She was looking forward to relaxing and chatting with her friend over shiitake mushroom soup and a couple of sushi rolls.

Alexis shook her head. "No, and I can't say I'm surprised, given the way the whole thing ended. It was just . . . weird."

She might not be surprised, but she had to admit to herself that she was also so damn disappointed. She had thought about Marcus all weekend long—couldn't shake him, as much as she wanted to. With other men, even Paul, it had taken much more time for her to feel anywhere near this smitten. Everything about Marcus felt different. He had impressed her in ways no man ever had before.

Still, she had no business falling for a man who might already be involved. Not to mention that she wasn't exactly single. Michelle had been the one who'd introduced her to Paul. The two had been close friends since college. Alexis wasn't sure Michelle would understand or approve, so she was reluctant to admit to her feelings.

Michelle had been happily married for two decades to a man named Franklin until he died of cancer about three years earlier. White and fifteen years older than Michelle, Franklin was a well-established businessman; he left Michelle a pile of cash and real estate investments, enough for her to live off comfortably for the rest of her life, provided she spent it cautiously. Which Michelle said she fully intended to do. She planned to work for about five more years and then retire at the relatively young age of fifty and travel the world.

"You're talking about the woman he was with?" Michelle asked.

"Claudia."

"Well, I agree with your decision," Michelle said.

Alexis frowned. "What decision?"

"On Saturday after they left, you said you wouldn't go out with Marcus even if he asked."

"Oh, *that*." As soon as Marcus and Claudia had left the patio, Alexis went back inside the banquet hall and scanned the crowd for Michelle. It didn't take long to spot her big reddish Afro halfway across the room. After making her way over, she pried Michelle away from the wealthy-looking older woman she was chatting with.

"You won't believe what just happened," Alexis had said, still reeling from the unexpected encounter on the patio.

"What?" Michelle asked, her ring-clad fingers planted firmly on her hips in an obvious display of annoyance at being dragged away mid-conversation. "This better be good, girl. I was trying to convince Freda Douglas to donate more to . . ."

"Marcus was here with a woman."

"You mean like a date or a girlfriend? You met her?"

Alexis nodded. "Yes, and yes."

"Okay. So, what's the big deal? He has every right."

"He asked me for my number. He really came on to me, laid it on thick. I don't know. It feels almost like he was cheating on her. Or trying to. With me."

Michelle nodded, beginning to understand. "She might even be his wife."

"Exactly. But it doesn't matter," Alexis said. "I wouldn't go out with him even if he asked. I'm not interested in a man who would do that to his date. Wife or not."

"I hear you, but you know, just to play devil's advocate—maybe it was his sister or a cousin or something."

Alexis scoffed and gave Michelle a "no-way" look. "I seriously doubt that. Not the way she was clinging to him. She called him 'honey.'"

"Got it. Then at least you found out what he's really like before getting all emotionally involved and it's too late."

Alexis sighed, thinking about that conversation as they turned onto Wincopin Circle and walked up the stairs to the restaurant. Although she didn't say it, she realized it was kind of already too late. Despite initially feeling that she wanted absolutely nothing to do with the man, she had barely left the house all day Sunday, hoping for a text from him. She found herself checking her cell phone every thirty minutes when she should have been focusing on her novel. She kept remembering Marcus's playful smile and brown eyes as they chatted on the patio. And the way he'd looked at her when he brushed her hair aside.

By early evening, she was telling herself that she was being ridiculous, childish even. She threw on her running clothes and a pair of Nikes and jogged around the trail at Lake Kittamaqundi near her apartment building, doing an extra two miles to relieve her stress. She did stretches at one of the benches dotting the lake and tried to clear her head.

She realized that although Marcus had certainly seemed like a prize catch—minus the other woman—her feelings weren't only about him. They were also about Paul and all the others before him. About the disappointment piled up over years of one failed relationship after another, some falling apart even before getting off the ground. She was thirty-seven years old and getting damn tired of playing these games. Sometimes she thought she should swear off men altogether. It was exhausting.

She'd made her way back to her apartment and whipped up a tuna sandwich and her favorite homemade tomato soup from a recipe she'd gotten from her mom. She tinkered with a chapter, then finally gave up and binge-watched a few episodes of a mystery series on Netflix until she dozed off. That morning when she woke up, she checked her laptop while dressing for work and realized she had written a whopping four paragraphs of her novel. What a waste the weekend had turned out to be.

Her silence as she and Michelle walked toward the restaurant seemed to catch her friend's attention. "It's already too late for you, isn't it?" Michelle asked as she held the door to the restaurant open.

Alexis firmly shook her head "no." Then she caught herself and quickly changed to a reluctant nod. She was confused and hurt. She needed to talk to someone. "Is it that obvious?"

Michelle nodded. "Yeah, it is."

"I go back and forth," Alexis said after they were seated at an outdoor table, menus in hand. "One minute, I really want to hear from him. The next, I feel like I need to run a dozen miles if he calls. But it's not just about him. It's all the disappointments over the years. Marcus is just the latest, really. It's getting depressing."

"Tell me about it, girl. You're not the only one still searching. And I'm forty-five."

"At least you were married once. And I thought you said you were never getting married again?"

Michelle shrugged. "That doesn't mean I don't want a steady companion. Widows get lonely, too. God, I hate to even call myself that. It's been three years since Franklin died. I'm beginning to miss having a man around."

Alexis nodded with understanding. She couldn't imagine going that long without steady companionship. "I get it."

"What is it you see in this guy Marcus anyway? He's clearly gotten under your skin," Michelle said after they had placed their orders of soup, sushi, and sashimi.

"You didn't think he was good-looking?" Alexis asked, surprised that Michelle even had to raise such a question.

"I'll admit that. But you're gorgeous. You have good-looking guys wanting to meet you all the time. I've never seen you fall so fast. Paul had a crush on you for months before you even noticed. What's so special about *Marcus*?"

Alexis shrugged. "The way he looked at me. Gave me goosebumps. And he signs so well, so the conversation flows easily."

"True," Michelle said. "And that's important for you."

"Plus, he's a lawyer. I admit I find that interesting. And he's so charming." Alexis smiled. "It's everything about him, I guess."

"He's got that swag," Michelle said.

"Yes, but not too much. I hate when it practically oozes off a man."

Michelle waved her hand with nonchalance. "Okay, but don't get carried away. He puts his pants on one leg at a time; trust me."

Alexis laughed. "Facts." Trust Michelle to bring her back down to earth. "But it doesn't matter anyway, since he's never going to call me. He already has a girlfriend."

"Or a wife."

"Or a wife," Alexis repeated. She took a deep breath as the waitress placed their food on the table.

"And what about Paul?" Michelle asked. "I know you two have been struggling lately, but I still have my hopes up. You're a cool couple. Always doing outdoorsy stuff. Plus, he's crazy about you."

"I don't know. If I was still really all that into him, it shouldn't have been so easy for me to latch onto someone else, right? The cheating got to me more than I realized. Until he started talking marriage."

"That was a whole year ago. It hasn't happened since, has it?"

Alexis shook her head. "No. Not that I'm aware of."

"I doubt it. He knows he messed up and almost lost you. I think you two just need to talk it out."

"I'm probably going to end it."

Michelle held her chopsticks in midair. "Really? Damn."

"I haven't made up my mind completely but . . ."

"You're waiting to see what happens with Marcus."

Alexis frowned. "Why would you say that? I still have feelings for Paul. I'm just not sure it will work. Marcus has nothing to do with this."

"The hell he doesn't. I've seen this with you before. You didn't break up with your last boyfriend until you and Paul became an item."

Alexis shrugged. "That was just one time. I'm not that woman."

"Mm hmm," Michelle said.

Alexis didn't push back further. Who was she kidding? Certainly not Michelle, who knew her all too well. She and Paul *had* been dating others when they hooked up. Alexis had to admit, to herself only, that she detested going long periods without a man. The loneliness and boredom she could gladly live without. A good man always made her feel secure, desired, confident. The key word, though, was "good." That could truly be hard to find.

3

Alexis sat on the balcony of her apartment a week later, her bare feet resting comfortably on the railing as she pounded away at her laptop keyboard. She paused, checked her page count, and smiled as she gazed out over Lake Kittamaqundi just as the sun was going down. She was halfway to her goal of that one-hundred-page partial, so she could start searching for literary agents. Finally, she was making some real progress.

She still had a long way to go. There would be revisions and she needed to write a synopsis, but she was on a roll. These moments of success were not to be taken lightly. Especially after what she had gone through the past week, trying to shake all thoughts of men from her head and get on with her life.

She took a sip of Pinot Grigio and watched as the sun dropped further in the sky and dusk settled into night. She loved sitting out here during this part of the evening when the weather was warm. She'd even spent time here snuggled up in her down jacket and woolen hat in the midst of winter when there was snow on the ground. This was where she was most able to clear her head. It was where she did some of her best thinking.

Her cell phone lit up. She glanced down at the small patio table to see that she had yet another text message from Paul. The third one in the past hour. She'd lost count as to how many there had been since yesterday, when he suddenly started texting her again after weeks of silence between them. They were simple, "Hello, how are u?" messages, but she had ignored them all. She had been in the throes of self-pity, trying to sort her feelings, still even a tiny bit hopeful that she would hear from Marcus. She was over that now.

She picked up and saw that this text message was a little more involved. Paul wanted to know if she had a few moments to hook up on FaceTime. She frowned and sat up straight. She had to think about that. She wasn't sure she was ready to reconnect with him after their last dramatic meeting. But Paul's patience was likely wearing thin; she couldn't ignore him forever.

She texted back, **Sure**, then walked inside the apartment, sat on the steel-gray colored couch in the living room, and snuggled into the orange and yellow Southwestern embroidered throw pillows. She clicked to open FaceTime. He picked up almost immediately. She smiled brightly when she saw him on the screen. He had shaved his head completely bald, and his sexy lips were even more alluring. He wore a white short-sleeve t-shirt that showed off his powerful build. His whole appearance was ruggedly handsome. She felt a tiny tug on her heart. She had missed him.

"Hi, there," she said. "I'm loving the new look."

"You're looking pretty good yourself," he said, signing a little and speaking at the same time. "How are you? It's been a minute."

"Oh, alright, I guess. How have you been?"

"Hanging in there. How's the writing coming along?"

"Funny you should ask. I was working on it when you texted. It's going well."

He gave her a thumbs-up. "Good to hear. When do I get to read it?"

She chuckled. "In due time, Paul. Let me finish first."

He nodded and then something odd happened, especially for the two of them. An unusual moment of silence pierced the air as they sat and smiled at each other. In the past, the dynamic between them had always flowed with an electricity that was effortless. They never ran out of thoughts and ideas to share. If anything, they usually interrupted each other a lot with so much to say. It had been common for them to sit up into the wee hours of the morning, discussing everything from politics to art and travel. From sports to working out. Even during the silent moments, as they cuddled on the couch watching television or each reading a good book, the energy between them had been soothing and peaceful.

Not so much now, she thought. "Um . . ." She paused, not sure why she felt uneasy. Perhaps they needed a little time to warm up to each other again.

He smiled tightly in a way that suggested he also felt the unfamiliar strain. He cleared his throat. "Look, the reason I called was to see if you're ready to talk. We could get together on Friday, have dinner. Check out that seafood restaurant we used to go to all the time in Baltimore."

She swallowed hard. If they met, he would likely want a decision she wasn't ready to make. And he could be pushy. "Uh . . . I'm not sure it's time yet, Paul."

"It's been three weeks. How much longer do you need?"

"It's hard to say."

"I don't get it. We always have such good times together."

"We do but . . ."

"I miss that. I miss you."

She thought back to the moments they'd shared. They had been biking buddies for several months before they became intimate and then a couple. They had both left others to be together. They were that much in love.

She sighed deeply. "Well, I . . ."

"Is there someone else?" he asked suddenly.

She blinked, startled. "What?"

"Are you seeing someone else?" His voice was a little more urgent now. Tenser.

"No. Of course not," she said, feeling a tinge of disappointment. She was not dating Marcus. She would never be dating Marcus. She needed to banish all those thoughts from her head.

"Then what's the problem?" He looked confused, wounded.

"Okay," she said. "Let's meet. But I can't on Friday; I'm in the middle of a new project. Pretty sure I'll be working late that night. How about Saturday?"

He smiled and nodded. "Saturday works."

"Good. I'm looking forward to it." Which was true in a way. She missed his company, the laughter, and deep conversations. She missed their soul-stirring lovemaking. She just wasn't ready to commit to marriage with him. Not yet. Or children.

"I was thinking about that time we went to the Blue Ridge Mountains and left the trail like a couple of idiots. We were lost for, what? Two hours? You remember that?"

"Oh my God," she said as that day came flooding back. "I was scared to death. I just knew we were going to be devoured by a bear." Maybe she would change her mind by Saturday and be ready to commit. Maybe.

"I know. It's funny now," he said laughing. "There was nothing funny about it then. It started to get dark and . . ."

The strobe light for her doorbell flashed, and she held up a forefinger to get Paul to pause. "Be right back," she said.

When she looked through the peephole, all she saw was red. She cracked the door open to a huge bouquet of roses in a large glass vase. The flower arrangement was gigantic. She could barely see the man holding them until he stuck his head around. She released the chain on the door, and he held out a receipt for her to sign.

She brought the heavy vase in and placed it on the kitchen table. The flowers were incredible; there had to be three dozen of them. She needed to get back to Paul but was curious. Who had sent her such a lovely surprise? It wasn't her birthday or any other special occasion. For a second, she wondered if it could be a mistake and they had delivered to the wrong address. But that didn't make sense since her name had been on the receipt she just signed. Had Paul sent them? If so, that would be a first. Sweet, but a first. Paul's way of showing kindness would be more like repairing a flat tire on her bike or fixing a leak under the sink.

She found a little card buried among the petals, opened it, and gasped when she saw the note inside.

Sorry not to have been in touch sooner. Really busy at the office but haven't stopped thinking about you. I'll call you on FaceTime this evening around nine.—Sending love, Marcus.

She covered her heart with her hand as she shook her head in disbelief. She was torn between smiling with relief and feeling like she should run for the hills. It felt exciting to finally hear from Marcus but also unsettling. It had taken him all this time to reach out. *Now* he was "sending love"? And who was the woman with him at the fundraiser? Was she being jerked around for some reason?

She slipped the note back into the envelope and placed it on the table. She'd already kept Paul waiting too long. She would figure out what to do about Marcus later tonight. She had no idea how things would turn out when they chatted. The flowers and touching note of apology were endearing. But so many questions needed answers before she could relax her guard.

Still, the anticipation of chatting with him again was exciting. She glanced at her watch. It was eight thirty. She would get off with Paul so she'd have time to get ready. She needed to pick out a cute top and style her hair.

She composed herself and sat back down on the couch.

"Who was that?" Paul asked as soon as she picked the phone back up.

"That? Uh, just an Amazon delivery." She hated lying to him, but there was no way she was going to tell Paul about Marcus. Or the three dozen roses. She wasn't sure whether Paul would lash out or hang up on her. Neither prospect was pleasant.

"Listen, Paul, it's been nice catching up, but I really want to get back to my novel. Trying to reach a certain point before bed."

She could tell that he was uneasy by her sudden need to go, given that they were deep into reminiscing about the past, and now, so soon after her doorbell had rung, she wanted to rush off. But it couldn't be helped, she thought. She had so little time to prepare for Marcus. She wanted to use every minute of it.

"We'll see each other on Saturday," she added. "Really looking forward to it."

He nodded slowly, the way someone does when they sense they're being shoved aside and aren't sure why. He no doubt figured that her suddenly wanting to get back to her book sounded fishy. But she was too excited about hearing from Marcus to really care.

* * *

By 8:50 that night, Alexis was applying her favorite shade of rose-colored lip gloss. She had donned a royal-blue V-neck top that showed just a hint of cleavage and brushed her black hair down softly around her shoulders.

At 8:55, she picked up her cell phone and debated whether to sit up in her queen-size bed while they chatted or on the living room couch. She finally decided against the bed; she didn't want to look like she was trying to seduce him, especially since she wasn't sure exactly where his head was. He had sent roses, true enough. And she had carefully placed them on the coffee table in front of the couch. But he'd also ignored her for an entire week. She was not about to forget that.

She sat on the couch and placed the phone in a stand on the coffee table. Then she waited. At nine fifteen, beginning to feel edgy, she jumped up and started to pace the floor. Was he about to stand her up yet again? These men and their empty promises were enough to drive her insane.

The phone flashed at 9:17, and she saw Marcus's name appear on the screen. She breathed a momentary sigh of relief, then got jittery all over again at the prospect of seeing and talking to him. What would she say? How would he act? Would he be as good-looking as she remembered? She sat down, spruced up her hair, and took a deep breath. She pushed the button to accept the call.

"Hey there, gorgeous," he signed.

Her heart fluttered wildly. He was wearing a crisp white shirt and looked like he had just removed his necktie. She smiled and waved. "How are you?"

"Good. Even better now that I'm looking at your face again."

She loved that he signed as well as he spoke. Reading lips for long periods could be a real strain on the eyes. She angled the phone so that he could see the red roses in the shot with her.

"So, you got them," he said. "You like them?"

"I love them. They're perfect. Thank you."

She had a hard time believing that Marcus Roberts was sitting there on her cell phone and looking like a million dollars. Still, she had to stay calm and control her expectations. She didn't want to scare the man off before she got her questions answered. She was tempted to shout: Where the hell have you been? But that would never do. Patience, patience, patience, she reminded herself.

He seemed to sense her coolness. "Look, I know you were probably expecting me to contact you sooner. But it couldn't be helped. I had a big case dropped on me last week. A senior manager at a large telecommunications firm headquartered in Maryland was sued for sexual harassment. I've been working around the clock."

She lifted her brows. That did sound big and important. And she understood being busy with work, especially since he was an attorney. But too busy to take a moment to drop a quick text? She wasn't so sure she understood that. The biggest issue, though—the elephant on the airwaves between them—was the other woman. What about *her*? Again, Alexis held her thoughts in check, waiting for the right moment. "I understand."

He smiled. "I appreciate that. So, what have you been up to?"

Her thoughts immediately turned to the book proposal—the one hundred pages, the synopsis, her bio. But she decided against telling him about that. It was too close and dear to her heart to share with him just yet. He was practically a stranger. She had no idea how he would receive it. She remembered sharing her early dreams of writing someday with her boyfriend shortly after college. They had just come in from frolicking in the ocean at Virginia Beach and were lying around on a blanket in the sand. Mary J. Blige played softly on her iPod as she stared out at the waves. He rested, his dark brown muscles glistening in the sun.

"Not self-published," she had said. "I mean with one of the big New York publishers. The real deal."

Ross had lifted his cap from his eyes, glanced up, and stared at her like he'd thought she was some creature that just walked out of the sea. In those days, her hearing loss had been mild, and no one around her signed. "Do you have any idea how hard it is to get a novel published?"

"Of course. Give me some credit."

He kept talking as if he hadn't heard her. "Something like one in every, I don't know, gazillion people who try are successful."

"I think I have a chance." She fixed him with a hard stare. "A little encouragement would be nice."

"I'm just trying to keep it real. I don't want to see you get your hopes up, only to be disappointed."

This was way before she'd put a single word on paper. Before she even had a solid idea what to write about. So, she didn't push. Ross had been absolutely right that her chances were slim. Still, the lack of confidence and harsh words coming from her then-boyfriend had stung badly. Now, she rarely talked about her writing ambitions. The only two people she had mentioned it to currently were Michelle and Paul. Not even her parents knew. She wouldn't want to disappoint them if it were rejected. And even with Michelle and Paul, she had casually shared only vague details.

For all she knew, Marcus might also think she was some kind of delusional nut for believing she could ever get published. So, she decided to keep it to herself. "I've been putting in a lot of overtime lately. I'm working on a new project that I'm really excited about to help children with disabilities improve their motor skills."

"Oh? I really admire that. You'll have to tell me more when we get together."

Get together? She wasn't sure how to take that. She let it slide. "How about you? Do you work for a firm or independently?"

"A firm in DC. I mainly deal with criminal cases, which can get ugly at times. Like with this new case. Some people can't stomach the details."

She thought about all the murder and mayhem she was conjuring up in her plotting. "I'm tougher than I look."

He laughed. "I don't doubt that. We'll talk more about my work another time. The reason I called, other than to see and hear from you . . . Have you been to the new Smithsonian African American Museum of History and Culture?"

She nodded. "When it first opened back in 2016, I went with my parents when they visited. But it was so packed we couldn't really enjoy it. I've been meaning to go back."

He nodded. "Where's your family?"

"Atlanta."

"So, the ATL? That where you grew up?"

She shook her head. "I was born there, but we moved to Maryland when I was four. My parents moved back down there a few years ago, after they both retired. Just about all my family lives there."

"I went to college in that area. My roommate's from there, too." He went on to talk about his college days studying, partying, and pledging a fraternity around Morehouse and Spelman Colleges and Clark Atlanta University. Alexis knew that area of Atlanta well. It was known as the Atlanta University Center Consortium, the oldest and largest consortium of African American higher education institutions in the United States. From there, Marcus said he had gone on to attend law school in Virginia.

"Anyway," he said. "Back to what I was saying. Some of us at the office were invited to a private tour of the museum. I'd love for you to join me."

A private tour of the museum sounded spectacular, Alexis thought. "Oh, nice. When is it?"

"This coming Saturday at three. It's a small group. That should make it easier for you to hear the tour guide, right?"

She immediately realized that Saturday was when she and Paul were planning to meet for dinner. Damn it! She almost laughed out loud. She could go for months without being asked out, and now she had two offers for the same night. Still, nothing was going down with Marcus until she got the answers to her questions.

"Um, right," she said. "Thanks for thinking of that. It sounds really special, Marcus. But I need to ask you something first."

He leaned forward in his seat as if he hadn't the slightest concern. "Ask away."

"About the night we met at the fundraising event."

"Yes?"

"When we were out on the patio. Do you remember?"

"Of course."

"Who was the woman with you?"

"Oh. You mean Claudia."

"Yes, that's it. Claudia." No, she had not forgotten the name. But he didn't need to know that.

He sighed. "It's complicated. It was a short relationship, lasted less than six months, and was always off and on. We must have broken up at least three times. It's over now. We ended things last week."

Hmm, Alexis thought, still feeling unsure. "Off and on?" What the hell did that mean, exactly? And what's to say it couldn't be on again soon?

"For good," Marcus added, as if reading her mind. "We're done. She was way too possessive. And clingy. And I would never ask you out if I was not sure that was over. I'm not that kind of guy."

Alexis eyed him closely. The usual playful expression in his eyes had changed to a serious one. That made her feel better about going out with him. His words weren't a sure guarantee that he and Claudia would never again be an item. From the looks of her, she wasn't going to give up on Marcus easily. But then again, nothing about dating was ever a sure thing. There were always complications and risks involved. If anyone was worth a risk, though, it was Marcus.

"Thanks for clearing that up," she said, letting out a breath of air. "That helps a lot."

Now that the other woman was out of the way, or at least seemed to be, what was she supposed to do about Paul? If she turned Marcus down for this big affair at the museum, there was no telling when he'd ask her out again. Perhaps never.

"So," he said. "Should I pick you up around two? We can get dinner in DC afterwards."

"Um, that could work." Her brain was going a hundred miles a minute as she tried to sort this. She would have to call Paul and make up an excuse to postpone their date. She felt guilty about it. But she'd feel worse about missing this opportunity to go out with Marcus. To get a feel for whether there could really be something between them.

"Yes," she said, having worked out the details in her head. "That sounds good."

"Perfect," he said. "I think you're really going to enjoy this, and I know I'm looking forward to seeing you again."

"I'm looking forward to it, too."

"And, Alexis, don't ever hesitate to ask me about something that's on your mind from now on. Deal?"

How considerate, she thought. "It's a deal."

"Good," he said. The twinkle was back in his eyes as he smiled at her warmly.

4

The National Museum of African American History and Culture in Northwest DC was nothing short of spectacular. The towering structure of gleaming bronze lattice seemed to soar from earth to the heavens. Alexis had goosebumps as she and Marcus approached the building on a warm yet breezy Saturday afternoon. They held hands as they walked around the side and met up with a small group standing near the entrance. Marcus knew most of them—attorneys from his law firm with their spouses and dates—and he took the time to make introductions to Alexis one by one. Everyone was dressed casually yet stylishly, the women in slacks or sundresses, the men in pressed jeans or khakis.

The tour guide, a young Black woman dressed neatly in a dark linen skirt and fresh white blouse, arrived and introduced herself. Marcus took Alexis and the guide aside and mentioned that Alexis was hearing impaired and read lips. And that she should be near the front as they toured the exhibits. The guide smiled with understanding. Alexis was very pleasantly surprised. These were things she often had to navigate on her own as best she could. Yet Marcus had been mindful of her needs and known just how to handle the situation. It felt good to know she could count on him to look out for her.

The group followed the guide past the line at the entrance and entered the building. It was a massive, open, and airy space filled with bright natural light streaming through the glass walls. Marcus took her hand and held it tightly for almost the entirety of the two-hour tour. They visited exhibits on topics ranging from slavery and the Civil Rights Movement to African American arts, crafts, and culture.

And he was so knowledgeable about everything, sharing extra details and insights with her and the others. The guide explained that the building had been designed by Sir David Adjaye OBE, an award-winning Ghanaian-British architect. Marcus further elaborated to everyone that in 2017, *Time* magazine had named Adjaye one of the 100 most influential people of the year. And that he was known for infusing his modern structures of cement, stones, glass, and bronze with a sense of history and culture. Alexis found Marcus's attentiveness endearing and his extensive knowledge admirable.

At the end of the tour, the group returned to the main level and entered the small, busy museum shop. They eagerly browsed the African American books, crafts, and accessories on display. Alexis stopped at a glass counter and admired a pair of gold heart-shaped dangle earrings.

"Let's see those," Marcus said to the clerk, who removed them from the case and handed them to Alexis.

She held them up, then took a look at the price tag; they were way too rich for her budget. She handed them back, but Marcus urged her to try them on. Why not? she thought. It would be fun even if she didn't plan to buy them.

"They're beautiful on you," he said.

"Thank you." She gave them back to the clerk, expecting him to return them to the case.

"Wrap them up," Marcus said. "We'll take them."

Her eyes grew wide. She shook her head firmly. "No. I . . ."

Marcus squeezed her hand reassuringly. "I'll take care of it."

"You don't have to do this."

"I insist. They're perfect for you."

She blinked, not sure how to proceed. No way could she take such an expensive gift from him so early in their relationship. But she didn't want to create a scene in front of all these people.

"Thanks, Marcus. I really appreciate the offer. But no." She moved away from the counter and strolled over to check out the history books, thinking he would give up and move on. She couldn't hear what they were saying, but out of the corner of her eye, she saw Marcus hand the clerk a black credit card. Oh crap, she thought. The man was obviously headstrong. Well, she could be equally determined. She would refuse to accept them.

She thumbed through the pages of a book, but her thoughts were elsewhere, picturing him trying to give her the earrings and her stubbornly holding her hands aloft in protest. She realized that would seem rude. He was trying to do something nice for her. She should probably just accept it. Besides, a few hundred dollars for a pair of earrings would not make nearly as big of a dent in his wallet as it would have in hers. Not to mention that the earrings were exquisite.

She replaced the book and walked back to the counter. The clerk was handing the wrapped package to Marcus. She stood next to him. "Thank you," she whispered. He took her hand and they exited the shop.

Soon they were seated in a swanky restaurant on Wisconsin Avenue in Georgetown, and Marcus was asking her to wear the earrings. She slipped into the restroom and happily switched her sixty-dollar sterling hoops for her new solid-gold hearts.

"Stunning," he said as she returned and he helped her back into her seat.

"Thank you again." She couldn't remember the last time a man had made her feel so attractive. She could easily get used to this kind of treatment.

"I took the liberty of ordering a rum and Coke for you," he said. "I hope that's alright."

"Um, yes, sure. Sounds good." She really would have preferred something lighter, like a glass of wine. She always tried to go easy with the drinking on first dates. The last thing she wanted was to feel tipsy around a new man, especially one she wanted to impress. But Marcus was being such a sweetheart. She would just sip it real slowly.

"Do you always spoil your dates like this?" she asked teasingly, as she placed her cloth napkin in her lap.

"Actually, no, I don't. I can honestly say that you're the only woman who has gotten jewelry out of me on the first date. Or the second or the third."

They both laughed.

She loved the sparkle that played around his brown eyes when he laughed or smiled. "Then thank you for making me feel special."

"That's easy to do. Because you *are* special. I'm surprised that you're unattached." He paused. "Or maybe I should ask before assuming. Are you seeing anyone?"

She coughed lightly, covered her mouth with her napkin. That had come out of nowhere. "Um, no. Not really," she said, trying to buy a moment to figure out how best to handle this.

"Not really? What does that mean, if you don't mind?"

"Just that it's been a while. I mean, I date, but nothing serious."

She was lying through her teeth and was ashamed that it came so easily for her. But what else could she do? Marcus didn't seem like the kind of man who would go for a woman who was attached elsewhere. Why should he? He could get any woman he wanted.

He lifted an eyebrow. "I'm happy to hear that but surprised. You're too pretty and engaging to be single."

Just then, the waiter brought their drinks. Thank God, Alexis thought. Saved by the bell. Or the waiter. She cleared her throat and took a generous sip of her rum and Coke as soon as it landed on the table. "Just haven't met the right man, I guess."

Marcus nodded with understanding. "Lucky for me."

"How about you?" she asked, eager to get the focus off herself.

"Divorced from way back. I have two boys, well, men actually. Both are adults now, living on their own."

She was about to question him about his sons when the waiter approached again and asked if they were ready to order. She'd had her eye on a shrimp dish, but Marcus suggested the sea bass and she decided to try it.

"Do you have children?" he asked as soon as the waiter left.

"No," she said hurriedly. *Another* topic she was anxious to move on from. She didn't want to have to explain why she did not think she ever wanted children. Not yet. There would be time to get into that later if things progressed far enough. And that was still a big if, given how new this all was. For now, she wouldn't mention anything that might turn him off before they even got a chance to get to know one another. Marcus already having children was a good omen. He might be open to not having more. Unlike Paul.

"So, tell me," she said, in a deliberate attempt to change the subject, "were you born here in . . ."

Marcus suddenly held up a forefinger to signal her to pause, then reached into a pocket and pulled out his cell phone. "Excuse me," he signed to her as he stood up. "It's a client. I need to take this."

She nodded and took a tiny sip of her drink as he walked off. She was really getting into this guy. He was generous and extremely considerate of her needs. He was successful, hardworking, and certainly easy on the eyes. And the way he looked at her when they talked made her feel like the most important person in his universe. He seemed perfect—almost too good to be true. But she wasn't going to knock it. She was going to count her blessings and enjoy every moment.

The only thing she regretted about this enchanting evening was that she'd had to lie to Paul to be here. Naturally, she couldn't tell him she was cancelling for an evening out with a hot new man. Paul would have been pissed. She didn't even want to think about how he might have reacted. Even though he'd cheated on her for months and this was only one date, there was a rotten double standard when it came to things like this.

She'd simply told him she had to work, and they agreed to meet the following week at Cold Stone Creamery in Columbia, pick up ice cream, and walk the three-quarters of a mile or so to Lake Kittamaqundi. She hadn't decided yet about their future. She would figure that out later, possibly depending on how things went tonight. That sounded calculating, she knew. But she was honestly torn between these two men. Paul had been a big part of her life for more than a year. They shared the same interests and enjoyed each other's company. They had some of the same friends, and her parents really liked him. So why wasn't she more excited about trying to work out their differences so they could take the next step together?

Then there was Marcus. She barely knew the man, yet she was well on the way to being hooked. Sure, he checked all the boxes—successful, handsome, charming. But it was more than that. His laser-like attentiveness to her needs was so flattering. She felt special in his presence.

Just then, a couple nearby caught her eye. The woman had red hair and a face full of freckles. She appeared to be in her early thirties. She hastily slapped her napkin down on the table, and her blue eyes flashed with fury at her male companion, whose back was facing Alexis. Alexis caught the words "You're a fucking asshole" on her lips and glanced around to see if anyone else had noticed the outburst. An older couple seated next to the red-haired woman seemed aware momentarily. But the upset woman calmed down a bit and the other couple quickly went back to their meals. Alexis tried to catch more of the heated conversation, but the words on the woman's lips were now mostly a rapid blur. All Alexis could make out was an occasional "you" and "no." Then the woman stood abruptly and stomped off toward the restroom.

Whatever that had been all about, Alexis was thankful to be having a far better evening with Marcus. She tucked her hair behind her new earrings. It had been so thoughtful of him to buy them for her. Still, she didn't know him that well and couldn't help but wonder if he would make a move on her later tonight. If he would expect something in exchange for such a precious gift. He certainly didn't seem the type. He could easily get just about any woman he wanted between the sheets without bearing gifts. Then again, as cool as Marcus was, she was still getting to know him. And some men, even seemingly decent men, could be such assholes when it came to sex.

She would find out soon enough. They pulled up in front of her apartment building in Marcus's late-model BMW convertible around ten o'clock and chatted for several minutes. Then he walked her from the parking lot to the door of her unit on the second floor. She had decided that as alluring as Marcus was, she was not going to sleep with him tonight. It was too soon. This was a man who likely had women throwing themselves at him. She did not plan to become a mere notch on his belt. But she enjoyed his company and didn't want the night to end yet. She invited him in for a cup of coffee.

"Thank you," he said as she unlocked her door. "As tempted as I am to take you up on the offer, I'm going to have to pass. I have an early meeting. And if I go in there with you, I'm never going to want to leave."

Huh? This was one of the rare times she wished she hadn't heard correctly. In all her years of dating, she could never remember a man turning down an offer to come inside her apartment. It felt like a rejection, a slap in the face. It was humiliating and it stung. Did this mean he hadn't enjoyed their time together as much as she had? Or was he being a gentleman and saying things he believed were appropriate? These thoughts filled her head and nearly took the breath out of her.

She cracked the door and turned to face him. "Um, okay. I understand," she said, straining hard to keep the disappointment off her face.

He kissed her gently on the corner of her lips. Really? she thought. That was it? A tiny peck on the edges of her mouth? She thought to reach out and give him a real kiss but stopped herself. What if he rebuffed it? She didn't want to make a fool of herself, acting needy and pathetic.

"I had a really good time tonight," he said. "I'll call you tomorrow."

Uh-huh, Alexis thought. A minute ago, she would have found those words a lot more believable. Now, she wasn't so sure.

"Right. Thanks," she said weakly.

She entered her apartment and stood with her back against the door. What the hell had just happened?

She kicked off her heels and poured herself a large glass of red wine, then sank down on her couch. She picked up one of the pillows and hugged it tightly. This felt crummy, no doubt about it. But she vowed not to let a puzzling ending to an enchanting evening throw her. The man had bought her an expensive pair of earrings, hadn't he? That had to mean something.

Tomorrow she would wake up early and get back to her writing, just as planned. She was not going to allow herself to sit around waiting and hoping to hear from him again. She would be bummed if he didn't call. Really bummed. But it would not be the end of her life. She still had Paul.

5

She didn't have to wait long at all to find out if or when she would hear from Marcus. It happened way sooner than she expected. She was pouring a cup of black tea while taking a break from watching reruns of *CSI* the next evening when his first text message pinged her phone. Then came another and many more in the days following, along with FaceTime chats. They talked about everything—their jobs, their families, the places they had traveled. The places they wanted to travel.

She learned that he was an only child, just as she was, and that he and his mom, Zenora, had been very close until she'd passed away about a year earlier. His dad, Alfred, left the family when Marcus was only four years old. He just walked out of the house one day and never returned. There was a rumor that Alfred had gotten into some kind of legal trouble and taken off for parts unknown, but Marcus never had any contact with him again.

Surprisingly, he said he'd never missed his father, rarely even thought about him. He had been so young when it happened, and his mother had stepped up and become everything he needed as a child. Even though deaf, Zenora worked two, sometimes three jobs, cleaning houses during the day and stocking the shelves of big-box department stores at night to give him a good life and send him to college. She was proud and overjoyed when she learned that he had won a full-ride scholarship to law school.

Marcus held his cell phone with one hand and placed the other over his heart as he shared the exact moment when he had informed his mom about the scholarship. "I remember she had tears in her eyes," he said. Alexis smiled. She was close to tears herself just listening to him share the story.

By midweek, with all the texts flying back and forth between them during the workdays and hour-long chats in the evening—ranging from personal to funny to flirtatious—Alexis began to feel like they were on the verge of becoming a "couple." The feeling was further cemented on Thursday afternoon when he texted to invite her to his house for dinner on Saturday. Outdoor grilling was his thing, and he wanted to prepare something special for her.

Ever had cedar plank salmon cooked on the grill? he texted.

No, can't say that I have.

Then you're in for a real treat. Saturday, my place at seven? After dinner, we can watch the sun go down from my balcony.

She knew from his address that his house overlooked Wilde Lake, another of Columbia's several man-made bodies of water and, in her opinion, the most picturesque. Can't wait, she told him, eagerly thinking about what she'd wear and anticipating their first real kiss.

* * *

Later that evening, still abuzz about all the good things happening with Marcus, she whipped up a tuna salad for dinner and ate it with a tall glass of iced tea. She was going to hit Stone Cold Creamery to meet Paul in ninety minutes and didn't want to have to hold back on the ice cream and toppings; hence, the light meal.

Around seven fifteen, she slipped into shorts and her favorite pair of Nikes and began the ten-minute walk to the restaurant. As she ventured farther away from Marcus and closer to her meeting with Paul, she realized that her spirits were sagging. She knew what she had to do, and it filled her heart with dread. Not only because she suspected he was going to take it badly, but it also meant that she was likely going to lose someone she considered her closest friend after Michelle.

She remembered the moment things between them had changed from friendship to romance like it had happened yesterday. They were relaxing in lounge chairs and sipping wine on her balcony after biking around Columbia's trails all day when she had turned to go inside for a jacket as the fall evening turned chilly. Paul had stood suddenly, blocked her path, and kissed her full on the lips. It caught her completely off-guard. She gasped and froze. All she could think was that they were both seeing others. What about Reggie? What about Rosea?

Paul must have read her mind. He released her, stepped back, looking embarrassed, and started to apologize. Until she pulled him in close for another kiss. A long, ardent kiss full of all the desire that had been seething beneath the surface between them for weeks. Next thing she knew, they were thrusting and thrashing around in her queen-size bed, unable to get enough of each other. They spent a long, memorable night of passionate lovemaking. The next morning, they discussed what had to happen next.

"I've been wanting this since forever," Paul had admitted as she lay snuggled in the crook of his arm. "Not going to lie."

"What took you so long?" she asked. "Never mind. I think I know. Reggie and Rosea." Their significant others.

"Well, yeah. But I also worried what it might do to our friendship if you rejected me. I thought I couldn't take that."

"I get it. So, what do we do now?"

"Whatever we need to do to make this work," he said, squeezing her tightly. "I'm not letting you go."

They broke up with Reggie and Rosea the following day. The next few months with him had felt like a dream. It abruptly turned into a nightmare when she found out that Rosea was still very much in the picture. Had never left, really. Rosea had made sure she knew it through a stream of nasty text messages. The whole sordid episode had nearly crushed Alexis. And her relationship with Paul. They didn't speak for weeks. She only forgave him after countless apologies and a whole lot of openness and patience on his part. Besides, she was tired of all the lonely nights and deeply missed having him around. Things went back to the way they were—minus Rosea—for several months. She was happy, even falling in love.

Then came talk about marriage and children. And Marcus. Now everything between her and Paul was upside down. *She* was the one who wasn't being open. *She* was the one who wasn't being honest. And she didn't like the feeling one bit. She couldn't deal with juggling two lovers. She was pretty sure Marcus would be more than enough man for her to handle. She had to break up with Paul.

She approached the small restaurant and spotted him standing at the entrance waiting for her. He was wearing light gray track pants and a t-shirt that showed off his muscles.

"Hey, Alexis," he said, smiling when he saw her.

"Hey, yourself," she said, returning the smile.

They hugged and greeted each other warmly. She reached up

and rubbed his bald head teasingly and he laughed, but truthfully, the look suited him. They entered, and she ordered one of her favorites, the banana caramel crunch. He chose something chocolate loaded with berries.

They walked slowly back toward the lake, taking a popular wooded path, and caught up on their recent lives. She could barely believe that it had been weeks since they'd last seen each other in person. She shared what she could with him—a little about her progress on the novel, how she was starting to tire of her job—and waited for the right moment to reveal the break-up news to him.

The promenade area was buzzing with people fishing and moving back and forth among the restaurants and shops. They found an empty bench, sat shoulder to shoulder and chatted briefly, then fell into silence as they savored the last of their ice cream treats.

In their moment of quiet, it suddenly hit Alexis that this was absolutely the wrong place to tell him. Too many people out and about. Paul tended to raise his voice when upset. In part to make sure she heard him, but it was also just his nature. He easily got worked up. What had she been thinking?

"So," he said, breaking the long silence. "Have you given much more thought to what we discussed?"

She sighed deeply. "You mean about marriage? And children?" Yes, she thought. I can't do it. But she couldn't tell him that right now. Not here. "Some."

He nodded. "I have a suggestion."

She took her gaze off the water and looked directly at him, a question on her face. She was not so sure she wanted to hear what was coming.

"Why don't we get away to a cabin in the Blue Ridge Mountains? Like we used to. And talk it all over."

She turned back to face the lake, not wanting him to see her indifferent expression. In the past, she would have jumped eagerly at the chance to get away to the mountains with him. Or anywhere, for that matter. And he knew that. He would never understand if she turned him down. Or *when* she turned him down.

He began to sign and speak rapidly. "Did you not hear me? Or am I being ignored here?"

"Um . . ."

As if sensing reluctance, he quickly added, "Just for a weekend. It will do us both good to get away and talk without any distractions."

She swallowed the last bite of her ice cream. "Things are kind of crazy at work now."

"It doesn't have to be this weekend. We can wait until things ease up for you. We can go later this month. Or early in July. It'll be good to get to the mountains when it's hot and humid here."

He stood up as they finished their ice cream and reached for her paper cup. She watched as he strolled toward a wastebasket.

Damn it, she thought. She hated all the dodging and lying. She needed to get this breakup over and done with. Maybe she could invite him back to her place. Give him the news in private.

He sat back on the bench. "Thoughts?"

She shook her head. "I can't, Paul."

"Then when do you think you can?"

"No time soon."

He turned and glared at her. "What is going on with you?"

"What do you mean?"

"You're different. Evasive."

She couldn't deny that. "Look, let's go . . ."

"You're seeing someone else, aren't you?" He spat the words at her. "I know you said you weren't before, but it would explain a lot. I want the truth, Alexis."

"No, I'm not." She could feel his eyes boring into the side of her face. She gulped. Hard. Looked away. Should she go ahead and end it now? Even with all these people around?

"Look at me," he said.

"What?"

"*Look* at me, dammit." His voice was getting louder. "And tell me you're not seeing someone else. 'Cause I swear . . ."

"You don't have to shout. I'm right here."

"You can't do it, can you?" He was yelling now. "You can't fucking look me in the eye and tell me."

A man fishing at the water's edge glanced back at them. A young couple strolling by did a double take.

Alexis stood abruptly. "I'm not doing this now. Not here." She turned and started back toward the path.

He jumped up, followed her. "Where are you going? We haven't . . ."

She kept walking until he grabbed her elbow. She paused, yanked it away. "Get your hands off me."

He took a step back, held his hands up. "Okay. I didn't think you heard me," he said, voice lowered. "I just want to talk. Can you come back and talk to me?"

"Hell no," she said. "You're not talking. You're yelling. It's embarrassing."

"Alright, I stopped yelling. Just come back."

"I'm not going back there. Not with you acting like a fool in public."

"Look, I've calmed down. Don't you even want to try to fix this?"

She took a deep breath, then blew it out her mouth. The outburst had been a bit much, even for Paul. But it was unfair to keep putting this off. She should have him over to her apartment now and get it over with. No point dragging things out any longer. The sooner she got this done, the better. For both of them.

* * *

Paul went to the kitchen cabinet where she kept her wine, opened a bottle, and filled two stemless glasses. Alexis didn't try to stop him. He had been to her apartment countless times and knew his way around. Besides, they both needed a little something to calm their nerves. Plus, it would give her more time to think about exactly how she was going to tell Paul that their relationship was over.

She fluffed up the pillows and made herself comfortable on the couch. He joined and handed her a glass. Then he sat back, slipped out of his running shoes, and propped his sock-clad feet on the coffee table. Alexis took a swig of wine. And another. She knew this was not going to be easy. Not only because of the way Paul had gotten so amped up earlier simply because she didn't want to go away with him, but also because she still had feelings for him. She still found him attractive, especially with his new shaved-head look, and could remember how much fun he was when things were good between them. His emotions could some-times get the best of him, but she loved his passionate ways, for the most part. They simply had too many differences when it came to marriage and children. She couldn't see a future for them.

She cleared her throat, and he turned and looked at her calmly, lovingly. She swore he was intentionally fixing her with his innocent, doe-eyed look, the one that used to melt her heart like butter. But it was not going to work. Not tonight.

"Look, Paul. I've thought a lot about this. We have so many differences between . . ."

Before she could finish the sentence, he reached out and placed his hand on her bare thigh. "Let me say something first. I want to apologize for the way I acted back there. It was stupid. Way out of line. You're the best thing that ever happened to me, and the thought of losing you scares the crap out of me. Regardless, I had no right to carry on like that."

He sounded sincere enough, she thought. She wasn't expecting that. She smiled thinly. "Thank you. Apology accepted."

She took another sip of wine, placed her glass on the table. This was really going to hurt him. She hated that but felt she had no choice. She was ready to move on. She *needed* to move on. Even if things never went anywhere with Marcus—and there was no guarantee that they would—she and Paul were not right for each other. End of story. Caring about each other and being good for each other were very different things.

He must have mistaken her moment of silence and reflection for acceptance. He slid closer, pulled her head down to his shoulder. The position was so familiar to Alexis. And comforting. But she knew she couldn't linger.

She sat up. "Paul, this has . . ." He cupped the back of her head in his hand and brought her lips to his. Also familiar. Also comforting. Still, she resisted, pushed against his chest . . . for a second. It had been weeks since they'd been alone together. She had forgotten how good his sexy lips made her feel. Her brain told her to pull away, to put a stop to it. But she didn't.

He scooped her up by the legs and sat her in his lap. His embrace tightened; his kisses pressed harder. Any second now, she told herself, she was going to put a stop to this. His hand slipped beneath her top. Okay, now, she thought. This had to end now. She pulled away weakly. He pushed gently. They fell back onto the couch, and it was over. She let him take her to all the familiar places they had been so many times before.

* * *

She woke up in the wee hours of the morning to see them both lying naked in bed. The next thing she saw was an empty bottle of wine sitting on the nightstand. She lifted herself up on one elbow and peeked groggily at the clock. Seven forty-five.

She popped up. "Dammit!" She had to leave for work in thirty minutes. How the heck had she let this happen? And if her foggy memory from the night before was accurate, they had gone at it not once, not twice. But three times. It was as if they were trying to make up for lost time.

She shook his shoulder sharply. Partly to wake him, partly because she was pissed. At him. At herself. She stood and slipped into her robe, then walked around the room grabbing their clothes off the floor one by one. His t-shirt. Her panties and bra. She snatched his briefs and tossed them in his face.

"You need to get up. *Now.*"

"Huh?" Paul raised his head, blinking at her.

"Get the hell up and get dressed. It's almost eight o'clock. I have to go to work."

"Well, damn," he said, stumbling into his briefs. "Give me a second here. What's gotten into you? Big change from last night."

Alexis grimaced. Her stomach cramped up at the thought of the previous evening. She was supposed to break up with him and send him on his way. Instead, she'd slept with him. Again, and again. What the hell was wrong with her? She had made a rotten mess of everything.

This was not the time to beat herself up about it though. She had to get to work. She would have to straighten this all out another day.

6

Alexis had seen the dozen or so contemporary white stucco town-houses along the waterfront at Wilde Lake countless times while jogging along the trail nearby. It was hard to miss them. They'd been designed by Hugh Newell Jacobsen, a world-famous archi-tect, and featured in many promotional pieces for Columbia. But she had never actually visited any of them.

She drove through the neighborhood toward Marcus's town-house on Saturday evening and noted people of all races and ages out walking and working on their lawns. An older Asian-American couple steered what appeared to be their grandchild in a stroller. A middle-aged white man trimmed the hedges at the end of his driveway, and a Black woman tended to the flower bed in her garden.

This was fairly typical for neighborhoods in Columbia, Mary-land, where people of many races and ethnicities lived together. While not without problems and occasional skirmishes, for the most part, residents existed in relative harmony. This had been the vision of the town's founder, local businessman and activist James Rouse, who'd set out in the early 1960s to build a small city that fostered economic, racial, and cultural harmony. It was one of the reasons Alexis had decided to make it her home shortly after grad school.

She parked and entered the walkway to Marcus's unit. Next door, an attractive gray-haired white couple who appeared to be in their early fifties tended their small front lawn. It was immaculate, with carefully trimmed plants and hedges. The woman dug intently into a patch of dirt at the edge of the house as the man trimmed branches off a small nearby tree with an electric chain saw. Like a lot of homeowners throughout Columbia's villages, they had posted a Black Lives Matter sign front and center on the lawn. The man looked up, smiled, and nodded, his eyes following her until she reached Marcus's front door. His wife also nodded, and Alexis waved in return. They seemed curious but friendly enough.

She reached a small iron gate and pressed the buzzer. Marcus appeared in seconds, wearing taupe-colored slacks, a casual shirt, and an apron. She had decided on a yellow sleeveless sundress cut low in the front. She smiled as they kissed in greeting, then followed him across a sunny terrace and through a glass door to a large open space with pristine hardwood floors. The unit was sparsely decorated, as might be expected of a bachelor pad, especially since Marcus said he had moved in recently. Much of the furniture had belonged to his mother and was not at all what you would expect for a bachelor. The kitchen was compact but nicely appointed with white appliances.

The undisputed highlight, though, was the expansive balcony that ran across the entire back of the place. It had sandy-colored wood floors and a glass and white stucco railing. The view of the lake was unobstructed and so close that it felt like it was sitting in his backyard. Maybe too close, she thought, not being the best swimmer. But she wasn't going to let her anxiety get in the way tonight. She'd been eagerly awaiting this date and had long admired these townhouses. Now here she was standing on the balcony of one of them, the landscape spread out magnificently before her.

Back inside, Marcus gave her a tour of all three levels, each with a balcony or terrace. It ended on the lower level, where there was a home office, recreation area, and a room filled with exercise equipment. Double French doors led to the patio and backyard and then directly to the water's edge.

"This is incredible, Marcus," she said as they strolled across the lawn and stood on a gravel pathway a few short feet from the lake. It looked hauntingly beautiful under the dim light of the evening sky, even though the huge body of water was so close. Her mind pulsated back to the day she'd nearly lost her life in the bay at Sandy Point State Park as a small child. A shiver crept up her arms. Though she later became a fan of just about every sport and an active participant in many, she had never learned to be at ease around deep water.

He seemed to sense her anxiety. "You alright?"

She nodded. "I'm fine. I had no idea the backs of these houses were right on the lake. I confess, I'm not the best swimmer."

"Really? We'll have to do something about that. Get you some lessons. I'm hoping you'll spend a lot more time here."

She smiled. She liked the sound of that, she thought, happy to follow him back into the house and up to the balcony on the main level. Marcus's expression told her just how proud he was of his new home, and she couldn't blame him. "How long have you lived here again?" she asked, relieved to be a safe distance from the water.

"I moved in a few months ago." He poured two glasses of Cabernet and handed one to her. "Haven't had much time to decorate, as you can see. I have more furniture out here on the balcony than I do inside. This is where I spend most of my time when home. So, it works fine for me now."

"I can understand why you spend all your time out here. It's a little slice of heaven."

He nodded, then walked toward the heated grill, lifted the top, and placed a cedar block as she made herself comfy in one of the cushioned garden chairs surrounding the table. She watched and sipped her wine as he seasoned three salmon fillets with oil and lemon juice and placed them on the heat.

He sat down beside her and picked up his glass. "You have any trouble finding me?"

She shook her head. "None at all. I've seen this area many times before, so I had a good idea how to get here."

"They are hard to miss."

"Oh yes. Do you like living here?"

"I do. The people seem social, although I'm not here often enough to really get to know any of them."

"I saw your next-door neighbors as I came in. Working in the yard."

"Oh, Sylvie and Stanley. Yeah, they're out there most weekends. A strange couple, but they seem nice enough."

Alexis frowned. "Strange?"

He shrugged. "In a harmless sort of way. She's at home, an artist of some kind. Also, a busybody. Always knocking on the door meddling about this or that. Very involved in the neighborhood association. Stanley is actually a client of mine."

"Really?"

He nodded. "He likes the ladies. All the ladies. Young, old, Black, white." Marcus chuckled. "So, you might want to keep your distance a bit."

"Got it."

He lifted his glass toward her. "That's enough about my neighbors. Here's to us. And this beautiful evening."

"To us," she repeated. They clinked glasses.

"It smells delicious," she said. "Can't wait to try it."

"I think you'll enjoy it." He stood to check the fish. "This is about ready. Do you mind getting the salad out of the refrigerator? It's in a big glass bowl with a plastic top. Oh, and grab a couple bottles of dressing."

"No problem," she said, standing up just as her phone beeped. She lifted it off the table and glanced at the screen as she walked into the house. *It was Paul.* Texting her yet again. For about the twentieth time since they had parted two days ago, after their impromptu night together.

She rolled her eyes and pushed the button to ignore the call. *Again.* She wasn't ready to think about any of that now. She would deal with him later. She quickly tucked the phone into the recesses of her purse and dumped it back on a kitchen chair. Out of sight. Out of mind. For the rest of the evening.

When she returned a few minutes later with the salad, Marcus had already set the table. The fish had been garnished with lemon slices and rested on a large colorful platter.

"It looks so good," she said as he refilled their wineglasses and sat down to eat.

"Mmm," she mumbled after the first bite. "This is the best salmon I've ever had, by a mile."

He smiled. "Glad you like it. It's so important not to overcook salmon."

"Well, this is cooked and seasoned perfectly."

"I like a woman who can appreciate good cooking. I once fixed a similar salmon dish for someone who thought it was undercooked. She refused to take a second bite."

"You're kidding?"

"I kid you not. I actually had to put it in the microwave to get her to eat more. It was rubbery and dry, but hey, she was happy."

They both laughed.

"I've been meaning to ask about your sons. Are they in the area?"

Marcus shook his head somewhat sadly. "One of them lives in DC. The other one is on the West Coast. I don't really see them much. When I do, there's always tension 'cause they're looking for a handout. Or some kind of favor."

She frowned, not sure how to respond. "I'm really sorry to hear that."

"As I explained to both of them, I'm always here for emotional support, advice. But I'm not their personal money tree. Not anymore."

She nodded with understanding. "What about their mother? Is she in the area?"

He hesitated and seemed to be gathering his thoughts. "That's a complicated story. To make it short, she left us a long time ago. Ran off with someone when the boys were young. Ten and twelve. Last I heard, she was somewhere down in South America. Brazil, Chile."

Alexis's eyes grew wide. How awful. She covered her mouth with her napkin. "Good grief. That must have been terrible. Especially for the boys."

"It definitely was not a pretty picture. She was a good wife and mom, at least in the beginning. But she changed when she met him, became selfish, thinking only of herself. And her lover. It was tough for all of us when she left. I did the best I could raising two boys alone, but it was hard without their mother around."

"Of course." She reached out across the table and touched his hand briefly. "How old are they now?"

"Aaron is twenty-five and Owen is twenty-seven. Aaron is the one in California. He works as a gardener and cleans pools, last I heard. Owen paints houses. I tried to get them to go to college. Actually, that's the one thing I would still splurge on for them. They're smart boys. Just made some foolish choices."

Although that didn't sound so bad to her, it had to be hard for a successful man like Marcus. Many fathers saw their sons as reflections of themselves. Black men had the added burden of teaching their sons the strength and skills they needed to survive in a world that could be so hostile toward them. And Marcus had to do it all on his own.

"They're young," she said. "Especially for guys. They have time to pick things up."

He sighed doubtfully. "One can always hope." He looked into her eyes. "Do you plan on having children someday?"

She hesitated, still reluctant to go into that with him. Marcus didn't get along with his sons, but that didn't mean he never wanted to have more children in the future. Then again, he was so disappointed with the ones he had, it seemed plausible that he would not want more. She should probably be upfront with him now, before they got in too deeply.

"No. I don't."

"Oh?" he said, obviously stunned. "Wasn't expecting that."

"I know, surprising, right? It's something I've thought long and hard about. I'm deaf and Black. And a woman. I don't want to bring a Black child into the world who has a good chance of being deaf and has to face so many obstacles."

She braced herself for a negative comment from him or at least some sort of admonition telling her to reconsider. Instead, he nodded.

"I get it," he said. "I deeply admire that attitude. Not that there's anything wrong with being deaf. There isn't. My mother was deaf, and I adored her. But I also know she faced some real tough challenges. So, I understand your way of thinking."

"You learn to cope, but it can still be rough at times. The stories I could tell you, Marcus."

"I'm all ears."

"Another time maybe." She wanted to keep things light and upbeat on this second date. "What about you? Do you want more children?"

"For what it's worth, no. I'm done. Don't get me wrong, I love my sons, but raising them alone was the hardest job in the world. So, no, I definitely don't want to go through that again. Two is plenty."

Alexis let out a deep breath of air, only now realizing that she had been holding her breath for some time. She looked at him with a newfound appreciation, and his expression back toward her seemed filled with the exact same sentiment.

He took her hand and guided her gently to her feet. Then he pulled her tight. They exchanged a long, deep kiss that Alexis never wanted to end.

"Where have you been all my life?" he asked, gently brushing her hair off her shoulders.

The same thought about him crossed her mind as she stared into his eyes. "Looking for you."

He took her hand and led her back inside. He paused at the base of the stairs, turned to face her, and signed. "Tell me if I'm moving too quickly, baby."

Somehow, he managed to make signing look seductive. Her heart did a little dance.

"No. You're not. I'm more than ready."

7

Alexis spent a magnificent weekend with Marcus. And another and another. They attended an exhibit of Indian artifacts at the Walters Art Museum in Baltimore and dined at Miss Shirley's Cafe on East Pratt Street near the Inner Harbor. They spent lazy afternoons browsing in historic Georgetown and around Antique Row in Kensington, Maryland. Then, to celebrate one month together, they caught a happy hour jazz performance at the Chrysalis amphitheater at Symphony Woods in Columbia, ending the night at his place for a quiet romantic evening dancing to make-out music. And then making out.

The next morning, while dining in bathrobes over cheese omelets, smoked turkey bacon, and fresh coffee at his place, Marcus casually said he wanted to discuss something with her.

"We're both unattached," he said, smiling warmly at her across the table on the balcony. "We spend all our free time together lately. Let's make it official. You and me, exclusive."

She smiled widely. This was the moment she'd been waiting for. He wanted them to be a real couple. She quickly pushed aside the thoughts of recent secret encounters with Paul that popped into her head—weeknights together at their apartments when Marcus pored over legal briefs, hikes in Great Falls National Park a couple of Sunday afternoons when Marcus hit the golf course. Until now, she'd had no idea how serious Marcus might want to get. She wasn't one hundred percent certain there were no "Claudias" in the background. She didn't think so, but men could be really clever about hiding these things. Hell, if she could find time for Paul, Marcus could find time for other women. Justification to her mind for having held on to Paul.

Naturally, this changed everything. She was elated and readily agreed.

Now she *had* to end things with Paul. For real this time. Still, she kept postponing it all the following week. Not that she wasn't ready to let Paul go. She was. But his behavior at the lakefront when she first attempted to call it off had shaken her. She didn't think he would hurt her. In all the years she'd known him, he had never laid a hand on her in anger. She'd always known he was emotional, but that was part of the attraction. She liked a man who was tuned in to his feelings and unafraid to show them. It translated into back rubs in the tub for her, long, deep discussions about everything under the sun, and hot nights between the sheets. She thought of Paul as passionate, the most passionate man she'd ever dated. But his jarring reaction at the lakefront had taken her by surprise. She needed time to figure out how best to approach him.

Then on Thursday, Marcus surprised her with yet another delivery of three dozen roses to her office. This time, yellow. Michelle teased her that Marcus was turning the place into a flower shop.

"I can't remember ever seeing you so happy," Michelle said. "I admit I'm kind of jealous. You're so lucky."

Alexis laughed, picked out a rose from the bouquet, and danced around her office. It felt like she was floating on air. Marcus was calm, collected, attentive, and oh-so romantic. Their relationship lacked the fiery passion and drama that was always present with Paul, from the cheating early on to the tense talk near the Columbia lakefront to the all-night love marathons. With Marcus, things were more like an intense, steady hum. He made her feel safe, secure, and elegantly alluring. She was ready for the change.

No more excuses. No more delays. Otherwise, she'd be no better than Paul and too many other unfaithful men she'd been with. And that wasn't the kind of woman she wanted to be. Although she might have been semi-justified until she and Marcus had become "official," she still felt a little sleazy sneaking about. Once, she had even nearly gotten caught. She and Paul had been lounging around half-naked on her couch watching a movie when Marcus texted unexpectedly.

Leaving the office earlier than planned. Going to swing by.

She'd dashed into the bathroom at the pace of a world-class sprinter and quickly fired off a text, hastily explaining that she had work to get done for a meeting the following morning. Then she waited breathlessly until he responded: Okay, I'll call you later tonight.

She hated the lying and deception. The sneaking around. On their first date, she'd told Marcus that she wasn't seeing anyone else. She needed to make sure that was the truth from here on. Time to put her big-girl panties on and get this over with.

Just before she left the office that Friday evening, she picked up her cell phone and sent Paul a text message. Marcus had to work late; they weren't planning to see each other until the following day, when they were going to take a drive to Rehoboth Beach for an overnight stay. She had planned to go for drinks after work with Michelle and Jeffrey, a bookkeeper at AASNC. At the last minute, she'd begged off. She really wanted to get the talk done with Paul before the weekend. And tonight was the only chance.

Hey. What are you up to this evening? she texted as she tidied up her office desk.

Just leaving basketball practice. How about a movie
later?

She shut down her desktop. We need to talk.

I take that as a no thanks to the idea of a movie. Fine.
Is this talk going to bring a smile to my face or a frown?

Alexis ignored the comment. Say around eight?

Sounds good. Should I bring a bottle of wine?

No, she thought. No, no, no. She had to stay stone-cold sober and crystal clear so she could resist any come-ons. But she shouldn't tell him that.

I already have enough wine, she typed.

* * *

When Alexis opened the door, Paul reached out to embrace her. He tried to plant a kiss on her lips. She quickly turned her head and gave him her cheek.

"Damn. What's that about?" he said.

She stood next to the couch. As she'd changed into cutoff jeans and flip flops after work, she decided that the best approach would be to get straight to it. To be firm yet empathetic. "We should sit down. I have something I need to tell you." She sat and placed her cell phone on the end table next to her, upside down as usual.

He ignored the invitation to sit and strolled to the kitchen cabinet above the sink. It was empty. At least empty of wine bottles. "Didn't you say you had wine here?" Paul said, riffling through boxes of tea bags, a plastic bottle of clover honey, and a box of raw sugar. "I could easily have brought some."

He had his back to her, but it was a small apartment. She could easily understand his deep voice and see him as he opened and slammed door cabinets. She just pretended otherwise.

He came back into the living room, looking more than a little peeved. She glanced down at her hands. "Did you hear me?" he asked more loudly. "I thought you said you had wine?"

"I thought I did," she said. "My mistake."

"We were making progress getting things back on track. Now you're throwing me aside. You've been ignoring most of my texts the past few days."

"Can you sit so we can talk?"

"I'll take whatever's coming standing up." He shoved his hands into the pockets of his drawstring shorts and eyed her with obvious suspicion from across the black-and-white living room carpet. "What's going on?"

She shrugged. "I was busy."

He threw his arms in the air. "So busy you can't respond to a damn text message?"

Just say it, she thought. "Paul." She paused and looked directly into his eyes. "I'm afraid it's over between us." She lowered her voice. "I'm sorry."

He frowned. "What do you mean, 'over'? What the hell . . . ?"

"I mean we're done. Finished." She signed the word "finished" with an outward sweep of her hands twice for emphasis. "We both need to move on."

His expression changed again, eyes scrolling from defiant to puzzled to pleading. "What about the past month?" he asked. "Didn't that mean anything to you?"

She shook her head. "It should never have happened. We're not right for each other, Paul. We need to move on."

He looked crestfallen. "I don't get it, Alexis. You were into it as much as I was." He stepped closer, reaching out to touch her elbow. "What changed? If we just talk about it, we . . ."

She cringed, snatched her arm out of his reach. Perhaps more hastily than needed. But that was then. This was now. Paul had to wrap his head around that.

"I hope we can still be friends," she said softly. "Like we were before. We just can't continue as a couple."

He looked dumbfounded. His whole body—that well-honed athlete's body—seemed to droop from the neck down. She felt terrible doing this to him.

"Excuse me," she said. She needed to get away to calm her own nerves. In the bathroom, she wrung her hands and paced the floor. Up and down. She hated seeing Paul so hurt, so lost. At her expense. At the same time, she knew it was best to get this done.

She returned to the living room with more resolve than ever, only to see Paul glaring at her, body tense, fists clenched. "Who is he?" he said, his deep voice like a dagger.

"Who is who?" She looked directly into his eyes and instantly wished she hadn't. They had changed from pleading a moment ago to . . . what? Fear? Hurt? She had never seen this expression on his face before.

He took a step toward her, jabbing at the screen on her phone, now clutched in his hand. It was filled with Marcus's smiling face. And a comment where he called her "baby."

Alexis could feel the resolve draining from her body.

"Who the hell is this? And don't you fucking lie to me. Who is Marcus?"

Dammit! They'd always had each other's passwords but rarely used them to check each other's phones. She took a tiny step backward. Bit her bottom lip. "I . . . Alright. It's true. I met someone."

His expression hardened. And that's when she recognized it. Fury. *Pure, naked fury.* For the first time ever, Paul was scaring the crap out of her. She glanced away. "It's nothing serious. We just met and . . ."

"Are you fucking him?"

"What? Um . . . I. That's none of your business. I don't have . . ."

He moved quickly. Without warning, his hands wrapped around her neck in a tight, powerful grip. He began to squeeze. *Hard.* She reached up and clawed desperately at his fingers with all her might. But the more she tried to pull them away, the tighter he squeezed. His face was twisted, glaring down at her in a fierce scowl.

Her eyes pleaded with him to stop. All she got back was a snarl. *Who was this man?* She had no time to think. She needed air. *She needed it now.*

She pounded his big, muscular arms, now as stiff as rocks, and tried to scratch his face and shaved head. It was hopeless, she thought as every ounce of energy drained from her body. Her arms fell slowly, dropping limply to her sides. Her eyes shut; she sensed that she was fading and had only a few breaths left. Maybe two. Now one. She thought of her parents. Of Michelle and Jeffrey. And Marcus. They were all smiling at her. *This was how it felt when your life was being snuffed out.*

And then he let go. Just like that, he released her. She coughed and wheezed. Gasped for air. Opened her eyes. Paul was backing away slowly, his face now filled with shame. As her heart steadied, the fear of dying was replaced with anger. And sadness. How dare he do this to her? Had she just almost died? But she wouldn't lash out at him. Couldn't. He might lose it again. She needed to project a sense of calm if she wanted to get out of this alive.

"You're going to have to leave." She was surprised at how serene her hoarse voice was. When she really felt like lashing out with the tirade of curses swirling through her head. *Bastard. Asshole. Motherfucking freak.*

He nodded. "I understand. I'm sorry. I'm really sorry."

Without another word, she walked to the front door and opened it. To get him out but also in case she needed to flee.

"I . . . I don't know what came over me," he said as he approached the door.

Neither did she. But she didn't care at this point. She had only one question before he left. And, she promised herself, it would be the last thing she would say to him. Ever. "What made you stop?"

He blinked hard, thought for a second. "I . . . I could see that you were losing consciousness."

Hearing him say that really drove it home to Alexis. Sent chills up her spine. She had nearly died. At Paul's hands. He looked full of guilt. But she had zero sympathy for him at this point.

She slammed the door behind him and bolted it, pins and needles tingling all over her body. She rubbed her arms to soothe them, then went to the base cabinet under the sink, reached all the way back behind the pipes, and pulled out a fresh bottle of wine. She sank down on the couch, her eyes resting on the black carpet with its white speckles. She felt so thankful for this moment. Thankful to be alive, nestled among the pillows in her little apartment.

She wanted to call Marcus so badly, to tell him what had just happened. How she had nearly died. But she couldn't. How would she ever explain Paul and why he had gotten so angry? She wasn't supposed to be seeing anyone else. She wasn't supposed to have slept with anyone else.

She lifted the bottle and gulped it straight. Then she texted Michelle. She really needed to talk to someone tonight.

8

Michelle was still out on the town with Jeffrey, attending a street concert at Color Burst Park near Busboys and Poets, but they quickly agreed to stop by when Alexis texted that she and Paul had just had a huge blowup and she was freaking out. It wasn't the kind of thing to talk about in text messages. And the concert was far too noisy for a FaceTime chat.

Thirty minutes later, Alexis opened the door to see Michelle and Jeffrey standing there, still dressed in their Friday work casual wear. They greeted each other warmly despite having seen each other earlier that day at work.

"You look terrible," Michelle blurted with her usual characteristic bluntness.

"I *feel* terrible," Alexis said. She curled up in a corner of the couch and hugged a throw pillow.

"So, what happened?" Jeffrey signed, sitting in the armchair across from Alexis and Michelle. He was a bookkeeper at AASNC and had a mild hearing loss, the result of a spinal meningitis infection during childhood. He signed fluently. He was in his mid-thirties, wore glasses, and loved all things dealing with numbers and technology. He had curly hair and deep dimples. Several women at AASNC had crushes on Jeffrey. They joked about him being a cute chocolate version of Jeff Bezos or Mark Zuckerberg. They'd flirted with him shamelessly until he got engaged to a woman living in Baltimore about a month earlier. Some still did.

Alexis squeezed the pillow tightly for a minute while gathering her thoughts. It was all so raw, so unbelievable. She wasn't sure where to start.

"You're going to have a hard time believing this," she said.

"You did it," Michelle said. "You broke up with him."

Alexis nodded.

"He didn't take it so well?" Michelle asked.

Alexis scoffed. That was the understatement of the year. "He choked me."

"Excuse me?" Michelle said.

"You're not serious," Jeffrey said. He pushed his glasses up on his nose.

"You heard right."

"Shit!" Michelle said.

"Wait. You mean as in trying to . . . to kill you?" Jeffrey asked, speaking and signing animatedly. He sat up on the edge of his chair.

Alexis hesitated. As bad as it was, she had a hard time taking it that far. "I don't think he knew what he was doing at the time. Something came over him. When he realized I was losing it, he stopped."

"Damn," Michelle said, her eyes wide with astonishment.

"That's no excuse," Jeffrey said. "Touching you in anger was wrong. Period."

Michelle nodded in agreement.

"Well, I also admitted I was seeing someone else."

"Oh boy," Michelle said. "What the hell did you do that for?"

Alexis shrugged. "Didn't have much choice. He read my text messages while I was in the bathroom."

"That bastard," Michelle said.

"How bad did it get?" Jeffrey asked. "I mean, did he just grab you for a second and then let go or . . . ?"

"I almost lost consciousness. Like I said, he knew I was zoning out. That's why he stopped."

Michelle leaned back on the couch and closed her eyes. "Oh my God. This is too much."

Jeffrey whistled with disbelief.

"I am in complete shock," Michelle said. She looked closely at Alexis. "Are you okay?"

Hearing those words brought the terror of Paul's hands wrapped around her neck back to the surface. Her eyes filled with tears. "Why would he do this to me? I don't understand."

Michelle reached into her bag and retrieved a few tissues. She slid down the couch and handed them to Alexis.

"Thanks," Alexis said between sniffles. "I'll be okay. At least physically. Emotionally, I don't know. It's going to take a while."

"Do you think you should call the police?" Jeffrey asked.

Alexis shook her head adamantly. "I don't want to go through all that. It's not going to happen again 'cause that's the last time I'll ever be alone with him. You can believe that."

"I should hope so," Michelle said. "Do you want me to get you some water?"

"Oh, sorry," Alexis said, beginning to stand. "Let me get you all something to drink. I need to get up and move around anyway."

In the kitchen, she filled a pitcher with filtered ice and water and gathered three tall glasses. She figured she'd had enough wine for one day after draining half a bottle in minutes. She really appreciated her friends coming by on such short notice. It helped to have them to share all of this with.

She returned to see Michelle and Jeffrey sitting in silence. Unusual but understandable. The three of them often went out for lunch or met up after work, and the chatter and joking among them always went nonstop. This dark news about someone they'd all thought they knew, especially Michelle, had clearly shaken them badly.

"At least I got it over with," Alexis said, trying to lighten the mood as she placed the tray on the coffee table.

Michelle took a glass, nodding weakly.

"What does Marcus think about this?" Jeffrey asked.

"I haven't told him. Don't plan to."

Jeffrey frowned quizzically. Michelle nodded with understanding. Although Michelle knew all about her secretly seeing both Paul and Marcus in recent weeks, Jeffrey was completely unaware, and Alexis preferred to keep it that way. "It's complicated," Alexis said.

"Got it," Jeffrey said. "Anything we can do to help? You okay with being here alone tonight?"

Alexis waved her hand. "I'm fine. I doubt he'll come back. I could tell he felt bad and embarrassed about it when he left." At least she didn't *think* Paul would come back. There was a bit of anxiety about that, but she would keep it to herself. She didn't want her friends worrying about her.

"Call if you change your mind," Jeffrey said.

"Thanks, I will."

Alexis glanced at Michelle. She had become unusually quiet. Perhaps Michelle felt some guilt knowing that she had introduced Alexis to Paul. Which was silly.

"Don't blame yourself," Alexis said to Michelle. "It's not your fault."

"I had no idea he had this in him," Michelle said.

"How could you have known? This was so out of character for him."

They talked a few minutes longer, then walked to the front door.

"Please be careful," Michelle said, hugging Alexis.

"Lock the door immediately after we leave," Jeffrey added. He squeezed her hand gently.

"I will. Don't worry. I'll be fine."

As soon as they left, Alexis realized she'd been wrong about that. She was not so fine. It felt as if demons lurked in every corner of her apartment. She ran around to each room and made sure all the windows were locked, even though she was on the second floor. She closed all the blinds.

Just as she sat at the kitchen table to catch her breath, her stomach started to growl. At first, she thought it was fear playing tricks on her. Then she remembered she hadn't eaten since lunch, and it was 10:30 p.m. She was in no mood to cook, so she quickly threw some one-day-old Chinese takeout into the microwave. While waiting for it to heat, she walked around and double-checked the door and all the windows.

She picked at her food while sitting on the couch. CNN was on—something about a serial killer striking again in Northern Virginia—but her mind was anywhere but the TV. It kept wanting to relive the attack—his angry hands around her neck, his glaring, hard eyes, her struggling to catch her breath. She wondered if she'd ever feel completely safe in her apartment again.

She stood and picked up the empty takeout container, and that's when it happened. The strobe on the wall flashed.

Someone was ringing the doorbell.

She froze, container in midair. Oh God. Was he back? No, no, no. He wouldn't have the nerve. Or would he?

She quietly placed the container on the table and stood still, unsure what to do. Thank goodness she had bolted the door.

She was trying to decide whether to sneak up to the peephole when she heard it.

Thump, thump, thump.

The banging on the door was so loud her stomach did a somersault. She nearly shrieked, then threw her hand up to cover her mouth and silence herself. Her eyes darted to her cell phone sitting next to the food container. Should she call the police? She would feel like a fool if it wasn't Paul.

She heard the knocking again. Only more softly this time. She also noticed her phone vibrating. But she was fixated on the door. And whoever was behind it. She sucked in her breath, slithered slowly up to the door, and stood on her toes until her eyes reached the peephole.

She let out a giant sigh of relief. It was Michelle. Alexis had no idea why her friend was back so soon, but she had never been so happy to see her. She quickly undid the locks and chain and let Michelle in.

"Girl, you scared the hell out of me," Alexis said. "I was about to call the police."

Michelle blinked. "Didn't you get my text message? When you didn't answer me ringing and knocking, I figured you didn't hear it or you thought it might be him. So, I texted. I'm so sorry if I frightened you."

Alexis picked up her phone and saw the message from Michelle: **Hey, it's me at the door.** She nodded. "No problem. What brings you back here? Is everything okay?"

"Hell no," Michelle said, dropping her shoulder bag on the couch. "I need to talk to you. I didn't want to say anything in front of Jeffrey." She sank down and Alexis sat next to her.

"Is it about Paul?" Alexis asked as they sat down. She noticed that Michelle looked ashen; her eyes were deeply troubled.

Michelle nodded. "When you told me what happened, it all came flooding back to me."

"What came back to you?" Alexis cupped her hands in her lap and waited.

"Years ago, our senior year in college, Paul dated this woman. Gloria. I didn't know her that well, but . . . has he mentioned her?"

Alexis thought back. Paul had mentioned a couple of ex-girlfriends from college, but the name Gloria didn't ring any bells. She shook her head. "I don't think so."

"Probably not. They weren't together all that long. A few months at the most. Paul got around in those days. He was the resident bad boy, and just about every girl on campus wanted to hook up with him. Anyway, Gloria was a friend—maybe more like an acquaintance—but that's how I met Paul. Through Gloria. I mean, I knew him. He was in my PE classes, but we didn't become friends until he started seeing her. Then we all started double-dating with this guy I was seeing who was close to Paul . . ."

Get to the point, please. Alexis was tempted to jump in and ask: *What did Paul do?*

"She told me this weird stuff about him."

"About who?" Alexis asked.

"About Paul. I'm not making much sense, am I?"

"No, you're not."

"This whole thing with Paul is really getting to me. Gloria told me that Paul smacked her a couple of times. Toward the end of their relationship. He hit her supposedly. Threw her against the wall."

A thick glob got stuck in the middle of Alexis's throat. She tried to clear it. "Paul?"

Michelle nodded. "He denied it and I believed him. By that time, I had gotten to know him much better. He was never violent around me. And Gloria had a way of, well, blowing things out of proportion, imagining things. She even accused me of sleeping with Paul behind her back at one point."

"Did you?"

"No. But try telling Gloria that. Sorry I'm babbling on and on."

"No, no. Why didn't you tell me this before?"

"Honestly? I forgot all about it. This was so long ago. We were so young, and Paul insisted it was all a lie. He said they argued, but he never laid a hand on her. Now I'm not sure what to believe after what happened with you . . ."

Alexis sat back. "Oh boy."

"Gloria could have been lying. We just don't know. But I thought you needed to know about it."

"I agree. You're right. Thanks for telling me."

"Girl, you know you can't ever be alone with him after this. Hell, I'm scared to be alone with him now."

Alexis had no intention of ever being alone with a man who'd nearly choked the living daylights out of her, even before she knew about this. "You don't have to worry about that."

"You know, Jeffrey had a point. You should tell Marcus what happened."

Alexis shook her head firmly. "No way. It's too risky. He would probably dump me."

"Give him more credit than that. He might be upset at first, but in the end, he would probably want to protect you. And he could . . ."

Suddenly, Alexis's phone vibrated on the coffee table. They

both stopped talking and stared at it with dread. It was turned screen-side down, so they couldn't tell who it was.

"If that's Paul, do not answer it," Michelle said, her voice filled with apprehension.

Alexis took a deep breath, picked the phone up, and turned it over. It was Marcus calling on FaceTime. She almost laughed out loud with relief. So did Michelle. "I'm going to take this," Alexis said.

Michelle leaned over and waved at the screen. "Hi, Marcus," she said, smiling.

"Hello, Michelle," he said.

She grabbed her bag and stood up. "I'll let myself out. That's all I wanted to tell you. I'll see you Monday."

Alexis asked Marcus to hold, then carefully secured the door behind Michelle. She cleared her head of all thoughts of Paul and went back to Marcus. She was determined not to let her ex-boyfriend consume her thoughts or her life. Not if she could help it.

9

Marcus's proposal had to be the sweetest ever. Of course, it included roses. Lots and lots of roses. And the perfect John Legend song.

Alexis had arrived at his house expecting a cozy early fall dinner on the balcony overlooking Wilde Lake. They would eat and watch the sun dip below the horizon while sipping one of Marcus's homemade cocktails; he made a mean whiskey sour, with fresh lemon and lime juice. Then they would retreat upstairs.

On this eventful evening, she showed up in his favorite lavender sundress—as requested—to find him looking like a million dollars decked out in his black tuxedo. And wearing the cutest grin on his face.

"What's going on?" she asked, trying to make sense of it all. Marcus wasn't one for spontaneity or switching things up. He much preferred routine. Dinner and cocktails at seven on weekends whenever he could get away from work. An outing—movie, gallery, concert—once a month. Maybe twice. He phoned or texted almost the same time every night before bed whenever they couldn't be together. In their three months as a couple, she had gotten pretty comfy with it all.

Instead of explaining what he was up to, Marcus, eyes sparkling mischievously, asked her to step out onto the balcony and wait there for him. Then he disappeared, skipping down the stairs. She dropped her handbag on a chair in the dining room and headed toward the glass doors. It was a perfect, clear night; she glimpsed the sun dropping lazily toward the horizon. She stepped out and immediately got the first big surprise—dozens and dozens of roses. More than she'd ever seen outside of a flower shop. They sat atop the table, chairs, and grill in brilliant colors: red, yellow, pink, white.

She was taking it all in when Marcus walked out, a guitar in his hand. A guitar? She didn't even know he owned one. He strummed a few notes. It took her a minute to recognize the song; his guitar skills were obviously limited, and given the half-smile on his face, he knew it. But she soon recognized the music to "All of Me."

When he began to sing, her mouth dropped open. She quickly shut it and listened. He sounded pretty darn good, his voice rich and soulful. Why was she just hearing him sing now, after all this time? The whole thing was cute and corny. And she loved it. This was a side of Marcus she'd known nothing about but sincerely hoped to see much more often.

She was still wrapping her head around it all—the roses, the guitar, Marcus singing—when he dropped to one knee and sang the familiar lyrics:

"You're my end and my beginning; even when I lose, I'm winning."

Alexis thought she would burst with anticipation.

He placed the guitar down and pulled a small black and gold box from his inside jacket pocket. She could barely contain herself as he held it up to her. He popped the top open, revealing a glittering classic round diamond ring.

"Marry me, baby," he said, signing with one hand.

Her hands flew to her lips. She couldn't believe he was actually proposing. They had said the words "I love you" to each other for the first time only a couple of weeks earlier. True, they spent all their free moments together. Alexis could never remember feeling so secure, so complete, so happy. Marcus was stable, successful, considerate. He was a *real* man. Just what she'd always been looking for. She had fallen madly in love with him.

"Yes," she said breathlessly.

He stood and slipped the ring on her finger. "I can't believe this is happening." She laughed with joy as they embraced tenderly.

"Why haven't I heard you sing before?" she asked, poking him in the waist. "You have an incredible voice."

He smiled with a touch of shyness. "Saving it for the right moment, I guess."

"I'll say. What else have you been hiding from me?" She lifted her head and they kissed.

"I've already arranged for us to slip off to Cartagena, Colombia, in a few months."

"Cartagena? Why Cartagena?" Alexis knew that tourism there was on the upswing in recent years. Still, it seemed an odd choice.

"Believe it or not, it's one of the most romantic cities I've ever been to. I've visited a few times. They have everything: interesting culture, good food and shopping, white sandy beaches, a vibrant nightlife. And it's always been one of the safest cities in Colombia since it used to be where wealthy and well-connected Colombians went to vacation even when Americans stayed away. Now it's been discovered and has become more of a touristy hot spot, but it's still nice. I'm sure you'll come to appreciate it as much as I do."

"You've convinced me. When?"

"Mid-December. I worked my schedule, so I'll have some free time then. We can get married and make that our honeymoon."

Mid-December? That would be only six months since their first date. With such a quick engagement, it might make sense to take a little more time to get married. "Marcus, you don't think that's too soon? We've only been together a few months."

"It feels like much more than that though, doesn't it? And if we wait, it could be ages before I can get away for a honeymoon."

"White sandy beaches in December does sound nice. I've always wanted to go to South America." And she loved the idea of traveling with him as Mrs. Roberts. "We'll have to really push to make arrangements in so little time."

"We don't need a big wedding," he said. "I'd prefer something small and intimate anyway. That shouldn't take long to plan."

"How small is small?" She eyed him skeptically and held her breath.

"Around fifty people?"

Fifty? Her extended family alone would make up nearly fifty people. Aunts, uncles, cousins who would want to make the journey from Atlanta. Then there were her friends from college who were scattered across the country. She wanted them all there on such an important day. Unlike for him, this would be her first time marching down the aisle.

"C'mon, talk to me," he said, taking both her hands in his. "What's bothering you?"

"This would be my first wedding, Marcus. My *only* wedding. I don't need five hundred people, but I'd want more than what you seem to have in mind."

"So how big are we talking, then?"

Three hundred. That's what she wanted to say. "Two hundred people."

He thought for a moment. "Make it a hundred. How's that?"

She inhaled deeply. "How about a hundred twenty-five?"

"Can you arrange it in a few months?"

She swallowed. That would be tough. Really tough. A year would be more like it. Six months at least. But not impossible. She might not get her first choices when it came to venue or caterer. But at least they were talking December, not June. And Cartagena, Colombia, for the honeymoon sounded exciting. She would have to make it work, one way or another. "Okay. Three months."

He hugged her. "Then it's settled."

She smiled and immediately began making arrangements in her head. First, she would need a venue. A few rather out-of-the-way places came to mind. Then food, a dress, music, flowers. Whew! The thought of doing all that in three months was practically making her swoon. What she needed most was a good wedding planner, and even securing that would be iffy given the limited time. This was going to be maddening. She could already see that clearly.

But she was engaged. To Marcus. The man of her dreams. She loved the thought of waking up to those mesmerizing eyes for the rest of her life. Nothing was going to get in the way of this if she could help it. And that included Paul, her crazy ex. Marcus could never, ever find out about him. Fortunately, it had been several weeks since Paul had shown up unannounced at her apartment. She hadn't heard a peep since. Hopefully, it had finally sunk in that she was done with him. Had moved on. Although she still had her creepy moments—like every time the doorbell rang unexpectedly—she was beginning to feel that her life was getting back to normal.

"I'll make it work," she said. "But you gotta promise me one thing."

"Name it."

"You'll sing to me every night while we're in Cartagena."

He laughed, squeezing her hand. "You drive a hard bargain, baby. You got it."

10

It was a little more than two weeks after Marcus proposed, and planning for the wedding was going full steam ahead. Alexis sat in the dining room at her fiancé's house across from the wedding planner, a well-dressed woman named Valeria. She was fiftyish and had a short salt-and-pepper Afro. Her Louis Vuitton Speedy bag, bulging with brochures and notebooks, perched at the opposite end of the oblong table.

Valeria had been making brides happy for nearly thirty years and had her own wedding planning business. Michelle had recommended her enthusiastically. Valeria's schedule was already booked in the evenings and on weekends for the next several months, so to make things work in such a short span of time, Alexis had to leave work early on a weekday to catch her.

The wood table was buried beneath a mound of bridal magazines, planners, laptops, tablets, and lists of all sorts. This had to be a record for organizing weddings, Alexis thought. But Marcus wanted it to take place sooner rather than later. He had a couple of big cases coming up the following year that could drag out for months, years even. So here they were, planning a December wedding with ten weeks to get it all done. Flowers, caterers, music, and on and on. After dinner, Alexis was meeting Michelle at a bridal shop in Baltimore to check out wedding dresses. Timing was especially urgent since Michelle was leaving town the following day to visit family in Ohio for a week.

"By the way, that rock is a stunner," Valeria said.

Alexis fondled her ring the way she had countless times since Marcus had put it on her finger. She could not get past its beauty and all that it meant for her future as his wife. "Thanks," she said, beaming.

"Mind if I ask how many carats?"

"Three."

"Niiiice."

They went back to the guest list, already spilling past the one hundred twenty-five names she was able to get Marcus to agree to. "We have to cut this," Alexis said, running her finger down the list. "Marcus wants to keep it small and intimate." It was getting down to the wire, with every guest being scrutinized to determine whether they could safely be eliminated without offending anyone too much.

"What about Marcus's sons?" Valeria asked. "You said you weren't sure about them."

"I'm still not." Marcus had also left work early and was in his home office on the lower level. Alexis didn't like to disturb him when he was working there. She had hoped he would break and come up at some point before Valeria left. But he hadn't in ninety minutes, and this was kind of urgent. "You know what?" Alexis said. "Let me go ask him so we can get this list finalized."

She walked down the carpeted stairs, guest list in hand. She tapped softly on the door and opened it to Marcus's sanctuary, his man cave. He'd had it gutted and rebuilt from the ground up shortly after he purchased the house. Earthy scents of mahogany and leather still hung heavily in the air. This was the only room not furnished primarily with items taken from his mother's house upon her death fifteen months earlier. No expense had been spared, from the coffered ceiling to the wall paneling and built-in bookshelves. A huge Persian carpet was spread out beneath his executive desk.

"Marcus, honey, have you . . . ?" She paused mid-sentence at the sound of voices. She was startled to see Stanley, the next-door neighbor. His pale blond hair was noticeably thinning in the crown as he sat across from Marcus in the only colorful object in the room, a red leather armchair. She occasionally ran into Stanley and his wife, Sylvie, going to and from the house. They always seemed approachable. Yet she kept her distance, given what Marcus had said about Stanley being a skirt chaser, greeting them with nothing more than a brief smile and nod. He might be one of Marcus's clients, but she wanted no dealings with him.

Both men turned and stared at her in silence, their expressions anything but approachable. She nodded toward Stanley. "Sorry. I didn't realize anyone was here."

Stanley nodded back, peering at her over his reading glasses. The look on his face was vacant, distant. Nothing to suggest the overly friendly, chatty way he normally greeted her when she ran into him outside the house. He and Marcus were obviously deep into a difficult conversation.

She cleared her throat. "The wedding planner had a question, Marcus, but I guess it can wait."

"That's best." Marcus's mouth smiled, but his eyes said: "Do Not Disturb." She backed away. Shut the door.

How strange, she thought, as she walked slowly back up the stairs. When Valeria had arrived, the three of them chatted in the dining room for several minutes before Marcus went down to his office alone. Stanley must have arrived later and entered from the basement patio door. Why he hadn't used the front door was odd.

Something else nagged her. She was almost sure she'd heard a name she hadn't heard in months when she opened the door. Claudia. Marcus had mentioned it in the past, but she couldn't place it. Claudia, Claudia, she repeated to herself. When and where had she heard that name before?

Back in the dining room, Valeria was gathering her notebooks and planners. She glanced up. "What did he say?"

Alexis shrugged, mind elsewhere by now. "He's meeting with a client. I'll find out later tonight."

Valeria nodded. "Let me know. I need to finalize arrangements with the caterer soon. We're really tight on time."

"Tell me about it."

And then it hit her, just as she was closing the front door behind Valeria. Claudia was the name of the woman who was with Marcus the night they'd met at the fundraiser. The gorgeous chick wearing the flaming red dress that clung to her like spandex. Marcus's ex-girlfriend.

Alexis tried to clear her head, to reason with herself, before her thoughts got out of hand. There was no guarantee that Marcus's ex and the Claudia he and Stanley were just talking about were one and the same. Why in the world would Stanley and Marcus be discussing a long-gone former girlfriend of Marcus's?

On the other hand, Claudia wasn't exactly a common name. Could it really be a coincidence?

* * *

"Sorry to walk in on you earlier," Alexis said when Marcus finally came up about an hour after Valeria left. "I didn't realize you were meeting with anyone."

While Marcus wrapped up his meeting with Stanley, she had prepared one of his favorite meals—lamb chops, rosemary garlic potatoes, roasted Brussels sprouts. Although it was still warm enough to eat on the balcony, the weather had suddenly turned foul. Dark clouds hung over the lake as a hurricane raced up the east coast, with high winds and flooding predicted for the area. She hoped it would not get so bad she would have to postpone shopping for her wedding dress tonight.

"Not a problem," he said as he sat at the small round table in the kitchen. "Stanley called while you were meeting with the wedding planner, wanting to see me. I had him come in through the basement door so we wouldn't disturb you."

Alexis smiled. Seemed reasonable enough. She placed two glasses of Cabernet Sauvignon on the table and sat across from him. "Do you mind if I ask what Stanley needed to see you about?"

He hesitated for a moment. "It has to do with his job as a manager at a tech firm. He's being sued on a very delicate matter that I don't want to go into detail about now. That's all you need to know." Marcus smiled but in a way that meant no more questions need to be asked.

"Understood." As a lawyer, he likely dealt with lots of sensitive and confidential issues that he might not want to share with her. Over time, that could change as he learned to trust her.

"I came down to ask if you've given more thought to whether you want to invite Owen and Aaron to the wedding."

He shot her a look. One that made her feel a touch uneasy. "I didn't realize I was ever thinking about it."

She cleared her throat. "We talked about it briefly. You didn't say one way or the other. I guess since you don't speak to them much, probably not?" It was half comment, half question. His sons were such a sensitive topic. Although why wasn't clear since he usually dodged the subject whenever she tried to bring them up. She sensed it had to do with the strain in his first marriage. Whatever the reason, she had learned to tread lightly. Or not at all.

"So, you have your answer," he said flatly.

"Hmm." Still so guarded. Although now that she was about to become his wife, maybe she could press a little harder? "I thought perhaps you wanted more time to think about it. I'd love to meet . . ."

"Look, they wouldn't come anyway. They know nothing about you. Honestly, they'd probably see you as an interloper, someone trying to get her hands on their inheritance."

Whoa. She stared at him, speechless. Not only because of what he'd just said. That was startling enough. It was also the way he'd said it. Almost scolding her. He had never spoken to her so harshly before. What happened to the man who'd sung love songs to her on the balcony?

He exhaled. "Sorry, didn't mean to snap," he said more softly. "I just don't want to see you waste invitations on them. Aren't you already pressed when it comes to the list?"

She nodded. At least he had been quick to change his tune. "Apology accepted. And yes, very much so."

"There you have it."

She knew when to shut up. She had gone far enough with the boys. They ate in silence as the sky grew darker. Thunder clapped in the distance.

There was obviously a lot of pain surrounding Marcus and his sons and his first marriage. Perfectly understandable, given that his ex-wife had abandoned the three of them for another man. Even if it happened many years ago, it would be hard for a proud guy like Marcus to get past that kind of desertion.

"I appreciate your interest in them," he said. "I really do." He reached out to touch her hand. His eyes were tender. "When my ex-wife ran off, it was immeasurably difficult for us. I still had to work long hours. I probably didn't spend as much time with them as I should have to fill in the gap with their mother being absent. There was a lot of bitterness and resentment all around. But I got us through with help from babysitters and my mother. We don't have the coziest relationship now, and I pretty much leave them alone. It's better that way."

"You did the best you could under some trying circumstances."

"They know where to find me if they need me."

"And they've never heard from their mother in all these years?"

He shook his head. "I waited three years to file for divorce. I kept hoping she would come back, more for the sake of the boys than me. Then I had to prove to the judge that I made a genuine effort to find her. I sent letters to her employer, her family and friends. I searched on the internet, published notices. Never found a trace of her. After a certain amount of time elapsed without any contact, I got a hearing and was granted a divorce."

"So, she just vanished. Into thin air?"

"Well, I wouldn't say that. She's out there somewhere."

"Could she . . . I mean, it's horrible to think, but could she be dead?"

"There haven't been any signs of that."

It all sounded so gruesome, like something that would happen in a horror or suspense movie. But she had heard of people disappearing. At a previous job, a coworker's husband had walked out one afternoon to get a haircut and a decade later still hadn't returned.

"That must have been really hard on the boys. They were so young."

"It was bad. I never told them she ran off with someone else.

That would have made things ten times worse for them. I just said she left without an explanation."

How chivalrous of him, she thought, to want to protect the boys' feelings about their mother despite the horrible things she had done to him. She toyed with her Brussels sprouts as rain pummeled the sliding glass door. It was a lot to digest. She sensed that he was also deep in thought.

Still, she had something else to ask. "Marcus, um, one more question."

He sat back in his chair, holding his wineglass. "Why do I feel like I'm on the witness stand here?" he said jokingly.

She smiled. "Sorry."

"It's fine. Go on. It's natural to be curious about these things."

"When I walked in on you and Stanley earlier, I heard the name Claudia mentioned. I'm not sure if it was you or him who said it."

Marcus sat up, frowning. "Claudia?"

"Wasn't that the name of your ex-girlfriend? The one with you the night we met?"

"Whoa," he said. "No one said anything about a Claudia."

"I'm pretty sure that's what I heard, Marcus."

He shook his head firmly. "Nope, you didn't. Sorry, baby. You're mistaken."

"You're saying I heard wrong then?"

"Actually, I am. You said you weren't even sure who said it, right? Me or Stanley?"

She nodded slowly. "That's only because I can't always distinguish voices with my hearing aid."

"You need to turn that thing up then."

Ouch. That stung. She sat back in her chair, picking up her wineglass. She could have sworn she'd heard it. But Marcus insisted she hadn't. She didn't like his sarcastic comment, but this wouldn't be the first time she'd heard wrong. "If you say so. My mistake."

"So, interrogation over?" He smiled as he said it, but she could tell he was more than ready to move on. So was she. This was one of those times she was glad to have been wrong.

"Yes, over. Oh, I meant to tell you, I'm meeting Jeffrey tomorrow after work. I'll stop and get us dinner while I'm out. Chinese?"

"That's the bookkeeper at AASNC?"

"Yes."

"Will Michelle be joining the two of you?"

"She's leaving town tomorrow. Going to visit her family in Cincinnati."

"So, it will be just you and Jeffrey? Alone?"

Alexis sat up and put her glass back on the table. His probing questions made her a little tense. "Is that a problem?"

"You don't think so?"

She detected a patronizing tone that was cloying. "No. What's the big deal?"

"You're about to be married. Drinks with single men, not a good idea."

She couldn't believe she was hearing right. "I've known Jeffrey for years. He's engaged. Besides, he's not even my type."

"What is your type?" he asked.

"You are, silly."

He smiled. "Still, I don't like it. It's inappropriate. If Michelle or someone else were going with you, that would be one thing. But you and him alone? It's a bad idea."

"Are you telling me I can't go?"

He looked at her pointedly. "I'm asking you not to."

"Fine. If you feel so strongly. I don't get it, but I respect your feelings. How about I go tomorrow and make it the last time?"

His silence still said "no" loud and clear. She was stupefied. Marcus was older but not *that* much older. This conversation felt like something from her grandmother's era. "Don't you trust me?"

"Of course I trust you. It's him I'm not so sure about."

Suddenly, Paul popped into her head. Alexis swallowed hard. If Marcus knew how she had deceived him about Paul, it would be *her* he wouldn't trust. She had lied on their first date by telling Marcus she didn't have a boyfriend. Then she'd turned around and had sex with said boyfriend. Both huge errors in judgment. Her biggest fear in life these days was that Marcus would find out about Paul. And drop her.

"Fine," she said. "I'll cancel."

This had been the most contentious conversation ever for them. Still, their lovemaking after dinner was as tender as always. It was good to know that they could have strong disagreements and move on.

11

White or off-white? Long or short? Plunging neckline or something more demure? So many choices, Alexis thought as she sat in her bedroom and browsed a gazillion bridal gowns online. Too many choices. But this was her first marriage and, at thirty-seven, she was a more mature bride. She wanted her wedding dress to reflect that.

The planned trip to Baltimore to shop for dresses with Michelle had to be cancelled due to the stormy weather. Then the weekend had been full of engagements with Marcus. So, Sunday afternoon, after Marcus dropped her off at her apartment before heading to the driving range, she climbed on top of her bed and took to the cyber wires. She was surprised to find so much to her liking. She could order a dress and have it altered locally.

She was about to press send on a perfect off-white bead and lace number with a serious slit up the side—Marcus loved her athletic legs—when the doorbell rang. She was expecting Marcus again but not until later that evening, when he'd pick her up before they headed out to dinner and a movie. She closed the laptop in case he was arriving early. Bad luck and all for the groom to see the wedding dress ahead of time. She wasn't really superstitious, but why tempt fate? Better safe than sorry. Besides, she loved all the rules and traditions, the ceremoniousness and grandiosity of weddings. That was what made them fun and memorable. She dashed out to the living room in her bathrobe and placed her hand on the doorknob. At the last second, she paused and glanced through the peephole.

Her face went dark. She stepped back so fast she nearly tripped over her own bare feet. Paul was standing outside. Right there. At her door. Maybe it was her imagination, but he looked thin, haggard.

He was the last person she was expecting. She hadn't heard from him in weeks; he had even stopped texting. She knew because she'd blocked him for a few weeks, then unblocked him to see if he was still trying to reach her. He wasn't. She figured he'd finally gotten the message that they were done.

Her head throbbed something fierce. She rubbed both sides with her fingers. He had some nerve showing up here.

Thump! Thump!

She froze. Now he was knocking. Hard. Probably assuming that she had not heard the bell. Marcus was due any time. She wasn't sure what scared her more. Being alone with Paul or Marcus finding out about him. She had to get rid of Paul. Fast. She squeezed her fists at her sides, her fear quickly turning to anger. "Go away, Paul," she snapped.

She heard his deep voice respond but couldn't make out the words. She crept up and glanced through the peephole. "I'm not opening the door. Get out of here."

He signed. "You blocked me. I didn't have much choice."

Hell yes, you had a choice, she thought. He began to shout, and she struggled to make out the words. She was so sick of this. Sick of him. Throwing caution to the wind, she wrapped her robe tightly and undid the locks but kept the chain secured.

He peered at her through the crack with a weak, cheesy grin and awkwardly rubbed a hand across his scalp. "I just want to talk. Why won't you talk to me?"

Why the hell did he think? *You nearly killed me, you sick bastard.* She could barely stand the sight of him now. "If you don't leave this minute, I'm calling the police."

He simply ignored her and pushed on the door. The chain jerked and looked about ready to snap. It had been a big mistake to undo the locks. This man was nuts. Alexis pushed back with all her might, frantically trying to shove the door shut. He quickly stuck his sneaker in the gap.

Shit! She ran to the bedroom, grabbed her phone off the end table. She brought it back to the door and held it up so he could see that she meant business. "I'm texting them now," she said as she fake-dialed 911.

That was when she noticed it. *Her fat, shiny engagement ring.* Sitting there prominently on her third finger. She threw her left hand behind her back and twisted the diamond underneath. She looked at Paul. Thankfully, he hadn't seemed to notice. He was too intently focused on her face.

"Fuck, Alexis," he snapped. "Why are you doing this? All I need is . . ."

"Get out of here. Do you want to be arrested?" She was yelling now, loud enough for the neighbors to hear. On purpose.

Just then, Paul dropped his hands to his sides. He glanced down the hallway, as if he had heard something. A young couple with a small terrier walked quickly past him, staring strangely. Paul shoved his hands in his pockets, backing away. "Okay. Fine," he said. "If that's how you want to be." He turned and fled down the hallway.

Alexis slammed the door shut. Bolted it quickly. She dropped her phone gently to the floor, lifted her hands, and spread her fingers. They shook like Jell-O.

She slid down to the floor, her back against the wall. She had to get ahold of herself. Marcus would be here soon. He could not see her in this agitated state. How would she ever explain it? Hell, Marcus didn't even want her having lunch with other men. Never mind having slept with one.

And then another thought hit her. What if this behavior continued after she and Marcus were married? What if Paul told Marcus about them? Out of spite, jealousy, whatever. He could ruin everything.

She had to figure out how to get him to stop this obsessive madness. She grabbed her phone and dialed Michelle's number. Her older, wiser friend might have some suggestions. At the very least, Michelle could lend some emotional support, something she sorely needed right about now.

Michelle wasn't answering. She was still visiting her family and probably busy. The only other person who knew about Paul and his insane behavior of late was Jeffrey. He was analytical and good about getting right to the point. She had cancelled their plans at Marcus's insistence. That didn't mean she couldn't talk to him on the phone. She felt bad about going behind Marcus's back, but she was desperate. Besides, it was only a phone call. Marcus need never know.

She climbed back on the bed and dialed Jeffrey on FaceTime. He picked up immediately, filling the screen with his dimpled smile. He was wearing his glasses, which meant he may have been working from home.

"I hope I'm not interrupting anything important," she said.

"Not at all," he signed, removing his glasses. "What's going on?"

She jumped up and paced the floor with her phone, trying to soothe her rattled nerves. "I'm about to go out of my mind."

His eyes filled with concern. "Calm down. It's hard to hear with you moving all around."

She remembered Jeffrey's mild hearing loss. She sat down and exhaled. "It's Paul. He just came by."

Jeffrey raised his eyebrows with alarm. "What do you mean? He was there?"

"Yes. Not inside. I didn't let him in, but he came to the door. I had to threaten to call the police to get him to leave."

Jeffrey frowned. "What the hell is wrong with that dude?"

"I don't know." She made the universal sign for crazy, twirling her forefinger around near her head.

"You want me to come by?"

Alexis shook her head. It was nice of him to offer but no way, she thought. Not with Marcus due to arrive any minute. "I'll be okay. Marcus will be here soon."

"You should file a restraining order. I'm serious."

"I thought about it, but that will mean lawyers and court hearings. I worry that Marcus could find out what's going on."

"So? I'm surprised you haven't already told him. If someone were harassing my fiancé, I'd want to know about it."

Alexis hesitated, remembering that although Jeffrey knew that Paul had nearly choked her to death, he wasn't aware that she had slept with Paul early in her relationship with Marcus. In other words, Jeffrey didn't know she had cheated on Marcus with Paul. It was shameful, but she decided to go ahead and fill Jeffrey in so he would understand all that was going on. They were fast becoming friends at work since he and Michelle had come by the apartment the day Paul attacked her. Still, she braced herself for a negative reaction for her crummy behavior. She deserved it.

"Now I get it," Jeffrey said when she was done explaining.

"It was a dumb thing to do," she said. "I really regret it. I should have ended it with Paul a lot sooner."

He nodded. "I admit I'm surprised. It doesn't sound like you."

She sighed with regret. And a little embarrassment.

"But now it's important for you to protect yourself," he said. "You might still be able to file quietly without Marcus finding out about it."

Alexis so appreciated him for not judging her harshly. But she shook her head defiantly. "I can't take that risk."

"Your safety is involved."

"Maybe, maybe not. Paul's acting nuts but . . ."

"That's an understatement," Jeffrey said, interrupting.

"True, but I doubt he would harm me." She had calmed down somewhat; she felt like she was coming to her senses. It was important to protect her relationship with Marcus. "Besides, that would aggravate him. I really just want him to go away. Given time, he will."

Jeffrey looked at her doubtfully. "I think you're making a mistake."

"You don't know Paul like I do," she said.

"I know he choked you. You almost passed out. That's all I need to know to understand that he's dangerous."

Alexis had to admit that moment alone with Paul in her apartment had been the most frightening of her life. She got chills now just thinking back. "True. But he's never done anything remotely like that before. It was way out of character for him. He'll calm down eventually."

Jeffrey sighed and shook his head, as if realizing that he wasn't going to change her mind. "Promise me that if he does anything else to frighten you, that you'll file. That includes showing up at your door uninvited. Jeez."

She nodded. "I will."

After they hung up, she propped a chair against the door for extra security. She dug her old baseball bat out of the rear corner of her bedroom closet and placed it on the bed. Only then did she head for the bathroom to get ready for her date with Marcus.

PART 2

12

The swanky Country Club Mansion outside Baltimore featured a sweeping grand staircase, gleaming crystal chandeliers, and an elegant tulle-draped ceiling. Following the wedding ceremony and a four-course meal including fettuccine with salmon and custard soufflé cake, guests jammed through the evening on an expansive three-thousand-square-foot dance floor.

Alexis and Marcus were no exception. They spent hours shaking their booties and greeting guests. She couldn't stop smiling as he twirled her around the dance floor in her bead and lace gown. He generally preferred quiet dinners and the theater, so this was a welcome treat. She loved watching him dance in his all-black tuxedo. His movements were fluid, graceful, rhythmic.

Her dad eventually grabbed her by the hand and took her out, showing that he could still bust a few moves despite his seventy years. Her parents, John and Loretta, had arrived a week earlier to help with last-minute preparations. And for a chance to get to know Marcus. Their first meeting with him had been over dinner in Baltimore at Ruth's Chris Steak House—her father's favorite restaurant. They'd also spent an evening at Marcus's townhome.

Although courteous around Marcus, when alone with Alexis, her mother and father both expressed reservations. They thought she was rushing into things; it had been only six months since she'd met him.

"Are you sure you're ready for this?" Loretta had asked over lunch at a local diner in Laurel, Maryland, a few days earlier. They had just picked up Alexis's wedding gown from the seamstress. Alexis wore black jeans and a leather jacket. Still, her always well-groomed mother had been dressed in a wool suit, one she had probably owned for a couple of decades. Not a strand of her pearls or short hairdo were out of place. She believed in taking advantage of every youthful product she could get her hands on short of surgery—Botox, filler, black hair dye. She looked much younger than a retired schoolteacher of sixty-eight. Alexis's father was also a smooth dresser, nearly always wearing slacks with a matching or coordinating jacket. His slightly paunchy waistline, though, was that of a retired police officer who had finally given in to his hearty appetite.

"Yeah, what's the rush?" John had asked between bites of his Reuben sandwich and french fries. "If he's serious about you, he'll stick around even if you wait a few more months."

"She needs to wait longer than that," Loretta said.

Alexis was surprised by their strong reactions given that her parents had gotten hitched after even less time knowing each other. "I don't get it. You and Mama got married after four months."

"And it was hard, especially the early years," Loretta said. "We separated once or twice, you know."

Alexis gave her mother a double take as her dad took a big gulp of his Diet Coke. No, she didn't know. "You never told me that."

"Yes, well, you were never about to marry someone you just met," Loretta said.

Alexis shifted uncomfortably in her seat. She didn't like hearing that her parents' marriage had once been troubled. It immediately brought vague memories to mind of her mom crying alone in the bedroom during her father's frequent absences. Her mother had always said he was away on business trips. It wasn't until Alexis was college age that she realized cops didn't go on lengthy business trips several times a year.

As an only child, she hadn't had siblings to keep her company. She could remember attempting to climb into bed with her mother at around age five during a particularly bad snowstorm when her father was away and being hastily sent back to her room. That was so unlike what she experienced when her dad was home and they were both always welcoming. She had spent many nights snuggled securely between the two of them. Her mother's actions on that snowy night had taken her by surprise. She'd felt confused, hurt. She'd cried herself to sleep. The next morning, she woke up determined never to climb into their bed again.

The way her mother often turned into a different person when her father wasn't around in those early years had always puzzled Alexis. What had set her mother off? Why? Alexis had always assumed her mother just missed her father so terribly when he was away that she couldn't help herself. Now she wondered whether there may have been more to it than that. Could her mother's odd behavior have been related to Daddy giving her grief in the way too many unfaithful husbands do? In a way that no child wants to believe of their father?

"Well, things turned out okay for you two, obviously," Alexis said, trying to steer the conversation in the diner toward more pleasant thoughts.

"We were a lot younger than you and Marcus, in our early twenties," Loretta said. "We grew together. You could even say we grew up together. You're both much older and already set in your ways."

"Whatever happened to that last brother you were dating?" John asked. "Paul?"

Alexis bit her bottom lip.

"You two were together, what, more than a year?" Loretta continued.

That just went to prove you never really knew who you were dealing with, no matter the length of the relationship, Alexis thought. "It didn't work out."

"What happened?" Loretta asked.

"It's a long story." No way was she going to tell her parents what had transpired with Paul. They would worry sick about her safety. Her father, ever the police officer even though retired, might even dig him up and give him a piece of his mind. The last thing she needed was for her father to get Paul even more riled up. "Give yourselves time to get to know Marcus. He treats me so well."

"He does from what I can see," Loretta said. "I'll give you that. Very charming. He seems to adore you."

Alexis smiled.

John seemed skeptical. "They're always charming in the beginning. Tell me you still think he's charming a year from now. Then maybe I'll believe it."

Alexis had reached out and touched her father's arm. "We'll be fine."

Her father twirled her around on the dance floor during the wedding reception. When Jeffrey cut in, her dad dragged her mom out as Marcus and Michelle entered the dance floor together. Next thing Alexis knew, the band jumped into an Afro-Cuban beat, and they all broke away from their partners to join the conga line making its way around the room.

The band broke into a line dance number, and that's when Marcus begged off. "Not my thing," he claimed. So, she and Jeffrey joined in, swaying to the music, until they noticed Michelle beckoning animatedly from the sidelines. How strange, Alexis thought, frowning, as they quickly left the dance floor. Michelle asked them to follow her out into the foyer. Alexis scanned the ballroom for Marcus. She wanted to let him know she was stepping out for a minute. But she couldn't locate him among the throng of people.

"It's quieter out here," Michelle explained as they moved near the grand staircase. "I have to tell you something." She looked directly at Alexis. That's when Alexis noticed the worried expression on her friend's face.

"What's going on?" Jeffrey asked.

Alexis was silent. She almost didn't want to know the answer. The day had been flawless to this point, far better than she had hoped given all the hectic last-minute arrangements. Was it too much to ask that it end that way, too?

"Please don't bring me bad news," Alexis said.

Michelle sucked her breath in. "Sorry. It's all my fault. I just heard from Paul."

Alexis's heart jumped. That was the last name she wanted to hear. It was like a curse. And why did Michelle say, "It's all my fault?" *What* was her fault?

"You mean he called you?" Jeffrey asked.

Michelle shook her head. "He was here."

"Here, as in here at the mansion?" Jeffrey asked.

"Yes, outside." Michelle looked at Alexis. "I'm so sorry."

Alexis shook her head in stunned confusion. What the heck was Paul doing here? How did he even find out about the wedding?

She sure hadn't told him. Then she noticed that the anxious expression on Michelle's face was tinged with something else. Guilt. And she knew. "You told him, didn't you?"

"Yes," Michelle said weakly. "I mean, no, I didn't tell him the date or where. I just told him you were getting married."

"When?"

"A couple of weeks ago. I assume he found an announcement in the paper or online somewhere."

"Dammit," Alexis whispered under her breath. "How could you? Why are you even talking to him?"

"I don't know. He kept calling me. Wanting to know how you were doing. If you were still with Marcus. He's so in love with you. He seemed hopeful that you two might be able to work things out. I felt sorry for him, but when you and Marcus got engaged, I told him, thinking he would finally move on. I never expected this."

Alexis was horrified. Was she hearing her friend correctly? "What is wrong with you? Have you forgotten what he did to me?"

"Of course not. But good people make bad mistakes. He really regrets what happened. He . . ."

Alexis held her hand up to Michelle's face, palm out, to silence the insane words coming from her lips. "Please, Michelle. I don't know what's going on with you, but I damn sure don't want to deal with this nonsense now. Not on my wedding day." She shook her head with exasperation. This was the absolute worst she could imagine. Paul knew she was married. He likely knew who she had married. Perhaps even knew where they would live. It certainly wouldn't be hard for him to find out now that he probably knew Marcus's last name. "Now you see just how nuts this man is. I can't believe you could be so freaking stupid."

"I was only trying to help," Michelle said.

Alexis cut her eyes. "Pfft!"

"There's no point fussing about it now," Jeffrey said. "Is he still out there?"

"I'm pretty sure he left," Michelle said. "At least I hope so. He started texting me about twenty minutes ago asking all these questions. *What time would the wedding be over? How many people were here?* I got the feeling he might actually be here the way he was talking. So I looked out the back door. That's when I saw him pacing around the parking lot near his car. He didn't see me, so I went and got the security guard to tell him he had to leave. You know there's a guard here?"

Alexis nodded. "Marcus hired him."

"So, Marcus knows about Paul now?" Jeffrey asked.

"No. He knows nothing about Paul. He just thinks you can't be too safe these days with everyone having guns and all the mass shootings."

"That was smart of Marcus," Michelle said. "Seeing that beefy security guy probably got Paul to leave in a hurry. But I thought you should know he was here."

"He's obsessed with you," Jeffrey said.

"I'm starting to agree with Jeffrey," Michelle said. "You should tell Marcus before Paul does something else weird."

Alexis shook her head. "The last thing I need is for Marcus to find out about him. My biggest worry is that Paul will say something to him. I have nightmares about it."

"I doubt he'll say anything to Marcus," Michelle said.

"How can you be so sure of that, Michelle? Did you ever think he would choke me half to death?" She didn't want to snap at her friend, but she was furious with her.

Michelle twisted her lips. "No. But what would be the point in him doing that?"

"Just to be spiteful. To get back at . . ." Alexis paused as Jeffrey tapped her arm and pointed toward the main entrance. For a split second, Alexis was sure it was Paul returning to the reception to cause a scene. She turned, bracing herself for the worst. At least Jeffrey and Michelle were there with her. Instead, she was surprised to see a very familiar-looking man in his twenties stroll through the double doors of the main entrance.

"He looks just like Marcus," Michelle said, taking the words out of Alexis's mouth. This was a shorter, younger version of her husband. Maybe a touch more handsome, with a silky-smooth complexion. He was dressed casually but stylishly in blue jeans, a collared shirt, and a black leather bomber jacket.

"He must be related to Marcus," Jeffrey said.

Alexis recognized the young man from the few photos Marcus had of his sons. Had Marcus changed his mind and invited them at the last minute? "It's his oldest son, Owen," Alexis said.

"He's cute," Michelle said. "Have you met him before?"

Alexis ignored the question. "You two should go on back in. I'll be there shortly."

She approached the young man as he started to make his way toward the ballroom entrance. "Hello. You must be Owen. I'm Alexis." He paused and stared at her coldly. An odd expression crossed his face, one she couldn't quite place. One that made her uncomfortable. Apprehension? Anger? Fear?

He seemed to quickly recover, and she caught a brief, reluctant-looking smile.

She extended a hand. "I'm glad you came. I've been wanting to meet you. And your brother."

Owen's lips tightened. He looked at her doubtfully. Said nothing.

She took her hand back. "Um, did your father reach out to you? Tell you about the wedding?"

He looked at her incredulously. Guffawed scornfully. "Hell no."

Alexis blinked. The reaction was acrid, unexpected. It seemed things were every bit as bad between them as Marcus had made them out to be. Or worse. "I see."

"I saw an announcement," he signed before she could ask how he'd learned about it. "Was curious."

A million questions popped into Alexis's head. It wasn't surprising that he knew sign language; his grandmother had been deaf. But how did he know to sign *with her*?

"You knew I was hearing impaired?" she asked.

"Where the hell have you been? You can learn anything about anybody on social media these days."

She nodded. He had a point there. "So, what were you curious about?"

"I wanted to see who he got to replace my mother." He looked Alexis up and down. "I wasn't expecting to run straight into you like this. You're attractive, but she was a lot prettier."

Alexis swallowed hard. Took a deep breath. "I'm so sorry about what happened with her."

He shoved his hands in his jacket pockets. "And just what did he tell you?"

"Um. About your mother? That . . . that she ran off."

Another scornful chuckle. "So, he's filling you with that crap, too? Not surprised."

Alexis shook her head, dumbfounded, unsure how to respond.

Owen leaned down toward her. Got in her face. She wanted to take a step back but didn't. "My mom would never have left me and my brother. No fucking way."

She gasped. More so at the tone than the words. Of course that was what he believed, Alexis thought. She should never have mentioned his mother. Should have kept her big, stupid mouth shut. "I . . . I understand. I . . ."

The door to the ballroom swung wide open, and Marcus

stepped out. He did not look pleased. Alexis wasn't sure whether to be relieved to see him or worried. She certainly was curious to see these two interact.

Marcus brushed by her, almost as if she was not present. He walked directly up to Owen, who by now had taken a few steps away from Alexis. "You shouldn't be here," Marcus said.

Alexis was startled that he was so blunt. So hardened. Yes, their relationship was strained, but still, this was his son. This was their wedding day. Couldn't he ease up this once? She gently touched Marcus's arm. "It's okay. He can stay."

"Let me handle this," Marcus said to her curtly, never taking his eyes off Owen.

"It's not a problem," Owen said, backing further away, a nervous but defiant expression on his face. "I had no intention of staying anyway. Saw what I wanted to see. I'm out of here." He gave Alexis one last glance, turned abruptly, and left.

She looked up at Marcus, trying to make sense of what had just unfolded. Obviously, the relationship was far more strained than she'd ever imagined. It was sad to see. "Are you okay?"

He glanced down as if seeing her for the first time since entering the foyer. He put his arm around her shoulders, kissed her forehead. "It's best that he left."

She nodded. Probably true given Owen's mood and behavior. "He said his mother would never have left him and his brother."

"Naturally that's what he thinks. No child wants to believe their mother would willingly abandon them."

Alexis nodded. "What does he think happened to her?"

Marcus shrugged. "That she was in an accident somewhere. Or that she was abducted. He wanted me to launch an all-out search for her. Hire detectives, all that. I kept telling him that made no sense. She left willingly. If she wanted to come back, she would."

"And Aaron. What does he think?"

"Aaron was more accepting of the truth. But I haven't heard much from him since he moved out West several years ago."

Alexis realized that she was going to have to accept that Marcus was not close to his children and probably never would be.

"C'mon," he said. "Let's go back in. Everyone will wonder where we are."

They held hands and reentered the ballroom. But it didn't feel the same. A short while ago, she'd been dancing at her wedding with the man of her dreams, about to embark on a life of hope, excitement, happiness.

Then along came a resentful ex-boyfriend—thanks to her inconsiderate, blabbermouth girlfriend—and an embittered son. Was it an omen?

13

Alexis's mood after the craziness of her wedding day brightened considerably the closer they got to the shimmering shores of South America. As soon as they landed at Rafael Núñez International Airport, the private car and driver Marcus had hired whisked them off on a picturesque fifteen-minute drive to Cartagena. She could immediately sense why this was considered one of the most romantic cities in the world, her eyes eagerly soaking up the narrow cobblestone streets, colorful houses draped with pink bougainvillea, and rich orange, yellow, and aqua-colored buildings adorned with charming Juliet balconies.

The driver dropped them off at their boutique hotel in the Old Town, a part of the city built behind great stone walls during the sixteenth century to protect against repeated vicious pirate attacks. As Marcus had explained to her during the flight, the most famous of the many buccaneers to plunder the once wealthy city was none other than Sir Francis Drake, who had destroyed nearly a quarter of the town. Some believed Cartagena was the inspiration for the film, *Pirates of the Caribbean*.

Alexis found Marcus's tales of the violent history of the area chilling but intriguing. And you would never know it now. The interior of their hotel was nothing short of magical, decorated with soft earthy tones and colorful artwork. The crown jewel was an enticing courtyard with a mosaic tile pool and plush white lounge chairs. Marcus pointed out that the hotel had formerly been a collection of colonial houses that were combined and restored to create the sense of staying in a large private home.

The friendly staff at the front desk filled them in on the best street food vendors, shopping, and lively night spots nearby. Alexis was in for more treats as the bellhop opened the door to a suite adorned with wood beamed ceilings and a massive picture window overlooking sumptuous greenery and the deep aquamarine of the Caribbean Sea beyond. They spent that first evening dining on seafood at a highly rated restaurant nearby. Then they returned to the suite and lounged in their private garden. As Alexis gazed out at the palm trees and stars with her handsome husband beside her, she felt like she'd died and gone to heaven.

After a leisurely breakfast at the hotel the next morning, they spent the day browsing historic sites and sampling the empanadas and fruit juices that could be found at street stands on nearly every corner. That night, they dined and listened to music at a trendy restaurant overlooking the glittering city and sea beyond. In the days following, they hit beaches in the morning and visited museums in the afternoon. One of her favorite spots was The Sanctuary of St. Peter Claver, a Spanish Jesuit priest and missionary who'd dedicated his life to treating and ministering to enslaved Africans, located in a church dating from 1580.

The only downside to their glorious getaway were the calls constantly setting off Marcus's phone, sometimes hourly, prompting him to excuse himself in restaurants, on the beach, even inside the church. This was their honeymoon, for goodness' sake, she kept reminding him with more than a little annoyance. Whenever she complained, he simply brushed it off with a regretful smile and insisted that it was business that couldn't wait. Which frustrated her even more.

The day before their departure, as she stood before the dresser mirror pinning up her hair—the heat and humidity had done a real number on it—Marcus suddenly announced that he was dashing off to a nearby golf course to practice his swing. Alexis was baffled. She stopped brushing and stared at him. "You don't even play that often at home. Why now? On our last full day here?" She was whining, she knew, but she couldn't help it. This was unbelievably disappointing.

"It's a beautiful course. I go every time I come to Cartagena."

"But you weren't on your honeymoon before."

Just then, his phone rang. *Again.* Alexis moaned out loud. "Can you please shut that thing off?"

Amazingly, he glanced at the screen and did just that, then shoved the phone back into his pocket. "I won't be long, I promise," he said as he strolled out of the bedroom. She followed, now curious about who had just called. She didn't get a chance to ask. He kissed her briefly on the lips and strode to the front door. "We'll have lunch at that place on the water you really liked," he said as he shut the door behind him.

For a moment, she stood, her eyes glued to the door, barely able to comprehend what had just transpired. Then she decided that rather than sit around the room moping and torturing herself trying to figure him out, she would get out. She could use some retail therapy, and Maria at the front desk had recommended a boutique nearby as a place to shop for the brightly colored tropical dresses she'd seen women wearing around the city. She slipped into a dress with spaghetti sleeves, grabbed her shoulder bag, and hit the cobblestone streets.

After picking up a couple of outfits, she walked around, taking in the vibrant sights and sounds, until she came across Ábaco Libros y Café, a small but charming bookstore. She ducked inside, as much to check out their stock as to escape the muggy Colombian heat. The shop was delightful, bursting with volumes stacked from floor to ceiling, and instantly lifted her spirits. After browsing for about forty-five minutes, she picked out the English version of a novel by a Colombian author and a coffee-table book with dazzling photographs of the city.

Believing that Marcus would be out at least another hour, she ordered a latte at the bar and sat at a small table with her new novel and cup of fresh Colombian brew. She loved the friendly vibe and the rustic decor, she thought as she admired the exposed brick surrounding the bookshelves. The rhythm of the entire city was so lively; she only wished Marcus had come with her. He would have enjoyed this place. Then again, maybe he had been here before on one of his earlier visits. Now that she thought about it, she wondered exactly who had accompanied him on those trips. Probably a woman. It was such a romantic destination. A business trip seemed unlikely.

Her own job had been becoming more a source of aggravation than happiness or even contentment week by week. Some days she struggled to get out of bed and make the drive in, usually when she knew there would be yet another long, boring, unproductive meeting. To make matters worse, her relationship with Michelle had chilled drastically. They spoke cordially enough when needed, but that was about it. No more leisurely lunches. No more almost daily phone calls and texts.

She couldn't shake the nagging feeling that Michelle secretly had feelings for Marcus. Extra feelings. There was something different in her expression whenever his name was mentioned. Then there was the time Marcus had taken her to lunch a week before the wedding. Michelle walked by, saw him sitting in her office, and stopped in to say hello. That part was perfectly fine. That part was normal. What wasn't fine or normal was all the batting of her eyelashes and fondling of her hair at she gazed adoringly at him. Alexis had been shocked. Floored. This was above and beyond anything she'd seen before from Michelle. What had gotten into her? She understood that Michelle had been lonely since her husband's death, but that was no excuse. She hadn't said anything to Michelle or Marcus. Pointing it out would have embarrassed them all. She'd simply suggested to Marcus that it was time to leave for lunch.

After Michelle's questionable behavior at the wedding, Alexis even found herself wondering if she had tried to encourage Paul to think they could get back together in hopes that it would free up Marcus. Was she being unnecessarily suspicious? Perhaps. In fact, she would give anything to have her suspicions be wrong. She didn't want to think that Michelle would have encouraged Paul to pursue her for any reason knowing what he had done. She didn't want to think Michelle had that in her. Yet, she had a hard time shaking the persistent doubts.

She was looking forward to getting together with Natasha, a friend and former co-worker at AASNC, when they returned home. She and her husband Derrick were a fascinating couple. He was a physician with an interest in public health who'd landed work in Tanzania as part of a CDC program a few years back. Natasha had quit her job to travel with him, but she and Alexis had kept in touch.

She had actually been closer to Natasha than Michelle before Natasha took off for Africa. She and Natasha were more alike, both quieter and more introverted than Michelle, and they shared a similar sense of humor. Natasha could be a hoot at times with a quirky but endearing way of finding humor in the most mundane situations. She also had a hearing loss. At one time, it had been more severe than Alexis's. But several months before Natasha left, she got a cochlear implant. She wanted to be able to hear her best before moving to a foreign country. Alexis remembered her taking off work for a couple weeks and then waiting another month for the incision to heal before the implant was turned on. Then, Natasha's hearing had improved noticeably. She was able to understand better in meetings and on the phone. She'd joked that she now had bionic ears and encouraged Alexis to have the surgery.

"It will change your life," Natasha had said, abruptly switching topics as they sat in Alexis's office on Natasha's last day at work. They had been talking about Natasha's Afro, recently trimmed to less than an inch long in preparation for living where water and electricity could sometimes be in short supply.

Alexis shook her head firmly. "I'm happy for you, but I'm not ready for all that. Was the recovery painful?"

"Yeah, it was rough for a few days. I won't lie. Painkillers helped. And you have to change the dressing a lot."

"See. I live alone. I wouldn't want to deal with that all by myself."

"You could get your mother or someone to stay with you for a few days. After that, you could manage."

"Maybe if my hearing keeps getting worse, I'll consider it. I'm fine for now."

Natasha and Derrick had moved back to the DC metro area in late fall. They attended the wedding, where she and Natasha chatted for several minutes and agreed to meet up for lunch once Alexis returned from the honeymoon.

Alexis's co-worker Jeffrey was a real sweetheart, very support-ive and easy to get along with. She couldn't meet with him after work because of Marcus's old-fashioned notions about marriage, but she did slip out for lunch with him now and then. He had pretty much replaced Michelle as her best office buddy. Still, Jeffrey could never take the place of having a close girlfriend to gab and share the most intimate thoughts with.

When Alexis arrived back to the hotel suite and entered the bedroom, Marcus was standing at the picture window talking on the phone, his back to the door. She had planned to drop her packages on the bed and wait for him to end the call so she could tell him all about the bookstore. Until she realized that whomever Marcus was speaking to was shouting, barely allowing her new husband to get a word in. She frowned. Anytime she could hear someone through the phone, that someone had to be yelling. Really loudly. She couldn't understand what was being said but she picked up the angry, strident tone. Thinking it could be one of his clients, she quickly turned back toward the sitting room to give him some privacy.

But then she thought of the many phone calls interrupting their honeymoon. One after the other. Could they all have been business calls?

Instead of walking away, she stood just beyond the doorway, carefully out of sight, and strained to hear. Not surprisingly, she couldn't make out much. Just Marcus's raised voice and what sounded like a bunch of mumble jumble. Sure, it could be an irate client he was arguing with. But knowing that didn't stop her mind from darting to all the wrong places, such as Paul cheating on her with a previous girlfriend. Or believing she had heard the name Claudia when she'd entered Marcus's office that day as he met with Stanley. Could all the phone calls be signs of a romantic entanglement that Marcus was having on the side?

She reluctantly slid away from the doorway, tossed her packages onto a table, and sat on the couch. She took deep breaths in and out, determined to banish the dirty thoughts from her head. They had just gotten married. No one would cheat this soon.

Marcus was likely just on with a difficult client, perfectly normal for an attorney.

She picked up her newly acquired coffee-table book and flipped through the pages full of sights around Cartagena, trying to clear her head and calm the anxiety creeping up by the minute as she wondered who he was talking to. Nearly half an hour later, he finally entered the sitting room. As he leaned down to kiss her on the cheek, she realized she was chewing her bottom lip. She released it.

"Looks like your shopping trip was a success," he said, sitting down beside her.

She nodded. Tried to smile.

"So, what did you do today?" he asked.

"Walked around. Found a lovely bookstore." She pointed to the name on her shopping bag. "Have you been there?"

He glanced at the bag, shook his head. "Don't think I have."

"I wish you could have gone there with me. Maria at the front desk said it's very popular and well-known."

"We'll have to check it out together next time."

"Mm hmm. How was golfing?"

"Wonderful. It's one of the most stunning courses I've seen."

She nodded, her mind still stuck on the phone call. She wanted to move on but couldn't. Why so many calls all week long? Why all the yelling? "Is everything okay? Any problems at work?"

He stared at her, a puzzled expression on his face.

"I thought I heard someone shouting on your phone when I came in."

"Oh, that. One of my clients was complaining about something to do with his billing. Boring stuff for you but it comes with the territory. Nothing unusual. We'll work it out. So, have you given more thought to what we talked about yesterday?"

He had deftly changed the subject, but she decided to let it slide. His explanation was plausible, and she was probably overly fearful when it came to these things, given the cheating in her recent past. She certainly wanted to believe him. At least he hadn't tried to deny what she'd heard. Relax, she told herself.

"I have. Still thinking about it." For weeks now, he had been trying to persuade her to leave her job. He felt she didn't need to work full-time since he made more than enough to support them both. Although she hadn't brought it up, she was pretty sure it also had to do with his antiquated views about marriage roles. Man: breadwinner. Wife: home.

"What's holding you back?" he asked. "You don't even like it there anymore."

"I like it fine. Not as much as I once did. But I don't hate it." There was something essential about getting up every day and going out to earn a living. It made her feel self-sufficient, independent. She wasn't ready to give that up. Although she felt closer to Marcus with each passing day, they had known each other barely seven months. What if the marriage crashed and burned? He was a lawyer. Not someone you'd want to go up against in a divorce. She would be a fool to ever think she could count on any kind of alimony. She *didn't want* to count on alimony.

But Marcus was nothing if not persistent when he wanted something. He had even offered to have a postnuptial agreement drawn up that would ensure she'd get X number of dollars should they break up after at least a year of marriage.

"I worry that I'll get bored without a job to go to every morning."

He shrugged. "You could work on your novel full-time. Or do volunteer work with children with disabilities. Or both. You would probably find yourself busier than ever."

He put his arm around her and squeezed her shoulders. If he was trying to reassure her, he was doing a good job. She smiled.

"And I'm redoing the entire house. That's going to take a lot of time."

His eyes grew wide. "The entire house? Not sure the whole house needs redoing. Maybe just the main level. I've already done my office."

"The bedrooms and baths upstairs could use a facelift. Drapes, paint. I think we should switch the wall-to-wall carpeting to hardwood throughout and update the tile in all three and a half baths. And I'd love to replace the carpet in the rec room downstairs with an earthy Spanish tile." She smiled. "Cartagena is rubbing off on me."

His chuckle sounded more uneasy than anything. He had made it sound like the sky was the limit when it came to fixing up the house. Now he seemed to be backing off. "I thought that was what you wanted, Marcus. A complete renovation. Top to bottom."

He squeezed her shoulder. "Whew! Let's talk about it when we get back. I don't want to get into any disagreements. Not now."

This was perplexing to say the least, she thought. Why had he changed his mind? She took a breath. She'd let it go, just as she had the heated phone call. Sometimes she thought she was too passive with Marcus. But this was their honeymoon. She wanted it to end on a good note. On that they agreed. "That's fine."

14

It was Alexis's final day at the offices of Arts and Athletics for Special Needs Children. As she boxed the framed photo of Marcus, she thought how surreal it all felt. After spending more than eight hours a day, five days a week, in this building for six years, she would never again set foot in here. She folded the handknitted wool sweater from her mother that she kept draped across the back of her swivel chair. A part of her was really going to miss this tiny but oh-so-familiar office and the lunchroom where she and her co-workers often gathered and gossiped about everything under the sun. But she wasn't complaining. Spending lots more "me time" doing the things she loved, like writing and volunteering for organizations and causes she believed in, sounded good to her. She was lucky to be in this position.

She had slipped out of the conference room, where a big send-off party for her was in full swing, to pack these few last-minute items. Her co-workers had moved the big table up against the wall and filled it with sandwiches and salads from Wegmans and cakes from a local bakery. More than forty staff members had showed up as well as a few of her long-standing clients. Like her star pupil, a young deaf woman named Angel who first came to the attention of AASNC when she was twelve; she was assigned to Alexis. Angel had been painfully shy with low self-esteem. She was now going on nineteen, a star basketball player and straight A student at a local community college. Alexis beamed with pride as Angel stood and gave a short speech, raving about how much Alexis had helped her boost her confidence to become a winner.

She walked back into the party; Jeffrey called everyone to attention to speak about how they would all miss her even as they wished her well. Then the crowd glanced in the direction of Michelle sitting on the other side of the room, as if fully expecting to hear something similar, knowing how close the two of them had been. Alexis was mildly curious about exactly what Michelle would say, given that they were on strictly business terms of late.

Michelle stood from her seat, cleared her throat, and lifted her glass. She started speaking slowly and so softly that Alexis could barely hear her. Why on earth was Michelle talking this way, Alexis wondered? Was it intentional? She stepped closer to her with mounting annoyance. ". . . to one of the most hardworking people I've ever . . ." Michelle paused suddenly, and everyone followed her eyes to the sliding glass door as it swung wide open and Marcus strode in. Alexis smiled. So he had decided to come after all, she thought, thrilled that he had been able to get off work in the middle of the afternoon. She had barely taken a step in his direction when she heard Michelle's voice, now loud and clear. She glanced back to see a huge smile on Michelle's face.

"Here's the man of the hour," Michelle said. "Looking like a million bucks as always."

It was all Alexis could do not to go cross-eyed. Good grief, she thought. The woman sounded like she thought some megawatt celebrity had just entered the room. Alexis spotted Jeffrey and shot him an "I told you so" look. He smiled thinly and shrugged. Shortly after returning from the honeymoon a few weeks earlier, Alexis had confided in him about her suspicions that Michelle was smitten with her husband and asked if he had noticed it. Or if he thought she was just being paranoid. Jeffrey claimed he had not detected anything different or untoward in Michelle's behavior but promised to keep an eye out. Alexis wasn't entirely surprised—men were generally far less intuitive about these things.

She strolled up to Marcus and gave him a warm, slightly possessive hug and kiss on the lips. Then she looked back toward Michelle, expecting her to continue with her speech. But Michelle was nowhere in sight. How odd, Alexis thought. But she didn't want to waste time on her. She turned back to her husband and squeezed his hand. "You made it."

He squeezed back. "Of course. I know this is an important day for you."

Jeffrey approached with Kim, his fiancé, a petite, young-looking woman whom Alexis had assumed was about twenty, if that. She introduced Marcus and the four of them chatted about the usual small-talk topics that dominated social gatherings nowadays—the strange severe weather, pandemics, social issues.

"Want me to get you a bite to eat?" she asked Marcus during a lull in the conversation. He nodded and she slipped off to the refreshment table, her thoughts on Jeffrey's fiancé. She would never have pegged him as someone who liked women so young, she thought, as she picked out a cold cut sandwich, a slice of Bundt cake, and a small plastic cup of red wine. Then she turned to make her way back through the crowd toward Marcus. Only he wasn't where she'd left him. She frowned and struggled to balance the sandwich and cake in one hand, drink in the other. What the heck? Why would he walk off knowing she was returning with his food?

She stood on her toes, scanning the crowd until she saw him. And then dropped everything. Sandwich, cake, beverage all on the floor. At least that's what she imagined in her head when she saw Marcus standing in a corner of the room talking to Michelle. The two of them stood alone, chatting animatedly. Alexis could hardly believe her eyes. Michelle hadn't even been in the room a few minutes ago. Now she was wrapped around Marcus like a glove.

She steadied the food and drink and approached them. As she handed the sandwich to Marcus, she couldn't help but notice that something was different about Michelle's appearance. And then it smacked her. Michelle had changed her blouse. She didn't remember exactly what Michelle had been wearing before—something gray—but it was definitely not the clingy, bright white, low-cut top she was now showing off.

It took every ounce of restraint not to fling the red wine in Michelle's face—white top and all. Then she noticed that Michelle had also applied more makeup, including a siren red lip color. This was way different from her usual office look, consisting of a little blush and mascara. This was not even the touch-up job Michelle often applied when they went out for dinner or drinks after work. Not at all. This was the full-blown, glammed-up face with concealer, eyeliner, and shadow, usually reserved for big, fancy gatherings like their annual fundraiser.

Alexis didn't want to believe her eyes. What the hell had gotten into Michelle? She took a generous gulp of the wine.

"Here you go, honey," she said, pointedly interrupting Michelle's chatter as she handed Marcus his wine. She slipped a glimpse toward Jeffrey standing several feet away with Kim. His knowing return smile seemed to finally acknowledge what she had suspected all along. Michelle had the hots for her husband.

As Marcus sipped his drink, Michelle asked for legal advice

regarding a cousin who she thought was being sexually harassed by a superior at work. She pretty much ignored Alexis and even faced Marcus in a way that partially blocked her view. Alexis was convinced this was done purposefully, to make it difficult for her to understand and join in the conversation. And it was working, just as Michelle knew it would. Alexis could barely make out what they were saying other than a few words here and there. She wanted to interrupt, to say something smart and rude like, "Back off, bitch," or "What the hell is wrong with you?" She wanted to yank Michelle's big red bush and give her a piece of her mind. But she didn't want to look jealous or petty in front of Marcus. So, she stood there fuming, holding the slice of cake for him and suffering in silence as her husband and former friend continued their semi-private conversation.

Her mind wandered back to memories of Michelle announcing shortly after her husband died that she would never again get involved with a much older man. She had gone on and on about how younger wives eventually ended up as caretakers for their husbands at some point. She wanted her next man to be rich and not much older than she was. Marcus was only a few years older than Michelle. And also, rich.

She snapped back to the present as Michelle threw her head and laughed heartily. Marcus was smiling. What the fuck was so damn funny? Alexis wondered. It was everything she could do not to lash out. She found some of her bitterness slowly shifting from Michelle to Marcus as he stood there lapping in every drop of her coquettishness. He had to know what was going on by now. That he was being shamelessly flirted with. So why didn't he put a stop to it?

Alexis shifted from one heel to the other. She could not bear this a single second longer. "Michelle, I need to talk to you for a minute." Michelle turned and stared at her as if she had just been interrupted by an alien from outer space. "About what?"

"It's private. Let's go into my office."

Michelle blinked. "Uh. Okay. Fine."

Alexis touched Marcus's arm. "I'll be right back."

She led the way out of the conference room and into her soon-to-be former office. After shutting the door quietly, all the doubt and anxiety about confronting Michelle resurfaced.

"What's up?" Michelle said, placing her heavily ring-clad fingers on one hip as the two of them stood in front of Alexis's now barren desk. They couldn't sit, as both chairs were piled with boxes that she and Marcus would later load into their cars. Not that she and Michelle would have wanted to sit for this strained conversation anyway.

She faced Michelle and took a deep breath, summoning the courage she'd felt a moment ago. This woman, once a trusted confidante, was trying to seduce her husband. Right in front of her face. She needed to put her on notice. "Um, so, you've got a thing for Marcus now?" There. She'd said it. Straight up.

Michelle jerked her head back. Feigned innocence. "What are you talking about? Of course not."

Give me a break, Alexis thought. "You act all stupid whenever he's around. Out there just now, you can't take your eyes off him."

Michelle stood up straight. "That's ridiculous."

"You even changed your outfit when he got here. Put on all this makeup. Explain that."

"It just so happens that I'm going out after I leave work, so I decided to freshen up. Last I heard, that wasn't a crime. Not that I need to explain myself to you."

Alexis hesitated. She hadn't thought of that. They'd both gotten into the habit of keeping a couple of fresh, dressy tops in their offices for whenever they went out straight from work. Still, something did not feel right. "You're different around him. A lot more, I don't know, whorish." She wanted to take the word back as soon as it parted her lips. Sort of. Instead, she defiantly crossed her arms across her waist.

Michelle blinked. Hard. "Excuse me? Wow! I'm just being friendly."

Alexis pursed her lips doubtfully. "A *lot* friendly. *Too* friendly. You really need to back off."

"Are you serious?"

"Very."

"You're leaving. What the hell are you so worried about? I doubt I'll ever even see Marcus again after today anyway."

"I certainly hope not."

"Well, damn. I'll keep my distance from now on if it bothers you that much." Michelle marched to the door, grabbed the knob, and stomped out.

Alexis smacked her lips. The abrupt departure had caught her off-guard. But it was just as well. She'd made her point. Hopefully, Michelle meant what she said, and this would be the end of it.

She couldn't wait to get out of this place for good now, she thought as she walked back toward the conference room. Thankfully, Michelle and Marcus would never again cross paths after today. Thankfully, *she* would never again cross paths with Michelle after today. It was sad to lose a good friend but couldn't be helped, all things considered. Truth be told, she clearly hadn't been *that* good a friend, so maybe not so much of a loss. She wasn't even going to mention their talk to Marcus. If he asked, she would simply tell him it was something related to work. Like a lot of clueless men, he probably hadn't even noticed that Michelle was coming on to him.

15

As the wintery months rolled into spring, all her work redecorating the condo began to pay off. The living and dining rooms had been refurbished with newly polished hardwood floors and fresh coats of paint. The old furniture that Marcus had inherited from his mother had been replaced with sleek, contemporary pieces. The white kitchen appliances had been upgraded with stainless steel.

She'd had to plan and organize it all on her own, with only the help of a few home design magazines and websites. Initially, she'd hired an interior decorator, someone who came highly recommended. But Marcus quickly nixed that idea when she told him how many thousands it would cost, and no amount of cajoling or pleading would get him to change his mind. He didn't come right out and say it, but she distinctly got the impression that he figured he shouldn't have to pay a decorator when he had her.

Not only that, but she'd also had to defend every expense other than paint. And he had insisted she downgrade to a cheaper brand of that. She'd been forced to scale back on so many of her big ideas, like new kitchen countertops and cabinetry. Marcus had put his foot down, insisting there was nothing wrong with the old ones. So instead of the upscale mahogany cabinets she'd had her heart set on, she had to settle for simply refinishing the current maple ones and replacing the hardware. But what could she do? She was totally dependent on him when it came to finances, especially big-ticket items.

She quickly began to see Marcus in a whole new light when it came to money and began to fear that perhaps she'd quit her job too soon. She realized that although her husband brought in a solid living as an attorney, he was as tight as they came. He watched over every major expense like a hawk. Small ones, too. She was doing volunteer work three days a week with a deaf advocacy group, but now she was more determined than ever to find paid work. She needed her own money. Every minute she wasn't decorating the house or volunteering, she spent looking for a part-time job.

When the main level was far enough along, they decided it was time to show it off and invited Natasha and her husband for dinner. Marcus had met them at the wedding reception and was very impressed with Derrick and his passion for curbing diseases like HIV and malaria around the world. Their lively conversation took place over a meal consisting of roasted duck with a side dish of braised carrots, celery, and onions, all carefully prepared by Marcus with a little help from Alexis. She marveled at how good Natasha's hearing had become and how easily she kept up with the chatter. When Marcus went into the kitchen for more wine, Natasha could even make out some of what he was saying as Derrick continued to talk to him from the dining room. That would never have been possible before. Prior to the implant, Alexis had had better hearing. Now Natasha clearly heard best.

After the meal, Marcus invited Derrick down to his office to continue their discussion over his favorite brandy. Alexis and Natasha slipped into the living room with cups of hot tea.

"So, how's married life treating you?" Natasha asked, smiling as they settled in across from each other on the new contemporary couch. Natasha had always been laid-back and easygoing, never one to fuss over her appearance. Today she wore a simple pair of black slacks with an off-white top. Her short brown Afro, once barely an inch long, had grown out. Alexis also wore casual slacks along with a short-sleeve linen top.

"Good," Alexis said. "I'm getting used to it, you know. Busier than ever fixing up the house, volunteering, writing."

"I love what you've done here. It looks so fresh and modern." Natasha's eyes traveled to the small wooden African figurine that she and Derrick had given them as a wedding gift. Alexis had placed it prominently on the newly built shelves amid hardback and leather-bound books and other treasures that she and Marcus had accumulated over the years.

"Thanks. Still have a lot more to do upstairs. Then there's the rec room in the basement. But I'm enjoying it, and Marcus and I have similar tastes, fortunately."

"You mean he has taste?" Natasha said, chuckling. "Because I swear, Derrick couldn't care less what surrounds him as long as he has a roof over his head. I'm not even sure he needs that. It's a constant battle when we travel. I have to put my foot down and insist on the basics, like electricity, especially now that I have to charge the batteries to my implant every night. You're lucky that Marcus even cares."

Alexis smiled and nodded. No need to bring up his penny-pinching and the controlling ways beginning to creep up in their marriage, as much as she was tempted. They were still newlyweds; she didn't want to sound unhappy so soon. And she wasn't really unhappy. Maybe just a little disappointed. "Derrick is amazing in a lot of other ways," she said. "All the public health work he does."

Natasha nodded. "Yeah, he really is. He's the same kind, generous man he was the day we got married." She smiled and touched Alexis's arm gently. "Listen, I have some news to share."

Alexis leaned forward. Natasha was clearly excited.

"I'm pregnant."

Alexis's mouth dropped open. She leaned over and hugged Natasha. "Congratulations. I thought that might be why you asked for tea. How far along are you?"

"A little over three months. We just started sharing the news outside of our families. We wanted to be sure everything was, you know, going to be okay."

"I completely understand. That's so exciting."

"I'm looking forward to becoming a mom. Derrick will make an amazing dad. What about you two? Any plans for children?"

Alexis shook her head slowly. "Not really. He has two from his first marriage and doesn't want any more."

Natasha frowned. "And you're okay with that?"

"I'm more than okay. Although I admire and respect mothers for the important work they do—fathers, too—it's not for me." She didn't want to share all her negative thoughts about rearing children with an expectant mom.

"I get it. You'll probably change your mind after you've been married a while."

Alexis tightened her lips. "I doubt that."

"You say that now but . . ." Natasha shrugged.

"I'm really happy for you, though," Alexis said.

Natasha smiled. "Thank you so much! So, you mentioned writing. What are you working on?"

"Just dabbling with some ideas in my head. A novel."

"Oh. Interesting. What kind?"

"A mystery."

"Now that's fascinating. Your dad was a police officer. Yeah, I can see that. Can't wait to read it."

"I haven't had as much time to work on it as I'd like with all the other things going on, so it's been slow going. Even though I'm no longer at AASNC, I can't believe how fast my days fill up."

"How is Michelle?" Natasha asked. "I spoke to her briefly at your wedding. She looks good."

Alexis smiled stiffly. "Um, I'm sure she's fine. We don't talk much anymore, you know. In fact, not at all, to tell you the truth."

Natasha raised her eyebrows. "What happened?"

"It's kind of a long story."

Natasha leaned back. "We've got time. Unless it's something you don't want to share."

Alexis thought a moment. Natasha knew Michelle from work, of course. The three of them would sometimes go out to lunch together when Natasha was at AASNC. But since Natasha got married, she had never accompanied them on their little jaunts after office hours, and she and Michelle had never been friendly outside of work. Alexis decided to share a smidgen of what had happened. It would be good to confide in someone.

"It still feels strange," Alexis said. "Like something in a dream. Or a nightmare."

"Really?"

"I think she was starting to get feelings for Marcus. In fact, I know she was."

Natasha sat back. "You're talking romantic feelings?"

Alexis nodded. "Unfortunately, that would be a yes."

"But what made you think that? What did she do?"

"It became so obvious. Her face would light up whenever I talked about him. She flirted openly with him right in front of me. Not in the beginning. This happened over time. The more

I got involved with him and bragged about him, the more she seemed to latch on."

"Damn. Did you talk to her about it?"

Alexis realized that talking about it, releasing it, made her feel better. Other than briefly discussing it with Jeffrey, she hadn't told a single soul. "Not until the day of my going-away party. You wouldn't believe the way she came on to him. Batting her eyes. Ignoring me even when I was standing right there. I couldn't take it anymore. I took her to my office and told her I knew exactly what she was up to and that she needed to back off. She denied everything, of course."

Natasha shook her head with obvious disbelief.

"Even if she developed feelings for Marcus, she should have kept them to herself," Alexis said. "And stayed away from him. You don't do that to a good friend. That's just wrong."

"Facts," Natasha said. "What does Marcus think about all this?"

Alexis scoffed. "I don't think he even realized it was happening. You know how men are."

"Mmm, I actually think men are usually more in tune to this kind of thing than they let on. It could be that he didn't want to alarm you or cause problems with your friendship with her. But he was probably aware on some level. He may have figured he could handle her."

Alexis hadn't thought of that. "You know, you could be right." After all, Michelle's behavior at the office party had been brazen. Even Jeffrey had finally come around to realizing what was going on. Who knew how many other people had been aware? "I may ask him if he noticed it one of these days."

"You should. In case she, I don't know, is around him again or something."

"How would that happen? I don't work there anymore."

"I don't mean to worry you or anything, but what's to stop her from contacting him under the pretense of needing legal advice or whatever else she can think of?"

Something else Alexis hadn't thought about. And not so far-fetched since Michelle had sought his legal advice at the party. "Girl, you don't miss a thing, do you?"

Natasha waved her off. "It goes with the territory when you're married to a doctor. A lawyer, too, I would think. So you better get used to it. What ever happened to the guy you were into before Marcus? I remember at one point you all were talking marriage. What was his name? Paul?"

Alexis's arm jerked and she nearly spilled her tea. She hadn't seen or heard from Paul since her wedding day. Not a peep in five months. Thank goodness. "Yes, Paul. We weren't right for each other." She said it hastily, not wanting to dwell. Maybe someday she would tell Natasha more about him. Not today. She cleared her throat. "So, tell me more about your cochlear implant. Your hearing seems to be even better than it was when you all left for Tanzania."

"It's so amazing. Your hearing really does keep improving over time. I'm told it will do that for several years."

"Wow."

Natasha nodded eagerly. "It's not just that I hear speech so much better but also sounds in the environment like footsteps and doors shutting softly. The floor creaking and glasses clink-ing when they touch each other. Water running, birds singing." Natasha leaned in, a smile playing around her lips. She laughed even before getting the words out. "I had completely forgotten that pee makes this tinkling sound when it hits the toilet. The first time I heard that after I got the implant, it startled me. I was like, what the hell is that?" She covered her mouth and chuckled. Alexis joined in and tried to remember the sound, one she hadn't heard in years. As well as many of the others Natasha had mentioned.

"But the absolute best thing about it is no more 7–1–1 calls. The phone relay service was a lifesaver when I really needed to talk to someone who couldn't FaceTime, like for making a doctor's appointment. But it feels so good to be able to pick up the phone and talk directly without using a teletypewriter and a relay operator."

Alexis nodded with understanding. "I know. Marcus makes a lot of those calls for me now."

"But what about when he's not available or you can't wait around for him to make a call? Or if you ever want to travel out of the country? That's one of the main reasons I got it before we left. No telling how reliable relay services would be in other parts of the world. Derrick gets busy, and I can't always rely on him."

Natasha was right. It was nice having Marcus to help with phone calls, and he was more than willing whenever he could. But there were times when he simply wasn't available. That was when she still had to pull out her TTY device and use the relay service. And speaking of foreign countries, in many ways, her life had become foreign. So much of it was new and unfamiliar. Her lack of a job, her residence, her love life. Even her friendships. Who knew what sounds she was missing?

16

Alexis was delighted to finally land a part-time job as a coordinator at an after-school program for deaf children in Fredrick, Maryland. It didn't amount to a whole lot of money, since it was only three days a week, but it was better than nothing and would leave time for writing and her many other pursuits. At least she no longer had to run to Marcus for every dime she wanted to spend. Which was probably precisely why he wasn't pleased about her new job. After less than a week, he began to protest that she was a lot more tired and short-tempered with all she had going on.

She agreed. She was a lot more tired. But it was a good tired, coming along with regaining some control in her life. It was well worth it. Marcus, of course, didn't see it that way. He began complaining that she wasn't keeping the house as pristine. And that she was ordering a lot more takeout for dinner instead of cooking herself.

"Don't be such an old-fashioned stick in the mud," she'd said one evening as she plated the takeout food she had picked up on the way home from work for the second day that week, this time

Thai. Never mind that he loved Thai food or that she had been teasing him. He snatched up his plate and marched down the stairs to eat in his office. She ate alone in the kitchen. In the past this would have concerned her deeply, but she had come to accept Marcus's little temper tantrums when he didn't get his way. They would move past it and be back to normal in a day or two.

As for being short-tempered, she preferred to think that she was a little less patient with some of his nonsense. Her mind was going over all of that as she made up their brass queen-size bed one evening after work with crisp new sheets and a duvet cover she'd ordered online from Frette. She knew without a doubt that Marcus would have a big problem with such expensive bed linen, and as soon as she was done, she planned to hide all the evidence—the packaging, the labels, and especially the price tags.

She didn't get a chance. Marcus strode into the bedroom, unexpectedly arriving home from work an hour early. Oh crap, she thought. She held her breath in panic as he walked by and reached down to the arctic-blue chaise lounge where she had placed the packaging. He grabbed the receipt, took one look at the four-figure price tag, and went bananas.

"Damn! What is this?" he said, thrusting the receipt within inches of her nose. As if she hadn't already seen it.

"They're made in Italy," she said. Although she knew full well that Marcus wouldn't give a hoot where they were made. All he cared about was the cost.

"What the hell is wrong with bed linen from Target?" he said, sneering as threw the receipt on the bed. He dropped his wallet and keys on his chest of drawers. "Don't they sell the high-thread-count sheets there?"

She exhaled exasperatedly. She was no store snob. Plenty of stuff from Target had graced her apartment not all that long ago. But this was different. He was an attorney. She was an attorney's wife. They could afford finer things. "I paid for them myself. So please. Relax."

"No excuse. That money could have been better spent else-where on the household than on some silly-ass sheets."

She paused from her bed-making and turned to face him. "God, Marcus. I can't believe how cheap you are."

"I don't believe in wasting money on frills. Spending thousands on sheets is foolish. If that's cheap in your book, fine. I'm really disappointed in your wasteful spending habits."

"Don't worry. If we go broke due to my spending habits, we can always sell one of the crystal and sterling silver whiskey decanters in your office. Or those expensive golf clubs you hardly ever use." He obviously needed to be reminded that he had no problem splurging on personal items for himself.

"That's got nothing to do with this."

"You're right," she said, glaring at him. "That was far more fucking frivolous."

He gave her a look of surprise. For a split second, she regretted her little outburst. But only for a second. He had it coming.

"What's gotten into you lately?" he asked. "Why are you being so difficult? It's like you flipped a switch after we got back from the honeymoon."

"I'm the one who flipped a switch? What about you? You've gone from wining and dining me to moaning about every little dime I want to spend. We haven't gone out to eat in months. And you're the one who asked me to redecorate the house. Remember?" She didn't mention the increasing number of whispered phone conversations that suddenly stopped when she entered his office or the exercise room. If she asked about them, he always said it was work related. She wasn't so sure about that.

"I didn't expect you to spend all my money doing it."

She walked around him, snatched up one of the empty boxes

from the chaise lounge, and threw it on the bed. She grabbed a sheet and began folding it. "Fine. I'll send them all back. That make you happy?"

"It's best. I'm glad to see you've come to your senses."

He sounded awfully smug. Patronizing even. She gritted her teeth as she jerked the sheets around. She was sick of feeling like she had to fight him over every damn thing she wanted to do. This was far from what she had envisioned when she accepted his proposal. "No wonder your first wife left you for another man." She stopped folding the sheets. Now those words she did regret the minute they rolled off her tongue. She bit her bottom lip.

"What did you just say?" His bitter tone sliced through the air like a machete.

She had gone too far. "I . . . I shouldn't have said that. But you can be so demanding at times, Marcus. It makes me think, you know, that this must be some kind of pattern or . . ."

He walked up, got within inches of her face. She took a small step back. "Don't ever bring that up again. You have no right."

Her stomach flipped. She gulped.

He turned and exited the room hastily. She sank down on the bed, hugged a pillow. *What had just come over her? What had come over him?* They had never gone after each other like that. She shook her head. Perhaps it shouldn't be surprising. They had been tiptoeing around each other with little spats and disagreements here and there, trying to keep the peace. Just now, all the pent-up emotions had erupted and spewed to the surface like hot lava.

She didn't like the couple they had become. She lay back on the bed and closed her eyes. She would finish repacking the sheets later. For the first time ever, she was having real concerns about Marcus and their marriage.

* * *

It was after eleven o'clock that night when Marcus returned home. She was sitting in bed with a book, doing more thinking about the earlier blowup between them than reading. She had wanted nothing more than for her husband to return so she could apologize for the smart-aleck comment about his ex-wife. Marcus was controlling but not excessive. Perhaps over time, as they grew closer, he would ease up. Despite their recent problems, he was the best thing that had ever happened to her; when things were good, they were real good. She wanted to fix this and move on.

When he strolled into the room, the luxury sheets were packed, with the boxes stacked neatly on the chaise lounge, ready to be shipped back in the morning. Where he had been for nearly five hours, she had no idea. She was dying to ask, but for now she was just thankful to see him. And to see that his facial expression was much calmer.

He sat on the edge of the bed next to her, and she placed her book down. He gently covered her hand with his. "I'm sorry about going off on you earlier," he said. "I had a difficult day at work. A difficult week, actually."

She caught a distinct whiff of liquor on his breath. That had never happened before, and it caught her off-guard. She eyed him closely. He didn't appear intoxicated, so she decided to let it slide. She didn't want to say or do anything now that could lead to another quarrel. At least she had some idea where he had been. At the golf club, unwinding with a drink. Or a few.

"I appreciate that," she said. "I need to apologize, too. I should never have brought up your ex-wife that way. It was uncalled-for. It won't happened again."

"Thank you. Obviously, it's a sore spot for me. When she left, those were some of the darkest days of my life."

"I don't doubt that. I'm sorry it was so difficult for you."

They kissed on the lips briefly but tenderly. He stood, removed his suit jacket, and entered one of the two walk-in closets. She was relieved that they had made up. Hopefully, things would never get that ugly between them again.

He emerged a few minutes later wearing his white terrycloth bathrobe.

"Marcus, do you mind if I ask you something I've been curious about?"

He paused in the middle of the room and glanced at her warily.

"You don't have to answer if you don't want, but . . . where did Charlene meet the man she ran off with?" She could see his jaw tensing up, his thoughts racing. Maybe she had gone too far. "I'm sorry if . . ."

"No, it's fine." He sighed and sat at the foot of the bed. "We were going to need to talk about this sooner or later. At work. They met at work."

She nodded slowly. "I see. What kind of work did she do?"

"She was a web developer for a tech firm in Rockville. He was her boss, the IT manager."

"Oh wow."

"Yeah, it was as bad as you can imagine. I knew him, saw him at office gatherings several times, even while it was secretly going on. He and his wife once had us over for dinner with a small group from the office." He shook his head.

"So, he was married, too."

"Yep. They both covered it up, lied about everything. For nearly two years. I sensed something was off a few months before it all came out. I asked Charlene at least twice if she was having an affair. Then his wife found out and called me crying. Bitch had been lying to my face the whole time. They made us look like fools."

She could feel the lingering hostility in his voice. This would have been a big ego crusher for a proud man like Marcus. She was beginning to suspect that the affair was at least partly why he preferred she not work. And why he had objected so strongly to her spending time outside the office with Jeffrey. In Marcus's mind, the workplace was fertile ground for women to meet and start affairs with other men.

"That sounds terrible," she said just as his cell phone rang. He removed it from his robe pocket and glanced at the screen. He turned his face away from her. "I'll call you right back," he said quietly, then stood and slipped the phone back into his pocket. Alexis hadn't heard his words; he had lowered his voice and turned away, but she was able to read his lips, even from the side. After several months of marriage, she had learned to lip-read Marcus better than anyone. Although she kept that to herself.

"Who is that calling so late?" she asked, trying to keep her tone light. She hated questioning him, but it seemed odd that he wouldn't take the call in front of her. That he didn't utter as much as a "hello" to whoever was on the line. And that he whispered.

"Just a client."

A client you just met over drinks? That's what she wanted to ask, but she bit her tongue. "This late?"

He shrugged. "We have court tomorrow. He probably has questions. I'll call him back first thing in the morning."

"Mm hmm." She never questioned Marcus when a client was involved. At times, she wondered if that was a mistake. Perhaps she should be more curious about some of these "clients." But she didn't want to be one of those doubtful, insecure wives.

"I'm exhausted, can barely keep my eyes open," he said, stifling a yawn. "I have court in the morning. I'm going to go hop in the shower and then get some shut-eye. What are you up to tomorrow?"

"I'm off work. Think I'll go for a run in the morning if it

doesn't rain, then work on the novel, run a few errands. And I have to take the sheets to the post office." A tiny bit of her hoped he had changed his mind and would tell her to keep the sheets.

"Go ahead, baby. Keep them if that's what you really want. You're doing a kick-ass job fixing up the house."

No such luck, she realized as he disappeared into the bathroom without another word. He might be sorry for snapping at her, but he was not sorry about insisting she return them. She noticed that his phone was still in his robe pocket when he entered the bathroom. He normally turned it off and left it atop his chest of drawers whenever he showered. Had he simply forgotten to remove it?

* * *

Two hours later, Alexis was startled awake. She quickly realized that Marcus was tossing and turning restlessly, snoring the alcohol off. She could barely hear the snores with her hearing aid removed but could feel the bed trembling. And now she seriously needed to pee.

She stood and tiptoed in the darkness around him. As she reached the master bathroom door, she thought she heard a faint throbbing sound. She paused and cocked her head to the side. She heard it again, eased closer to the chair just outside the door, and waited for the sound to repeat. This time it was more distinct, and she knew exactly what and where it was—Marcus's cell phone in his bathrobe, which he had tossed over the back of the chair. He had probably forgotten to turn it off due to all the drinking and the late hour. Normally, she would have ignored it or awakened him. But curiosity got the better of her tonight. Who was blowing up his phone in the middle of the night?

She fished around the robe until she found the phone. Her actions felt sleazy and reminded her too much of all the uneasy feelings of mistrust that had consumed her when Paul had cheated on her. Still, she couldn't help herself. What if it wasn't a coincidence that she felt the same way now?

Her fingers trembled as the phone vibrated again and she turned it face up. Prickly goosebumps spread up and down her arms when a name popped up on the screen. Not one she had anticipated. Or was it?

Claudia.

She froze, unsure what to do. Marcus had sworn up and down that she hadn't heard this name that day in his office with Stanley. Now here it was. Coincidence? She thought not.

She ran into the bathroom, clutching the phone tightly in her hand. She shut the door softly and anxiously pressed the home button to answer. Then she remembered that she wasn't wearing her hearing aid and wouldn't be able to hear the voice on the other end. But it didn't matter anyway, she quickly realized. The phone had stopped ringing and asked for the code. She racked her brain, desperately trying to remember the four digits. Some numbers came to mind, and she punched them in. They didn't work. She tried again with fresh numbers. Nothing.

That was when it hit her. The phone in her hand was *not* Marcus's. She had never even seen it before. What was Marcus doing with someone else's cell phone?

Don't be stupid, she told herself. Don't be a fool. *Of course*, this was Marcus's phone. Just not the one she was familiar with. This was a second phone she knew nothing about.

A sharp pain shot across her brows. She sank down to the toilet seat and rubbed her forehead. "Lord help me," she whispered. What's going on? A Claudia was calling Marcus on a strange phone. This might explain all the whispered phone conversations of late. She squeezed the phone between her fingers. She had a fierce urge to smash it against the wall, but what good would that do?

None, she told herself. She jumped up, marched into the master bedroom, quickly inserted her hearing aid, and knocked Marcus's side of the bed with her knee. He stirred slowly, too damn slowly for her. She shook the bed again, this time more aggressively. He was going to be pissed at her for waking him up at this hour, but so what? He had been able to deny what she thought she'd heard that day in his office, but no way was he going to get away with this. Her vision was fine. He couldn't deny what she'd just *seen*.

His sleepy eyes glanced up at her, then toward his clock and back at her. "What the . . ."

She was tempted to slap him out of his stupor. Instead, she threw the phone down on the bed, barely missing his head.

He ducked and raised an arm, as if in defense. "What the hell are you doing?"

"What the hell is *that*?" She pointed sharply toward the phone.

He reached back, picked it up. His eyes flickered and she caught a fleeting glimpse of . . . something. Shock? Apprehension? Guilt?

"That's right. I found your little secret phone."

He paused. She could see the wheels turning in his head. "It's just my work phone. There's nothing secret about it."

"Don't act all innocent with me."

He scoffed. "It's the truth. I use it for sensitive clients. You've seen it before."

"I have *not* seen that phone before, Marcus."

"Yes, you have, Alexis. But whether you have or not, what's the problem? There's no crime in having two cell phones."

"Is Claudia one of your 'sensitive' clients?" She made little squiggly quote marks in the air.

He sat up abruptly and swung his feet to the floor as he checked the phone.

"That got you up, didn't it?"

"I see," he said. His tone was now annoyed. "Maybe you shouldn't be checking my work phone in the middle of the night."

"Excuse me? Maybe you shouldn't have ex-girlfriends calling you in the middle of the night."

His lips tightened. "I don't know why she called so late. Or at all. She shouldn't do that."

That was an odd comment, Alexis thought. Was he trying to throw her off? Well, he was not going to get away with it. "That's the same Claudia whose name I heard in your office that day when Stanley was here, isn't it? The same Claudia who was with you when we met?"

He nodded slowly. "Yes."

He was finally admitting the truth. Not that he had much choice; she'd caught him red-handed. "You're a real piece of work. So, you're still seeing her?"

"Of course not. Stop being silly. This was probably related to our court appearance tomorrow."

Alexis threw her hands in the air. He really thought she was dumb enough to believe anything he said. Why the hell would Claudia be attending court with him tomorrow? "Earlier you said it was a man calling you about court tomorrow. You're lying."

"Yes, I mean, no, I'm not lying. It was a man. Calm down for a minute and I'll try to explain."

Alexis folded her arms around her waist, eyeing him sharply. "Yes, try. I'm waiting."

"I'm representing Stanley in a sexual harassment lawsuit. He was the one who called earlier. The woman suing him is Claudia. Stanley was a senior manager and her supervisor until she left the job."

Alexis had to pause to take all this in. It was a bit much. "Even if I believe you, why is she calling you if he's your client, especially at this hour?"

"She shouldn't have called. But we do have court tomorrow. She could have called to talk about that. Or it could be that she pocket-dialed me."

Uh-huh. "Why does she have the number to a phone your wife doesn't even know about?"

"I . . . I've had the phone a while. Can't remember exactly why I gave her the number."

"Call her back."

He frowned. "What? Now? It's nearly three in the morning."

"If it was related to court tomorrow, it could be important."

Marcus shook his head firmly. "That would be unethical since Stanley is my client. Besides, like I said, she probably pocket-dialed me."

She paused in frustration. It felt as if they were doing a cat-and-mouse dance and he had just seized the upper hand. Of course he had. He was a lawyer. "I swear, Marcus. You have all the excuses. First, you lied when I was sure I heard her name that day. You even tried to convince me I was hearing things. Now she's back in the picture, and you're giving me some lame-ass story. For all I know, she never left."

"I admit I probably should have been up front about all of this sooner. But I didn't want you to worry about what was going on with the next-door neighbor."

"I don't know, Marcus. Give me one good reason why I should believe you now."

"I knew that was coming." He shrugged. "You're just going to have to trust me."

She didn't say anything, just tapped her foot anxiously while she thought. This was confusing. She desperately wanted to believe him. But there were so many oddities. So many coincidences. It filled her with alarm to think what it might all mean. Then again, what if he was telling the truth now? It wasn't far-fetched to believe that Stanley had reached out to Marcus if he was being sued for harassment. That was Marcus's specialty. And it would be absurd for him to lie about something like this when she could simply walk next door and ask.

"Come back to bed," Marcus said gently. "It's a lot to take in. You'll feel better in the morning."

He was probably right about that. It was best to let this go for the moment, for the sake of her sanity. She would deal with it tomorrow after she got some rest. She walked slowly around to her side of the bed and climbed in, intentionally keeping the gap between them as wide as she could.

17

The weather report for that morning called for sunny skies and mild temperatures. And it delivered. Alexis woke to a cool June breeze and barely a cloud in sight. Perfect for a long refreshing run, she thought as she sat on the balcony in her white terrycloth bathrobe, sipping from a mug of black Sumatra coffee. Although her husband had kissed her goodbye before departing for work, her head was still spinning wildly as she turned their middle of the night argument over and over in her mind.

Stanley, the next-door neighbor. Claudia, the ex. Ceaseless secretive phone calls. Sexual harassment lawsuit. Court dates. It was all so bizarre that she was beginning to think Marcus must be telling the truth. At least now. She wanted to believe him. She had to trust him if she wanted this marriage to work. If he was not being honest at this point, it would eventually come out. It was her belief that these things always did, one way or another.

She downed the last of her coffee and stood up. She was looking forward to that run. She dressed quickly in running tights and tee and was out the front door by seven. Despite the cool temperatures now, by late morning high heat and humidity would blanket the area with gooey mugginess, making any kind of outdoor exercise miserable. She wanted to get back to the house by eight thirty at the latest. She jogged a couple of blocks through the sleepy neighborhood, then started down one of her favorite wooded trails. Flanked by a canopy of dense trees and shrubbery, it would provide plenty of protection from the sun.

She had to find a way to put aside all the anxiety creeping up lately between herself and Marcus about everything—the house, her job, money, and now Claudia, who was back in his life due to a lawsuit. The constant bickering over things big and small needed to end; they butted heads way too often. But it was hard to see how to overcome it. Marcus seemed to want to challenge just about everything she did. After the kitchen cabinets were refinished and she had placed the food and dishes in them, he went behind her and rearranged it all, claiming his arrangements made more sense.

"Why do you even care about this stuff?" she had asked with exasperation as she watched him remove all the dishes and glasses and place them on the island countertop. Yes, it was once his house, but now it was theirs. He had put her name on the deed shortly after they were married.

"Why shouldn't I?" he'd responded with a shrug.

He had even challenged her on the kinds of flowers to plant in the front and back yards. She'd been going for blues and lavenders with a splash of yellow. He wanted a monochrome color scheme. They had bickered for nearly two weeks before she finally won that one. But only after she'd flung her gardening trowel on the ground and stormed back into the house. Stanley and Sylvie, working in their yard next door, had seen and heard the whole spat. That had probably shamed Marcus enough to allow her this one small victory.

Now there was the whole Claudia–Stanley lawsuit predicament. And what a predicament it seemed to be. She and Marcus would certainly have to discuss it. She still had questions even as she was coming around to believing him. If this marriage were to have a chance, she would have to trust him when he told her something was related to business. And he was going to have to trust her judgment and decision-making.

As difficult as he could be at times, she needed to always remember the broad picture and how fortunate she really was. They lived in a luxurious townhouse on a lake. They both loved to travel, had recently returned from a memorable trip to Colombia, and were considering a European jaunt next. They enjoyed dining and museum hopping and each other's company. And though it had been a while, Marcus could be incredibly romantic, surprising her with flowers and elegant jewelry out of the blue, for no reason. Their love life, although not as fiery or passionate as she might have hoped, was warm and fulfilling. No marriage was perfect. Theirs certainly wasn't. She would have to learn to appreciate the good and deal with the bad.

As she rounded a bend in the pathway, her thoughts were interrupted by what felt like raindrops splashing on the back of her hand. She glanced down to check just as the bright sky above her disappeared behind a veil of darkness. That had indeed been rain, she thought, glancing up at the clouds as she wiped her hand on her jogging tights. She had been so preoccupied with thoughts about Marcus as she left the townhouse that she completely forgot the hoodie she usually wrapped around her waist for her runs. She was tempted to turn back toward the safety of her house but decided to press on. She could duck into the deli once she reached the plaza a mile or so beyond. So what if she got a little wet. It was only water. She picked up her pace.

It wasn't long before she began to question her decision. The rain that started as a drizzle rapidly descended into a relentless downpour, pounding her face and neck. The path beneath her feet turned wet and dangerously slippery, rendering her white tennis shoes and socks a soggy mess. Where the heck had this nastiness come from all of a sudden? It certainly was not in the forecast, but unforeseen downpours were not unusual in late spring. She cursed herself for forgetting her jacket, yet trudged on, growing more and more miserable with each step.

The slick path soon forced her to slow down. She slid over to the stability of the grassy edge and debated whether to pause at one of the benches scattered along the path until things let up. She had no idea how long it would last. It could be a few minutes or go on for another hour. Or longer. She moved back onto the paved path, deciding to take her chances and make a beeline for the plaza and the dryness of the deli.

She stopped dead in her tracks and jumped back as a man on a bike whizzed by within inches of colliding with her. He seemed to come out of nowhere and had nearly knocked her flat. "Damn it!" she hissed, clutching her heart. Hearing sounds behind her while jogging had always been difficult. The pounding of this rain made it practically impossible. But that jerk who nearly ran her over had certainly seen her. She fumed as she watched him peddle off into the distance.

Before taking off again, she wiped the slick hair from her face and glanced back to make sure all was clear. It wasn't. A lone figure far in the distance was approaching on foot. She squinted. It was hard to make it out through the gloomy weather, but something felt eerily recognizable. She strained to see and finally began to make out a tall, muscular frame jogging her way. He wore a dark jacket, the hood pulled way down over his forehead, and she couldn't see his face. But the physique was familiar, maybe too familiar for comfort.

Paul? Oh shit! Her chest nearly exploded.

Her eyes scanned up and down the path to see if anyone else was around, but there was not a soul. She was entirely alone except for the man coming toward her, now much closer. She whirled around and hit the path, taking off in the opposite direction. The rain still pounded fiercely, and the pathway ahead was almost invisible. She found herself running off the edge a few times but quickly stumbled back. Praying that she wouldn't trip and fall, she pushed one leg after the other, desperately trying to put more distance between them.

She was too frightened to glance back even once. That would slow her pace and she had no time to lose. She willed her water-logged sneakers to move faster, to get to the plaza now, where there would be other people. Hopefully. Her stomach quivered as it dawned on her that at this early hour, the shops and restaurants, including the deli, had likely not yet opened. It would be another hour or more before the place came to life. Ugh! she thought, chills racing up her arms. Still anything, anywhere had to be safer than this dreary, deserted path.

She realized she could hear her own breath as she ran, very unusual since she was in such good shape. Then it dawned on her: her breathlessness was entirely due to fear. Fear of the figure behind, likely closing in on her, inch by inch. Any second she expected to feel a hand grab her arm. *Or fingers clutch her throat.* She grunted as she pushed herself forward, using all her might to reach the end before he caught up to her. Push, push, push.

The rain finally began to lighten, and the path opened up ahead, renewing her will to keep going, no matter how tired, breathless, or scared. Nothing could stop her now.

She hit the plaza at breakneck speed. Although the rain had nearly stopped, the area was void of people, just as she had expected. Then she noticed two middle-aged men approaching the lake, bearing fishing gear. They glanced in her direction with a puzzled expression as she whizzed by. It was not customary to see someone running full speed onto the plaza, but Alexis didn't care how weird it looked. She had never in her life been so damn thankful to see anyone. She stopped several feet away from the men and bent over at the waist, huffing and puffing hard as she fought to catch her breath. Then she stood and glanced back, fully expecting to see Paul. At least now she wasn't alone.

She was shocked to see that no one was behind her. She looked left and right and all around. The only other people in sight were the two men fishing. She wiped her hair from her brow. Where could he have gone? Maybe when he saw that she had made it to the plaza, he slipped off in another direction or turned back. Whatever. It didn't matter. He was gone now. She was safe.

She walked slowly to a nearby bench. It was soaking wet, but she was too exhausted to care. Her backside immediately got drenched, but it was nothing compared to the ordeal she had just endured. Her body and mind begged for a moment of calm to try and process what had just happened. She thought back to the figure she had seen on the path, now with the benefit of distance and time. And other people. Could she be certain it was Paul? No, but it sure looked like him. And the way he had mysteriously disappeared as she came out in the open made her doubly suspicious. And if it was Paul, had he been stalking her all along? She'd thought the whole dreadful episode with him was done. That he had finally seen the light and moved on, especially now that he knew she was married.

She shivered, a mixture of being chilly and wet and jittery nerves. She lifted her hands, stretched her fingers, which were shaking uncontrollably. Her whole body was shaking. She hugged her waistline to warm herself up as she tried to figure out how to deal with this going forward. If she wanted to ensure that she would never go through anything similar again, she couldn't ignore what just happened and hope it had not been Paul. Or that it had only been her overworked imagination.

She so badly wished she could tell Marcus. She would love to be able to confide in her husband about this looming threat in her life. But Marcus would be absolutely furious if he ever learned or even suspected that she had continued to see Paul long after they'd started dating. He might even leave her. And that she could not have. She had to come up with something else. Any woman would be at a huge disadvantage alone with a man who was obsessed and angry with her. She was even more vulnerable with her hearing loss. Even with a hearing aid, she often didn't realize someone was approaching from behind until they were right up on her. When it could be too late.

The only real solution? Probably a cochlear implant. At least to her mind. She had been reading up on them ever since talking to Natasha and had come across encouraging stories of people hearing sounds for the first time after the surgery. And late-deafened people like her, who had lost their hearing after birth and learning speech, made the best candidates. It was a fairly major surgery, which was why she had kept putting it off. She had learned to manage well enough, and it hadn't seemed worth the risk.

This frightful incident changed everything.

She stood with a new sense of resolve. Johns Hopkins Hospital in Baltimore had a major, top-notch hearing center where doctors performed the surgery. Hopkins was practically in her backyard and could not be more convenient. As soon as she got back home, she was going to give them a call. She wasn't sure the surgery would work for her. But she had to check it out. If successful, it could help with so many things she had learned to accept but still found challenging even with hearing aids. Like talking on the phone without video. Understanding voices and sounds in the distance. Her husband whispering on his cell phone.

She whirled her water-soaked derriere around and headed in the opposite direction of the wooded path. She had vague memories of once being able to hear wet tennis shoes squeaking when she was younger. It excited her to think that she might soon be able to hear that again, and a whole lot more.

One thing was certain, she thought, as the sun peeked out from behind the clouds. She was going to take a much more well-traveled route back.

18

"And exactly how much will this gizmo surgery cost?"

Those were the first words out of her husband's mouth as they relaxed on the patio a few days later, discussing the cochlear implant. Not, how much would it help her hearing? Or what were the risks? But how many of his hard-earned dollars—no, their dollars since they were married now—would it set him back? She was not surprised. After being married to the man for six months, it was exactly what she should have expected.

She wished he'd take it more seriously. They were talking about her hearing. "It ain't cheap," she said, mockingly. "Around fifty thousand dollars."

He whistled. "Excuse me?"

She took a generous sip of iced tea to hide her smirk. That ought to shut him up. It was hardly a "gizmo" at fifty grand. She had made phone calls and knew that their insurance would cover the bulk of it, but she wouldn't reveal that little piece of information just yet. Shame on her, but she got a thrill out of seeing Marcus squirm over money, even if only for a few seconds.

"That's a lot," he said.

"I think it's worth it. It would make a big difference in what I'm able to hear."

"Will insurance cover it?"

She nodded. "Yes, it should cover most of it. All but a few thousand."

He looked somewhat relieved but still uncertain. "They cut your head open, don't they? To insert the gizmo?"

She twisted her mouth with deep disapproval, gave him a "quit it" look.

"Okay. Implant. Cochlear implant."

"Yes, they cut. But it's outpatient surgery. I won't need to stay overnight."

"Really? That's good to know. Wonder why it costs so much."

She shrugged. "It's pretty advanced technology. And there are follow-up visits and testing."

"Everything is so damn expensive these days. How risky is it?"

"Like with any surgery, there are risks. Nerve damage for one. And I'd have to be vaccinated for meningitis. But I think the risks are low compared to the benefits."

"Those sound like pretty significant risks to me, Alexis. You sure you've given enough thought to this?"

"I've been researching it for several days. And I talked to Natasha. She says it pretty much changed her life."

"Actually, that's part of what bothers me. You know, how much it might change you."

"What do you mean? Natasha is still the same person if that's what you're worried about. But it would make my life so much easier. Yours, too. I won't have to depend on you as much for help with phone calls or understanding other people in noisy environ-ments. Things like that." She didn't add that she hoped it would help her hear Marcus speaking in hushed tones on the phone, among other things that made her uneasy. Yes, she was trying to trust him. But what was that saying? Trust but verify.

"I don't mind helping you," he said. "You know that."

She smiled. "And I appreciate it. I really do. But this will allow me to be more independent, Marcus, if you can understand that."

He nodded weakly. "I'm trying to."

She sat back in her chair. He had said that with a touch of sadness. It had never dawned on her that he would be so resistant to the surgery. She was beginning to realize just how uneasy he was about the prospect of her becoming more self-reliant. He probably loved knowing who she was in contact with from day to day. Well, he'd need to get past that.

"Marcus, I haven't completely made up my mind to have it yet. I was just updating you on my thinking. But I am honestly disappointed in what I'm hearing. You sound selfish."

"Would you go ahead with it even if you knew I was against it?"

She thought for a second. Probably. But she would keep that to herself for now. "Are you even listening to what I'm saying? Why would you object to something that will help me hear better? It makes no sense."

"There could be real complications. You said so yourself. And again, it'll probably change the dynamic between us. I like the way things are now. I like the way you are now."

Of course, he did, she thought. Almost totally dependent on him. "The dynamic will only change for the better."

"I'm not as certain about that as you seem to be," he said, shaking his head. "I need some time to think. It's a big decision."

She grimaced. She was tempted to point out that she was not asking for his permission. She firmly believed that the decision was hers. And that he should understand why it was important and support her. But she would keep those thoughts to herself for the time being and gently try to get him to come around. "I really want to do this, Marcus. And I want your support."

"I hear you. But you can't dump this on me and expect me to say yes or no just like that." He snapped his fingers for added effect.

"Mm hmm." She would give him a few days to see the light.

"And to think," he said, smiling, "that I married you because dating you was getting so expensive. That was nothing compared to how much you're spending now. First, all the renovations. Now, this. What you got planned next? A vacation home in the mountains or on an island somewhere?"

"That's actually not a bad idea," she said jokingly. Yet another wisecrack about how miserly he could be lingered on the edge of her lips, but she held it back. One thing she had come to realize was that although her husband could dish out the smart-aleck comments, he had a real hard time taking them.

19

It took a few weeks, way too long, but Marcus finally came around to her way of thinking about the cochlear implant. Not only did he come around, to her delight, he became an absolute sweetheart about it. For the first time in months, he brought her a dozen red roses and then apologized for not being more understanding.

"What changed your mind?" Alexis asked, inhaling the scent.

"I could see how important this was to you."

She suspected that he realized how determined she was to have the surgery. She was normally passive with him, always giving in and letting things slide. This had not been one of those times. She nagged him relentlessly, day after day. He had probably figured that the only way to have some peace was to get with the program. Her program.

Three nights before her surgery at the Johns Hopkins Outpatient Center, he took her to dinner at the Georgetown restaurant where they had dined on their first date. Then at the dinner table, he surprised her with a stunning pair of 18k gold and tanzanite stud earrings from Tiffany. This was definitely the most elegant jewelry he had ever given her. Still, the heart-shaped dangle earrings he'd purchased for her on that first date would always have a special place. After dinner, they went home and spent a sexy night in bed. And again the following night. This was the first time in many months that they had made love two nights in a row.

The Monday of the surgery, he took off work to take her to the outpatient center, then stuck around and waited nearly all day before driving her home. He took off two more days to nurse her back to health, changing her bloody head dressings several times a day, preparing nutritious meals for her to eat in bed, even scrubbing her back while she soaked in the tub. It was the first time since their honeymoon that he had missed work. This was the man she had fallen in love with, she thought as he rinsed her back and helped her from the tub. She felt a little guilty for ever doubting him, for suspecting that he might still be involved romantically with Claudia.

"Who are you and what did you do with my husband?" she asked. "'Cause I sure hope you stick around."

He laughed as he tucked her into bed, then went down to his office while she slept.

By the time he went back to the office on Thursday, the dressing had been removed and she was able to tend to the site on her own. Marcus checked up on her throughout the days following. It would take another month of healing before she was hooked up to the sound processor; for now, she still had to wear a hearing aid in the opposite ear.

She and Marcus had just disconnected from a FaceTime chat when the strobe light on the kitchen wall flashed, indicating that the doorbell was ringing. She flinched and nearly dropped the phone on the floor. Ever since that day jogging in the rain, doorbells gave her the creeps when she was home alone and not expecting anyone. Paul always came to mind; she could feel the nerves tingling all through her arms. She rubbed them briskly to soothe the surge of anxiety that had hit her, even though she found it hard to believe that he would be brazen enough to knock on the door of the house she shared with her husband.

She had tried to persuade Marcus to have an alarm system installed, but he insisted it would be a waste of money given there was so little crime in the neighborhood. She had started saving from her part-time job, but that would take time.

She slipped quietly to the door. The bell rang again just as she perched on her toes to look out the peephole. It was not Paul, thank goodness. But who she saw standing there filled her gut with a different kind of anxiety. Sylvie, their next-door neighbor. Wife of Stanley, the accused sexual offender. The only times she had spoken to Sylvie were always outside the house, when they were both coming and going. And always brief encounters: "Hello. How are you? Nice weather we're having." What could possibly have brought Sylvie to their door? Could it have something to do with Stanley? She certainly hoped not. If so, she would keep her comments brief and let her husband deal with it later.

It was only 9:30 a.m. and she was still wearing her nightgown and bathrobe. She pulled the robe tighter and opened the door. Sylvie stood there smiling, holding a Saran-Wrapped plate piled high with delicious-looking cookies and a small package covered in brown paper. Her thin, wispy brown hair dangled softly at her shoulders. Seeing Sylvie up close for the first time made Alexis realize that she had silky smooth skin and was pretty in a gentle sort of way.

"Hi, Sylvie. How nice to see you. Come on in."

Alexis stepped aside and Sylvie strode in wearing a pair of loose-fitting faded blue jeans and a white shirt. She turned to face Alexis. "I baked these for you, honey," she said, pronouncing every syllable loudly and carefully and using her spare hand in an awkward imitation of sign language. "Oatmeal raisin. I ran into Marcus earlier this week. He told me you had surgery. A cochlear implant. How are you feeling?"

Alexis took the plate of goodies. "Thank you. You didn't have to do this, but I really appreciate it. I'm doing well. A little tired but feeling better each day."

Alexis placed the cookies on the countertop as Sylvie followed her to the kitchen. "Can I get you something?" Alexis asked, indicating that Sylvie should sit at the kitchen table. "Coffee? Water?"

Sylvie waved her hands as she sat down. "Oh no, thank you. I'm good. I try to stick to one cup in the morning or I get crazy, you know. Too hyper. And I don't want to trouble you."

"It's no trouble," Alexis said. She filled two glasses with ice water and placed them on the table along with the cookies. "Listen, you really don't have to shout," Alexis said as she sat down across from Sylvie. "I wear a hearing aid, and I'm pretty good at reading lips close up."

"Oh, okay. I didn't know that."

"It's fine. It's understandable."

Sylvie unwrapped the brown package and pulled out a small framed watercolor seascape painted in bright, cheerful blues and yellows. "This is for you," she said, handing it to Alexis.

"Really?" Alexis was deeply touched. No one had ever created a painting for her before. "It's lovely," she said, holding it out as she admired it. "Thank you so much. Marcus told me you were an artist."

Sylvie waved a hand nonchalantly. "Oh, I just dabble. But I enjoy it. Relaxes me. So, you read lips? Bet that's a lot of fun. Eavesdropping on conversations."

Alexis smiled. "It's not as easy as it sounds. If someone is on the other side of the room, I might be able to catch a few words here and there, but not an entire conversation. And some people are hard to lip-read. Men with mustaches or anyone who talks fast, forget it. Radio commentators are the worst."

"I could see that. I have trouble understanding them myself sometimes. Tell me about this cochlear implant. How does that work?"

Alexis went into the full drill, explaining what the process involved and how they improved sound over and above hearing aids.

"That's fascinating. I'm so happy for you. Although you seem to hear me fine now."

"That's because we're sitting directly across from each other, and the surroundings are quiet. Makes it easier to hear and read."

Sylvie nodded. "How does it feel being a newlywed? Getting used to it?"

Marcus wasn't kidding when he had said Sylvie was a busybody. But she didn't mind all the questions. Probably because Sylvie asked them with a smile, and they were innocuous. At least so far.

"I'm not sure we're still newlyweds," Alexis said, chuckling. "We've been married seven months now. We have our ups and downs, you know, but all in all, it's been good." She didn't mention that the lows could get a lot deeper and came far more often than she would ever have imagined. "Fortunately, there are more ups than downs."

"I get it," Sylvie said. "That's what marriage is all about. Working through the bad times."

Alexis nodded in agreement. This was the point in the conversation where she would normally ask about the other person's marriage. And she *was* curious. But she couldn't bring herself to do that given what Marcus had told her about Stanley. She wondered if Sylvie were even aware that her husband was being sued for sexual harassment and that Marcus was representing him. It seemed odd that Sylvie would have popped in for a casual visit, if so.

"Stanley took a leave of absence from work, so he's at home a lot more these days. I admit that while I like having him around, for the most part, at times it gets to be a bit much." Sylvie laughed. Alexis returned the gesture. Marcus had already revealed that Stanley had taken a leave from his job. His firm had insisted he do so until his legal issues were resolved. Did Sylvie know the reason her husband was home all day with her now? The real reason? That was the million-dollar question.

"I see," Alexis said.

"He was burned out and needed a break to recuperate," Sylvie added. "He plans to go back in about six months."

Guess she had the answer to her question now, Alexis thought. Sylvie was in the dark about Stanley's alleged behavior and his time off. Either that or she was a talented actress in addition to being an artist; she seemed completely unfazed. "I understand," Alexis said. "Technology can be a demanding career."

Sylvie nodded. "And Stanley was a senior manager. I could tell work was starting to take a toll on him the past few months."

Alexis nodded silently. She was ready to move past this topic. "I really appreciate the cookies, Sylvie. And especially the painting. That was so nice of you. But I'm starting to feel a little tired. I still nap a couple of times a day."

"Oh, of course," Sylvie said, standing abruptly. "Where are my manners? Of course you need your rest."

"This was so nice of you," Alexis said as they walked toward the front door. "Thanks again for everything."

"You're welcome, honey. You take care of yourself."

"I will."

"Oh. There's something I meant to ask," Sylvie said just as Alexis placed her hand on the doorknob.

"Yes?" Alexis asked.

"Have you met Stanley?" Alexis noticed Sylvie's fingers clench tightly together at her waistline. The movement was subtle, and if she hadn't been on guard the minute Sylvie mentioned Stanley's name, she might have missed it.

"I mean, other than running into him out front. Has he been by here?"

What an odd question, Alexis thought. If Sylvie knew about the lawsuit, Stanley would have no reason to hide his visits here to meet with Marcus. Then she remembered the time Marcus had called Stanley a skirt chaser. That was more than likely what this was about. Sylvie might know or have suspicions about her husband's philandering ways. She had to tread carefully.

"He came by to see Marcus a couple of times," Alexis said. "That was it." And if he did ever come by when Marcus was not around, she would not let him place a single toe inside her doorway. That much was certain. One creepy man in her life was more than enough.

Sylvie's hands relaxed. Her smile returned. In a way, Alexis felt sorry for her. It must be hard living with a man like that.

20

Alexis felt like dancing as she scanned the clothing racks for an outfit for tomorrow's visit to the John Hopkins Cochlear Implant Center. Finally, the long-awaited and much-anticipated day had arrived. She was going to get her processor, the external device that would bring a whole new world of hearing into her life. It would allow her to turn the implant on and off, adjust the volume, select programs for music and hearing in noisy environments, and much more. It was so exciting.

She brought home a pair of black leggings and a sleeveless lemongrass-colored top with flared sides and hung them near the closet entrance. Marcus was working late, and she was about to head downstairs to throw some leftovers in the microwave for a late dinner alone when the phone lit up indicating an incoming text message. It was 8:30 p.m. Dusk was descending over the room. Rather than switch on the bedroom light, she held the phone up to the glow coming through the window from the streetlamp below. A text message from Marcus letting her know that he was leaving the office and should be home in about fifteen minutes. He asked if she needed anything for the following day. She smiled as she responded that all she needed was him. She loved the way he had come around and now embraced the implant full-on.

She was about to turn away from the window when something outside caught her attention. Something moving on the street below. She pulled the partially open drapes back further and glanced down. Her eyes scanned up the block until they hit on a tree just beyond the yellowish glow coming from the streetlamp. Something seemed odd about the tree, right around the dark trunk. She stared for a minute as her eyes adjusted.

Then she saw it; at least she thought she had. A shadowy figure mostly hidden behind the tree. Her guard immediately went up. Was someone lurking back there, a prowler, perhaps, casing the block? It was hard to be sure. She walked out to the hallway and switched the light off. Then she crept back up to the window in the darkened room, stood off to the side and peeked out from behind the floor-length drapes. A lone figure was there, still partly hidden by the tree, but clearly, unmistakably, someone was standing there. She watched quietly, anxiously, her chest rising and falling as she tried to figure out what to do. Should she call the police?

Finally, the figure stepped out into the open, directly into the light. He was wearing a dark jacket with the hood pulled down starkly over his forehead, concealing his face. It was very similar to what that man on the path a month ago had been wearing.

Paul?

She gasped. Jumped back behind the curtain. No, no, no. He would never be so bold. Her eyes must be playing nasty tricks on her. She took several deep breaths to steady her rapidly pulsating heartbeat. Then slowly, inch by inch, she eased from behind the curtain until she had a clear view. At that moment, he looked up directly at the house.

Shit! She darted back behind the drapes. Had he seen her? He had some nerve showing up here. She hastily pressed the number nine on her phone, intending to call the police. Then she stopped cold. Marcus would be home any minute. The last thing she needed was for him to pull up to flashing police lights directly in front of their house, along with cops questioning the ex-boyfriend she had cheated on him with. She would never be able to explain that. She had to find another way to get rid of this out-of-control man. She was so sick and tired of him. She unblocked Paul's number and sent off a text.

I know you're here Paul. And I know that was you following me in the rain that day. Get the hell away from my house this minute or I will call the police.

She pulled the drapes back and looked down as he reached into his jacket pocket. He glanced at his phone, then quickly began to type.

Alexis, do you know where your husband is?

She frowned as she typed. What the hell kind of question is that?

I've been trying to contact you. I even told Michelle to tell you.

To tell me what?

I saw Marcus. In DC back in June.

So what? Alexis thought, feeling extremely annoyed. It was a free country. Marcus could go anywhere he pleased. This man was stalking her and getting on her last nerve. She pounded out a message telling him to mind his damn business and leave. But she paused as another message from Paul hit her screen before she could send it.

Coming out of a condo with another woman.

She froze, shook her head. Claudia instantly popped into her thoughts. Then she laughed at the absurdity of it all. He was lying, plain and simple. Trying to start something between her and Marcus. It was not going to work. She erased the message she had been typing. She had to get him away from the house before her husband came home. No telling what this desperado might say or do if he ran into Marcus. Jeez!

You're a fool if you think I believe you. I am not stupid. I know what you're doing. So just stop it.

I'm telling you the truth.

She looked anxiously up the block, praying not to see Marcus's car approaching.

You're lying. Tell me what day and time you saw him. Hopefully he would pick a day when she and Marcus were together, and she could prove he was lying.

It was a while ago. I don't remember the exact date.

Of course you don't, Paul, because you're lying.

Why the fuck would I lie about this?

"Pfft," she scoffed. She could think of plenty of reasons. Trying to break them up. Trying to win her back. Because he was frigging nuts. But none of that mattered. All that mattered was getting him off that curb before Marcus drove up.

I'm two seconds away from blocking your ass again and calling the police. Don't try me.

Long pause as he stared at her message. Then.

Fine, but don't say I didn't warn you. And I have not been following you. Maybe it was your asshole husband.

Recoiling, she was about to insist he leave again when he quickly turned on his heels and sprinted down the block. It wasn't until he was out of sight that she sank slowly down onto the bed. She lay on her back, closed her eyes, and went over what had just happened. No matter how much she tried, she couldn't make sense of it because it was all nonsense. All lies. This was Paul's pathetic, twisted way of trying to lure her back into his life. She was married now, yet he still kept trying. When would he ever learn that it was never going to happen?

Something was not right with him; it made her sick to her stomach to think that he simply could not get over her. How had she ever been so attracted to him? He had even attempted to bring Michelle into his twisted reality. She hadn't spoken to that sorry woman since the day she'd left her job. Although they were no longer friendly, she was pretty sure Michelle would have called if Paul had told her any such thing about Marcus.

She needed to get up and get dinner started. Tomorrow would be a long but rewarding day. Goodbye hearing aid. Hello implant. She was going to put this bizarre episode with Paul out of her head and not let him ruin her happiness. Eventually somehow, someway, she would find a way get him out of her life for good.

"Is everything okay?"

Her eyes popped open, her entire being momentarily startled by the voice. The bedroom light came on and she quickly realized Marcus was home. She had been so preoccupied with Paul that she hadn't heard him enter the room. She shuddered, thinking how close Marcus and Paul had come to crossing each other's paths.

She sat up, forced a smile. "I'm fine," she said. "How was your day?"

"Busy but good."

She stood. "Have you eaten? I can heat up some leftovers."

"No, thanks. I grabbed a bite at work. You sure you're okay?"

She nodded. "Yeah, just a mild headache. Probably from all the excitement and anticipation about tomorrow." Not entirely a lie, she thought. She did feel a headache coming on. But she was pretty sure it was thanks to Paul and all the anxiety surrounding him. "I'm going to get myself something to eat. That might help."

"Sounds good," he said. "That'll give me time to get a quick shower."

He kissed her briefly on the lips and walked off to his closet while she headed down the stairs. He didn't usually shower after work, but they had an early start tomorrow. Maybe he wanted to get that out of the way tonight. She entered the kitchen and shook her head to clear it of any oncoming negative thoughts. She was going to focus on the good stuff happening in her life.

PART 3

21

The following few months were some of the most blissful ever for Alexis and for their marriage. She coasted from one day to the next, feeling like she was on a natural high. The implant was a miracle maker. The minute Monica, the audiologist, had placed the processor on her ear and attached the small coil to the back of her head, all sorts of new sounds came rushing forth. The rumble of the air conditioning system, the clatter of a pencil dropping from Monica's desk to the floor, the rustle of papers. These were noises Alexis hadn't heard in forever. They felt at once strange yet familiar.

Marcus's voice, the first familiar one she'd heard after Monica spoke, sounded deeper and crisper. She could make out the S's and T's as well as other soft sounds. They weren't perfect based on what she could remember before losing her hearing, but Monica said her hearing would continue to improve noticeably week by week and then more slowly and subtly for years to come. She remembered Natasha saying that she still noticed slight improvements occasionally, even to this day.

Her happy mood must have been infectious. Marcus became

more upbeat, too, and they began to get along better than ever. He even complimented her on the townhouse renovations as she wrapped up the bedrooms and baths on the second floor. When she shared her plans for paint colors and flooring in the recreation room on the lower level—his office was still hands-off as he reminded her often enough—he approved her choices without a single objection. She was shocked and nearly asked if he was sure but decided to keep her mouth shut. No point pushing her luck.

They began to dine out and attend concerts regularly again. He brought her flowers almost weekly for no reason. All just as it had been when they dated and during the early weeks of their marriage. She bought sexy new lingerie, and they made love nightly. Which was entirely new for them. Eventually, she was even able to get Paul out of her head. She hadn't heard anything from him for several months, since she'd caught him lurking outside the window. Her life was perfect.

When she first missed her period, she was immediately concerned. She was normally so regular. Like clockwork. But shortly after the wedding, she had switched from the pill to a diaphragm. The pill had always caused occasional but annoying headaches, but she'd stuck with it for convenience and ease. After she was married, she figured she could take the time needed to work with a diaphragm and say goodbye to the headaches. They had stopped almost instantly, and she had felt so relieved. But the diaphragm did lead to an occasional slip-up. Perhaps it had been a mistake to switch.

All this was swirling around in her head as she sat at the desk in her small office on the second floor, a week after she first missed her period. She was trying to work on her novel, but not much was happening. She moved from her word processor to a browser and Googled "missed period" and "birth control failures." Lots of hits popped up and she spent a good forty-five minutes poring over them. It put her at ease somewhat to learn that missing a period was not that uncommon. Several things could be at work besides pregnancy, such as a very early menopause. Or lifestyle changes. Or stress. All of the above could be the case for her. She sat back in her swivel chair with relief. This was nothing to freak out about. Not yet anyway. She should get her visit from Mother Nature any day now.

When another week passed by, her short-lived relief slowly turned to sheer panic. She could think of nothing besides her missed period. Morning, noon, and night. Marcus had even caught her staring into space a couple of times and asked what was on her mind. Whether at her desk at work or at home trying to focus on her book or preparing dinner, her mind always pivoted back. Whenever she felt anything at all down there, she flew to the bathroom to check. And, always, she was disappointed. This was a complete change. She used to dread getting her period. Now, she couldn't wait.

Finally, a week later, she caved. She couldn't put it off any longer. Futilely trying to convince herself that it would happen any day was foolish. As soon as Marcus left for work, she slipped off to the drug store and bought a home pregnancy test. Still, she held off using it. It felt like the act of taking the test would guarantee pregnancy. So, she stuck it in the top drawer of her bathroom vanity and hoped she would never need to use it.

She didn't even want to think what she would do if the result was positive. She had nothing against children; she just didn't want to bring any of her own into this messy world. And it seemed to get messier day by day. Drugs, violence, hatred, reckless social media. And on and on. She had made this decision while in her twenties, and nothing happening in the world today had tempted her to change it. Marcus didn't want children either. Their marriage was really starting to jell, and they were building a fulfilling life together. They were even planning a trip to the Caribbean in December to celebrate their first wedding anniversary. She didn't want anything to spoil all the progress they'd made.

Two days later, as she measured out brown sugar for an apple pie, she realized she was going to have to do it. She was going to have to take the damn pregnancy test. Baking was something she rarely did—she was following an online recipe on her laptop—but she had recently discovered that Marcus loved pies. His mother had baked them all the time—apple, sweet potato, lemon meringue—and she wanted to keep the fire going in their marriage. But this pregnancy thing was troubling her to the point where she was forgetting she had added ingredients to the bowl and ended up using them twice. So she placed the brown sugar down on the countertop, wiped her hands on her apron, and marched upstairs to the master bathroom.

She opened the vanity drawer and eyed the pregnancy test kit sitting there next to her diaphragm. She bit her bottom lip and picked it up. What in the world would she do if the result was positive? She'd simply have to deal with it, that's what, she told herself. Continuing to avoid this wasn't going to change a thing. She was either pregnant or she wasn't. She shut the bathroom door and opened the box.

A few minutes later, she stood tapping her foot on the tile, fully convinced that the line would not appear. This was all a fluke. A one-time thing. She'd heard of women even skipping an entire period or two and not being pregnant.

She grabbed the stick and glanced down. She gasped. Her breath caught in her throat. She coughed to clear it.

Two lines.

Oh hell.

With a jolt, she realized that everything was about to change. Her life. Her marriage. Her future. Every damned thing.

How had this happened? *Why* was this happening? She sank down onto the toilet lid, numb with confusion. A tear slid slowly down her cheek.

22

She didn't say a word to Marcus about the baby. She needed time to wrap her head around this news before sharing it with anyone else. Including her husband. Especially her husband. She did make an appointment with her gynecologist to get tested. The home pregnancy tests these days were pretty accurate, but she wanted to be absolutely, one-hundred-percent certain. Before working herself into a bigger frenzy, she needed confirmation.

She sat on the exam table in the gynecologist's office, naked except for a flimsy paper gown, swinging her bare feet back and forth as she waited breathlessly for the doctor. She wasn't devoutly religious. Attended church maybe once a month at best. But she found herself praying passionately for good news. The news she wanted. The news she needed. That she was not pregnant. That the home test kit was wrong, a piece of junk.

The door swung open, and Dr. Wesley walked in. Alexis had been seeing her for a decade now yet always marveled at how tall she was for a woman, probably around six feet. Her towering height was tempered considerably by the soft gray hair that framed her warm brown complexion, big round eyes, and ready smile. She reminded Alexis of one of her aunts on her mother's side.

Alexis gritted her teeth. Tried to return the smile. Braced herself.

"Congratulations!"

Alexis stared into the doctor's smiley face, speechless. *Fuck.* Her chest deflated like a popped balloon.

"You're about six weeks along," Dr. Wesley continued. "I want to see you again in a month. And then you should . . ."

All the words she did not want to hear tumbled rapidly from the doctor's lips. The words she'd dreaded. The words she knew Marcus definitely would not want to hear. They felt like a ton of bricks crushing her alive. Was she really at the point of having to decide between abortion or having and raising a child in this unmerciful world?

"Alexis?"

She jumped at the sound of her name and realized she had drifted off. The doctor had been talking and was now trying to get her attention.

"Yes," Alexis said, shaking her head. "Sorry."

"How are you doing?" Dr. Wesley asked, a touch of concern in her voice.

"I've been better."

"Morning sickness?"

Alexis shook her head. That was why she had continued to believe for the longest time that she was not pregnant. She'd had no symptoms, at least until just days ago. She sighed. "Well, yes. It started the day before yesterday."

"I can prescribe something for that. Tell me, did you and your husband plan for this?"

Alexis shook her head. "No. Not at all. This completely caught me by surprise."

"And now that you know? How are you feeling about it?"

"Floored. I never expected this. I was using birth control."

"I see. And your husband? How does he feel about it?"

"I haven't told him yet. I wanted to be sure first. I'll tell him tonight."

The doctor nodded with understanding as she wrote the prescription. "This kind of news is always stunning, even when planned. A child changes your life."

"Tell me about it," Alexis said.

Dr. Wesley handed her the prescription and gave her a maternal pat on the knee. "I'm sure you'll feel better once you discuss it with your husband. Remember, I'm always here if you need to talk."

Alexis nodded and tried to smile, her thoughts racing forward with apprehension about breaking the news to Marcus.

23

Alexis held back. Kept putting off that talk with Marcus. I'll tell him tomorrow, she told herself, day after day. She needed time. Her mind had started to play devious little tricks on her, entertaining thoughts of keeping the baby. Of raising the child. Of being a mom. She wasn't sure where the thoughts were coming from. Or why they kept popping up. When writing or showering or cooking, she found herself pondering what the child might be like. Whether it was a boy or a girl. Whether it would it look like her or Marcus.

One afternoon, she grabbed a down jacket from the hallway closet, slipped into a pair of furry boots, and left the house. It was freezing cold, the ground covered with several inches of an unusual but not unheard-of early April snow from the night before. But she desperately needed to try and gain some clarity. The outdoors often helped with that. She walked over to the Birches, a semi-wooded community on the other side of Wilde Lake, and weaved in and out among the short blocks of contemporary houses.

She had always thought it would make no sense to bring a

vulnerable, possibly deaf, child into this world. It scared her to think of trying to rear any child, much less one who was hearing impaired, amid so much misery. Just the other night she'd heard a report about a high school girl who had committed suicide because of relentless bullying on social media. She'd seen reports citing suicide as a leading cause of death for teens in the United States. And with her hearing issues, she was at a distinct disadvantage. How would she help her child cope with all of this? What kind of mother would she be?

She rounded a corner and approached a small group of children laughing and yelling in their yards as they played in the snow. Before the implant, she would never have been able to make out much of what they were saying. Now she could pick out many of the words as they gleefully challenged and teased each other. "I dare you to throw it." "Wanna race to that hill?"

She smiled. She had to admit that her cochlear implant gave her a tiny sliver of hope when it came to raising a child. She'd been reading up since finding out she was pregnant and had learned that surgeons implanted children as young as twelve months old, sometimes even younger. It seemed that the earlier a child had the surgery, the better. Children who got their implants before the age of acquiring speech—around eighteen months— were better able to hear and speak than those who got them later in life. All of this was encouraging. Definitely something to keep in mind. With her child having normal or close to normal hearing, she would worry so much less about him or her coping in the world.

She paused when she reached the Wilde Lake barn, a historical two-story white board and stone structure with a red gable roof. She had always thought the old-fashioned barn was out of place in a neighborhood of modern houses. But it had withstood the test of time. It was still standing, its red roof gleaming proudly against the blue winter sky. Somehow, at this moment, that thought filled her with an inner sense of strength and peace. And a feeling that she could endure anything.

It was exciting to think of possibly keeping the child and all that would mean, she thought as she headed back toward the house. She wouldn't put off telling Marcus any longer. She really wanted to discuss this with him. She would share all that she had discovered in her research about children and cochlear implants. The two of them could visit her audiologist and implant surgeon to learn even more. She knew Marcus didn't exactly relish the idea of having more children now, but they were getting on so nicely. He had come around on the implant once he realized she was dead set on it. Maybe if he saw that she was hopeful about the prospect of having a child—and serious about it—he would reconsider.

She was going to tell him tonight as soon as he got home from work. He was her husband. He should know and be in on her thinking. She was actually beginning to feel excited to tell him.

* * *

"You have got to be kidding me," Marcus said looking up sharply from his desk. "How the hell did you get pregnant?"

His tone, brusque and strident, instantly wiped the smile off Alexis's face. She flinched. She had anticipated hesitation, doubt, anxiety from Marcus. She was ready and armed with facts and suggestions for obtaining more advice. But she never expected this. Now she wondered if she should have waited until dinner and some wine to soften his mood instead of disturbing him as he worked. But she had been so eager to share her thoughts, and as soon as the chicken was in the oven, she had marched down the stairs and into his office.

"I wouldn't make up something like this," she said warily. "I'm about six weeks along."

He sucked in a loud, aggravated gust of air. Loud enough for her to hear clearly with her implant. "But how?" he said, glaring at her. "Aren't you still using birth control?"

"Of course. You know that."

He slammed his pen down on his desk. Cracked his knuckles. She was surprised to be able to hear that, too. "How far along are you again?"

"A little over six weeks."

"And you're just now telling me?"

"I just found out and I was as shocked to hear this from my doctor as you are hearing it from me," she said. "I didn't believe it at first. I kept thinking I would get my period. I didn't."

He twisted his lips. She could see that his mind was racing and waited in silence for his response.

"Do you know someone you can go to?" he finally asked.

"What do you mean?" She had an idea what he meant, of course, but wanted clarification.

"A doctor. Someone who will perform an abortion."

She folded her arms across her waist. "No. I don't."

"I'll ask around then. You do the same. Talk to your doctor. And do it soon. Goddammit!"

He said it with such fury that she jumped. But she couldn't back down. She had to let him know what she was thinking. That she was reconsidering her opinion about having children. She cleared her throat. "Marcus, I, um . . ." She pushed a lock of hair behind her ear. Why was she so nervous? Because she was going back on something they had agreed on before their marriage. Something that would be life-changing for them both.

"What?" he said, interrupting before she could get the words out.

She swallowed. "I . . . I've been giving this a lot of thought. I'm not sure that's where I am now. At least not yet." Probably not ever, she thought. But she would have to break that to him slowly.

He stood and stared at her in disbelief.

"I mean, I've done a lot of research and keeping the child might not be as . . ."

He held his hand up to silence her. "Wait a minute. Stop right there. I distinctly remember you telling me before we got married that you did *not* want children."

"Yes, yes I did. But that was before . . ."

Now he held both hands up. "No. No buts. I don't want to hear but. That was what we agreed on."

She closed her eyes. Opened them. "If you would just listen for a minute." She paused to wait for his reaction. And to choose her words carefully.

"I'm listening."

"My biggest reason for not wanting children was that I had concerns about raising a hearing-impaired child. Now that I've had the cochlear implant and found information showing how much implants help deaf children, I . . ."

"I don't give a fuck about your goddamn research."

She stopped. The words were harsh enough. His expression was even worse. He was furious.

"You don't get to change your mind about something like this," he said, obviously trying to calm his voice. "This is about my life, too. I'm nearly fifty years old. I'll be approaching seventy by the time they go to college. I do not want to spend my remaining good years raising another child."

"I hear you. But you're in great shape, Marcus. You'll be fine. And it's different now that I'm carrying a child. Our child. I want us to at least consider all the options. We can go see my doctor together."

He shook his head emphatically. "Forget it. I don't even want to hear this. I told you, no more children. I won't be changing my mind about that. So, you need to wrap your head around getting an abortion."

She clenched her fists at her side. "Why are you being so stubborn?"

"Why are you flipping on me? I expect you to keep your promise."

"Promise? I didn't promise anything. I simply stated I didn't want children at the time."

"And how the hell was I supposed to take that? Was I to assume that you would change your mind?"

"Well, maybe."

He scoffed. "I don't believe I'm hearing this."

"I don't believe I'm hearing you."

He walked around his desk, pointed his finger at her. "Now you listen to me. A child is out of the question."

She clenched her fists at her side. Yes, she had changed her mind. But this was her child. She was the one carrying the child. She had every right to change her mind. And he owed it to her to at least consider her feelings. But no, he refused. Bastard. "We'll see about that. You don't get to tell me what to do with my body or my baby."

He stared at her, obviously stunned by her defiance. She turned on her heels and headed toward the door. She had nothing more to say.

"Alexis," he said.

She paused, her back still toward him.

"Don't do this," he said, his tone serious but quieter. "Don't even think about it. You're going to ruin everything."

She turned and stared at him. "No, you're the one who's about to ruin everything."

24

The minute Stanley and Sylvie saw Alexis getting out of her Mazda, they hastily dumped their shovels onto their front stoop, turned their backs, and all but ran into the house. How odd, Alexis thought, staring after them as she made her way up the pathway to her house. They were usually so friendly, especially Sylvie. Only days ago, her next-door neighbor had shared a recipe for strawberry pie after learning that Alexis had taken up baking. Alexis had begun to look forward to Sylvie's smiling face and friendly chats over the past week. She and Marcus had talked little since the day she told him she was pregnant. They ate dinner in separate rooms, slept at the edges on their respective sides of the bed. Marriage in Siberia was how she'd started to think of it.

Once inside the doorway, she set down her briefcase and hung up her jacket. Something was way off with her neighbors. But what? She asked Marcus what he thought when he returned home from the office. He pretty much told her to stop concerning herself about Stanley and his wife, to mind her own business. "All sorts of women are coming out of the woodwork accusing Stanley of harassment," Marcus said as he dropped his briefcase on a kitchen chair. "Or worse. Stay away from him, from both of them."

"Stanley?" she asked, lifting her eyebrows with surprise. "You told me about the harassment lawsuit, but now you're saying he's been accused of . . . ?"

"Assault."

She was stunned, momentarily speechless. Stanley had to be well into his fifties. And he was married. Obviously, Alexis knew that it was entirely possible for married men to attack women, but this was their next-door neighbor. It was so close to home. Too close. "Why didn't you tell me before, Marcus? I think I should have been warned."

"We have so much else going on now. It slipped my mind."

"Still, I would . . ."

He shook his head exasperatedly. "Have you looked into terminating the pregnancy?"

She froze mid-sentence, not sure how to respond. Truthfully, no, she hadn't. Quite the opposite. Her thoughts were preoccupied with trying to find a way to *keep* the baby. But she didn't want to tell him that. "Not yet."

He scoffed. "I figured as much." He tossed a blank envelope onto the countertop. "Open it," he said curtly.

She picked it up. Inside was the name and address of a family planning clinic in Baltimore. She clenched her teeth, shot Marcus a sharp, silent glance.

"Don't give me that look," he said. "It's still early. You should have time to get an abortion by pill. But you need to do it soon. Call them tomorrow."

She replaced the paper and dropped the envelope on the countertop. She was not going to be pushed into anything she wasn't sure about. Certainly not when it came to this.

"Say something," he said with impatience.

"I have nothing to say."

"We talked about this, Alexis."

She folded her arms around her waist firmly. "We did. And I told you I need more time. Since we're going to Jamaica in a couple of weeks for a late one-year anniversary, we can discuss it then."

"I cancelled that."

Her arms fell to her side. "You what?!"

"You heard me. The trip is off until we get this out of the way. There's nothing to talk about until then. Unless you want to discuss divorce."

She clenched her fists and stared at him. "Really, Marcus? You're going to divorce me over this?"

"It's not what I want," he said sincerely. "You know that. I want what we have now. Or had before all this."

Though stung, she reached out across the countertop, touched his hand. "We should be able to find a way . . ."

He pulled his hand out of her reach, shook his head. "I will not be changing my mind."

"Marcus . . ."

"Let me know when your appointment is," he said with finality. "I'll drive you to the clinic."

She watched silently as he picked up his briefcase and bounded down the stairs. Then she walked to the balcony doors and stared into the darkness, her mind turning his words over and over in her head. Her husband had just threatened divorce if she refused to do exactly as he insisted. She didn't want their marriage to end. Despite his stubbornness, she still loved him. In all fairness, she had led Marcus to believe that she did not want children. It was one of the many reasons they had clicked early on. They'd both envisioned a childless life focusing on their careers and interests and traveling the world together. He had just recently turned fifty. Was it fair to force a child on him? Would he even have married her if she'd told him she wanted children someday? Probably not.

She walked back to the kitchen, stared at the envelope for a few seconds, then picked it up. She took a deep breath and headed down the stairs to let Marcus know that she understood and would do as he wished.

25

The day started as a blur for Alexis. They rode together to Baltimore in silence—Marcus focusing intently on I-95N through blinding rain and gnarly traffic, she gazing out the foggy passenger side window. All during the drive, she silently questioned her decision. Here they were barely a year after their wedding date, headed for an abortion clinic. Was she making a drastic mistake she would live to regret? Or was she doing the right thing? She certainly hoped the latter. She didn't think she could deal with losing Marcus and caring for a child on her own. Parenthood was one of the hardest jobs on earth, and the thought of going about it all alone as a single, hearing-impaired mom terrified her. Besides, she kept reminding herself, it wouldn't be fair to burden Marcus with a child at his age after she had led him to believe that she never wanted any.

As Marcus searched for a parking space, she closed her eyes and told herself that this was needed to keep her marriage intact. While they waited to be buzzed into the multi-story redbrick building, Alexis kept reminding herself of that to keep from turning and running for dear life. Where she would go and how she would get there she had no clue. She knew next to nothing about Baltimore outside of the waterfront and Johns Hopkins Hospital. She had been to the city only once to meet Marcus for lunch and that was an entirely different part of the city. Marcus must have sensed her skittishness. He opened the door and held her firmly by the elbow, not letting go until they reached the front desk.

Inside, it was clean and modern, and she tried to relax. She nodded and responded almost by rote as the middle-aged woman behind the reception desk asked questions and handed her paper-work. Her thoughts were scattered, and she had a terrible time trying to focus on filling out the forms. It seemed to take her forever. Finally, Marcus took over, completing them himself with an occasional question for her, while she fiddled with her cell phone in an attempt to settle her rattled nerves. The next thing she knew, Marcus was tapping her shoulder and telling her that they had called her name. Whether she missed it due to her hearing loss or because her attention was elsewhere, Alexis wasn't sure. She stood and glanced down at him, expecting he would stand.

"Sorry, he can't accompany you into the exam room," the young assistant said, smiling.

Alexis frowned. "Why not? He's my husband."

"Doesn't matter," came the response. "That was explained to you earlier."

Maybe so, Alexis thought. She didn't remember. Everything was happening so fast. All she knew was that without Marcus by her side, she wasn't sure she would go through with it. She glanced back at him as she followed the assistant, hoping he would insist they allow him in.

"You'll be fine," he said. "I'll be waiting when you get out."

It didn't take her long to realize that she had been right. All through the ultrasound, the blood work, and the questions, she found herself toying with the notion of not going through with it. Of fleeing with her baby. The thoughts came gently, slowly at first, then grew into a raging torrent as the nurse described the process from beginning to end—from the in-office injection and the pills to be taken and the follow-up visit. Every little detail was explained. Again and again. Instead of feeling grateful for the thoroughness, she became more and more alarmed. By the time the doctor entered the room, she had made up her mind.

She could not do it, she told him. Not now. She needed more time. She had to get out of here, needed some air.

The doctor got the nurse, who gently explained that abortion by pill could be done up to week eleven. That meant she had a few weeks to think it over. She sighed with relief. Hugged the nurse. She would not utter a word about backing out to Marcus, she thought as she gathered her bag and stuffed the literature from the clinic inside. Only if she made a final decision not to go through with terminating the pregnancy would she let him in on this.

She smiled weakly at Marcus as she approached him in the reception area.

He stood. "All done?"

She nodded faintly and walked out the front door, down the block, and through the parking lot, all the while thinking on her feet. What exactly should she tell him? How should she act?

"Everything went well?" he asked, opening the car door for her as if unsure whether they should be leaving quite yet. "That's it?"

She had asked enough questions during the visit to have a good idea of what would have happened had she seen it through to the end. "Yes. He gave me a couple of shots."

"I see," Marcus said, starting the car. "How do you feel?"

"Fine now. I may get some cramping later." She felt horrible about all this lying, but it would only be for a few more weeks at most. By then she will have made up her mind to either come back to the clinic on her own or tell him the truth: that the termination hadn't happened. And wasn't going to. Now *that* was a conversation she dreaded even thinking about.

"So, you should rest?" he asked as they pulled off.

She nodded. "I go back in about a week. To make sure it worked."

"Good. I'll rebook Jamaica. When do you want to go? Same time?"

"Um, let me think about that. I'll let you know."

He dropped her off at the house, then headed to work. She went straight up to bed, the emotional agony of the near-impossible choice she had to make within such a short time already getting to her. Whenever she believed she'd made up her mind one way or the other, she thought about the consequences and backed down. Lose her husband or lose her baby was what it came down to. Either way, she couldn't win. She didn't want to imagine a life without Marcus or a life without the baby growing inside her. And she had no one to talk to about it. Not her mother, not her friends. It was too private, too personal. If she decided to go through with the procedure, it should be no one else's business except hers and her husband's.

Attempts to go about her daily routine or to write were impossible. If Marcus already thought they ate too much takeout, it only got worse as she was loathe to cook and clean. And she was unable to focus long enough to make any meaningful progress on her novel. Within minutes of sitting at her laptop, her mind would begin to wander. Even her job with youth with disabilities, something she had once found fulfilling, had taken on a different meaning. The thought of working so closely with children when she might never have her own only made her despondent. So, she quit within days of the clinic visit. Marcus didn't ask why. Regardless of the reason, it was fine with him. He had never wanted her to work anyway.

Marcus was patient at first, thinking she needed time to recover from the abortion. Which made her feel even worse about duping him. He suggested she ease back into decorating the house to lift her spirits, even telling her not to worry about the budget. He was trying to cheer her up, she knew, but it didn't work. The last thing she cared about now was decorating and budgets.

When she awoke one morning and realized a week had flown by and she was no closer to a decision, her anxiety spiraled. She could barely get out from beneath the bedcovers. She ate and watched TV in bed and became obsessed with counting the remaining days on her Google calendar. Should she end the pregnancy and keep her marriage together? Or should she keep the baby and . . . ? Well, that was the problem. She had no idea how Marcus would react if she flat-out refused to do what he wanted.

He'd begun to tire of her behavior, especially since she would not let him touch her. In the past, they had rarely gone more than a few days without intimacy unless they were really angry with each other. But the thought of Marcus's hands touching her body made her stomach turn.

26

His patience eventually wore off. That became obvious in his short tone when he spoke to her one evening. He snapped that it had been two weeks since the clinic visit, that it was time for her to break out of this behavior. As if she needed to be reminded. She knew exactly how long it had been.

Attempting to reason with her, Marcus suggested they go someplace romantic for dinner. At first, she had agreed, but when date night arrived, she was not feeling it. During all the time lounging around the house, she'd done so much thinking. Marcus's kindness was beginning to turn her off more than anything. It was easy to be nice when you thought you were getting your way. She didn't like how he could be kind to her yet so cold and uncaring about their child.

When she heard him coming up the stairs from work, she told herself to climb out of bed and at least greet him. To throw something decent on to replace the cotton pajamas she'd been wearing for the past two days. But she couldn't summon the will. She simply lay there and raised a hand to shield her eyes from the sudden blast of brightness she knew was coming before he greeted her.

The blast of light and the greeting never came.

Instead, he strode up to the bed in the darkness and yanked the covers off her. "This is insane. Get up."

She pulled the blanket back up over her shoulders and closed her eyes. "I'm too tired, Marcus. I . . ."

"If I didn't know better, I'd think you were still pregnant."

Her eyes popped open. A chill fluttered across her stomach. Where the hell had that come from?

"Are you?"

"No, of course not." His harshness made her feel like she had no alternative but to lie. She was protecting her baby as well as herself.

"Then what's your fucking excuse for all this laziness?"

She closed her eyes with relief. He believed her. "Nothing. It's just that I'm feeling tired. And I'll admit, a little down. I'm sure I'll be fine soon. I just need you to . . ."

Suddenly, she felt his warm body behind her, pulling her toward him. She reached back and could tell that he was naked. She elbowed him hard in the gut. Harder than she'd intended. "Marcus. I'm not in the mood for this. I . . ."

"Fuck. You're never in the mood." He reached under her pajama top. "You're still my wife," he mumbled as he twisted her around and climbed on top of her. She could push him off, keep resisting. But she decided against that. Maybe if she allowed him to continue, the mood would come over her. She shut her eyes and lay there listening to his breath coming directly into her cochlear implant. She felt nothing.

He rolled over on his back and stared at the ceiling for a moment. Then he stood and gathered his clothes off the floor. She turned onto her side, facing away from him. She didn't have to suggest he sleep in another bedroom that night. Or the following nights. Over the coming days, if she entered a room and he was there, she got what she needed and exited quickly; he did the same. He returned home from work later and later. Would they ever get past this? She began to wonder if she wanted to get past it.

The flowers arrived the next day. She was up by then, cooking for the first time in weeks. Marcus had not sent her three dozen roses since they had gotten married. She read the one-word apology on the card and tucked it back into the bouquet. She wasn't sure how she felt, certainly nowhere near as excited as the first time he'd sent flowers. She had come to realize that her husband could be downright ruthless when he wanted his way. But he could also be generous and loving.

She was placing her plate in the dishwasher when he walked in from work at eight, much earlier than usual. He spoke. She nodded. "Thank you," she said, trying to smile.

"How are you?" he asked.

"Better. I cooked. There's food in the fridge if you want it."

"Thanks," he said. "Something smells delicious."

She smiled thinly and turned to head for the book awaiting on her nightstand. He held out a small blue box in front of her as she passed by. She paused.

"Go ahead," he said. "Take it."

Should she? It was obviously jewelry and probably something precious. She was long past the point where that stuff mattered. But the gesture, his attempt at reconciliation, did touch her in some way. She opened the box to find a rose gold and diamond Cartier bracelet with a charm that read "Love, always." It was easily the most extravagant piece he'd ever given her. He took it, opened the clasp, and placed it on her arm.

"Like it?" he asked.

"It's very pretty."

"Sorry for the way I acted the other night, pushing myself on you. Not sure what got into me."

She nodded silently.

"I don't know," he continued. "With work, us lately. I've missed you. I want my wife back. I want our old life back. We have to try to get past this."

She inhaled, blew out. She missed their old life, too.

27

The door to Marcus's office was ajar so slightly that Alexis hadn't even noticed the first time she passed by, her arms juggling carpet samples and drape swatches as she headed for the fitness room. The only items she held now though, as she headed back upstairs, were a tape measure and notebook.

It was less than a week before the impending deadline, and she was coming around to doing as Marcus wished in order to save her marriage. She had already booked an appointment at the clinic. Until then, she wanted to clear her head, to distract herself from what she was about to do as much as possible, lest she change her mind. What better way than to get back to decorating the house as Marcus had suggested?

She paused at the door. It was a special lock that Marcus had installed only on that door, which he rarely left open when he wasn't around. The one time she'd found it like this, she had closed it without a moment's hesitation. It seemed almost unnatural for it to be open. Her first instinct now was to do the same—pull it shut. Instead, she touched the knob and found herself pushing. There was a time she would never have done this. Marcus was so protective of his office, he'd often said, because of the sensitive nature of his work. And she had respected that. Now, nearly eighteen months into their marriage and after so much happening between them, she no longer felt as much under his thrall.

She took a step in and glanced around, purely out of curiosity. This was his haven. He had lovingly furnished it with rich mahogany pieces, and the scent of leather-bound legal books permeated the air. The blinds were partially open; late-afternoon sunlight poured through the large picture window. She could see why he spent so much time between these walls.

Many weeks earlier—now what seemed a lifetime ago—he had talked about having new automatic blinds installed. She decided that since he was out, this would be a good time to take some measurements. She grabbed the small ladder from the storage room, placed the notebook down on his desk, and carefully measured. She had become something of an expert at this after all her work redecorating the main level.

As she climbed down and picked up the notebook to jot down the numbers, three letter-size envelopes wrapped in a rubber band fell to the floor. She picked them up and her eyes caught the word "overdue" stamped on the top envelope. And on the one beneath. That surprised her. Marcus did not seem like the type to let bills go unpaid to the point where he was getting warnings.

She was tempted to look inside, but that seemed like spying. Then again, she was his wife. She had every right to know about overdue bills. She pulled the top bill loose and realized it was still sealed. He hadn't even bothered to look at it. She frowned. What was he thinking? She had always left the finances up to Marcus. She'd trusted his judgment. He was a lawyer and a businessman after all. Had that been a mistake? She pulled the second bill out, and the envelope at the bottom of the pile came into full view. It felt like a card of some type, and the return name was one she hadn't come across in ages but was very familiar with. *Claudia.*

Before she had a chance to react, she heard a noise at the door. She glanced up to see Marcus standing there. Her heart skipped a beat.

"What the hell are you doing in here?" he asked, still holding his briefcase.

She quickly gestured toward the window. "I was taking measurements for the treat . . ."

Before she could finish the sentence, he marched over and snatched the envelopes out of her hand. "You have no business going through my things."

She swallowed hard, feeling guilty, like she'd been caught red-handed. But that was ridiculous. She brushed the feeling aside, determined not to let him intimidate her. "You don't have to be so rude."

"You shouldn't be so goddamn nosy. How did you even get in here?"

"The door was open."

"You're lying. I never leave it open."

"Well, you did this morning. How else would I have gotten in?"

He glared at her and pointed toward the doorway. "Leave," he said between tight lips. "I told you a hundred times, my work is confidential."

She hastily gathered the tape measure and notebook. She preferred not to take things too far when he got like this, but curiosity got the better of her. Not to mention that she was within her rights as his wife. "Marcus, why do we have so many overdue bills?"

"Those are personal. I'm taking care of it."

And the card from Claudia? Was that personal, too? She was tempted to ask but thought, why bother? He would tell her it was business whether that was true or not. She left the room and headed up the stairs, feeling totally baffled by his harsh reaction. She knew it was his sanctuary and they had both been short with each other lately, but this behavior seemed over the top. Could it have to do with Claudia? His continued correspondence with his ex-girlfriend was bothersome, to say the least. Also, probably unethical; she had accused one of his clients of harassing her. For the first time, Alexis seriously considered the possibility that something furtive could be going on between them. Like an affair. She thought back to the night Paul had showed up outside the window and warned her that he had seen Marcus with another woman in DC. Had she brushed Paul off too eagerly?

* * *

After tossing the idea of calling her mother around for more than an hour while sitting up in bed later that night, Alexis finally punched the number on her cell phone. She hadn't been paying attention to the TV anyway. She just kept rewinding on the remote, her focus only on Claudia. She had never reached out to her mother for advice about men before. Loretta had very traditional ideas about marriage, but she was the only one Alexis knew who had been through infidelity and was close enough to confide in.

"Marcus might be cheating on me, Ma." She blurted it right out, point blank, immediately after the exchange of "hellos."

"What makes you say that?" Alexis could hear the sewing machine in the background. Her mother was likely working on one of her patchwork quilts.

"He's so secretive. And I recently saw an envelope, probably with a card inside. From her."

Loretta sighed deeply as the hum of the sewing machine died down. "I see. Did you talk to him about it?"

"What's the point? He would deny it, of course."

"Of course. Hopefully, it's not what you think, but if it is, I'm really sorry you're going through this."

"How would I know if he is?"

"Pay attention to your gut," Loretta said. "You'll probably know before you're ready to admit it."

Alexis paused, let that sink in. Had she already reached that point? "How did you find out about Dad?" She hated going directly there with her mother. But desperate times called for desperate measures.

Loretta smacked her lips. "Now I'm not going to get into all that with you. I stuck it out and we made it but . . ." She paused. "I probably wouldn't go through that now."

Alexis was surprised to hear her mother say that rather than lecture her on how sacred marriage was and why she should tough it out. "Really?"

"Too much heartache," Loretta continued. "Back then, even if a woman had a job and could take care of herself like I did, you were expected to have a husband. Especially when children were involved. Things are different now. You don't have to put up with that."

"Thanks for being so forthcoming, Ma," she said before they exchanged goodbyes. She had decided before calling not to mention the pregnancy since she had been leaning toward termination, but now she wasn't so sure. Was her husband having an affair? If so, that would certainly change everything.

28

"Can you pick this lock?" Alexis asked as she stared into the young locksmith's eyes the following afternoon. He squinted at her outside the closed door to Marcus's office. She couldn't be sure, but he seemed wary. Alexis cleared her throat. "My husband is at work and asked me to check on something in there for him. This lock is different from the others inside the house, and he has the only key with him." Stop it, she told herself. Stop explaining. You have no reason to feel unentitled or guilty or embarrassed. This is your house. The locksmith is the hired help.

Steve examined the lock closely, then looked back at her. "Sure, I can do that."

"How long will it take you?"

"Five, ten minutes tops."

"Okay," she said.

Fifteen minutes later, she walked Steve to the front door. Then she quickly set the security system so that the chime would beep if anyone—namely Marcus—entered. She needed a warning system in case he came home early from his office, which he often now did before heading back out. She had always assumed he was returning to his office in Baltimore or to meet a client. Now she wondered if he was really hooking up with Claudia.

She knew exactly what she was searching for as she sat in Marcus's chair and combed through papers on and inside his desk. That envelope from Claudia and anything else she might find about her. She was also curious about the overdue bills. It didn't take very long. Tucked in the back of the middle desk drawer were the two sealed bills that she'd seen earlier, as well as several others that had been opened.

She was appalled as she flipped through notices for a Bentley sedan, a sixty-foot yacht, and jewelry, including items he had given her. She assumed most of the luxury items had been sold at some point. She had certainly never laid eyes on a yacht or Bentley. She sat still for a few seconds, numb with disbelief, then quickly replaced them. She didn't have a lot of time to sit and think. Marcus had separated the piece from Claudia from the pile, and that's what she really wanted to get her hands on.

In the bottom drawer, she noticed a folder marked "Mortgage" and pulled it out, thinking it was for their townhouse. Was he behind on those payments, too? She opened the file to find several overdue notices, but surprisingly they were not for their house but for a condominium in Chevy Chase, a very pricey part of Washington, DC. She frowned. A condo in DC? They had no property anywhere other than Columbia as far as she knew. She examined one of the notices, expecting to find an early date prior to their marriage but was stunned to see how very recent it was—just this past November. The other was for December. Only one and two months ago.

She leaned back. It wasn't so much that he owned a condo. It was that he had never told her about it. Not a word. And no wonder he was so frigging tight with money. He was spending it much faster than he was bringing it in. She stood abruptly. It felt like she was drowning in a sea of deception, and it was infuriating. What else was he hiding? And where was that damn card from Claudia?

She walked to the wood file cabinet against the wall, opened the top drawer, and immediately came across a thick file related to the condo purchase from two years back, just before they'd met. She also discovered files for a half dozen of Marcus's clients, including Stanley, as well as bank statements. It was too much to sit and look over now. Marcus could come in any second. So she spent the next twenty minutes at the copier, hoping the chime wouldn't go off before she got it all done. She stepped to the window repeatedly to check for his car.

She replaced the files and went back to the cabinet. There wasn't much of interest in the middle two drawers, mainly paperwork for his health and car insurance policies, birth and marriage certificates, and other mundane items. But she was in for yet another surprise when she reached the bottom drawer and came across folders with the name Charlene—Marcus's ex-wife—staring back at her. Two files were stuffed to the brim with tattered newspaper clippings, all about Charlene's disappearance. It stopped her dead in her tracks. This was the last thing she expected to find. It felt like a ghost had risen from the past to greet her. She picked out one of the clippings, opened it, and spread it on Marcus's desk, preparing to read it.

The chime went off.

She gasped aloud and quickly covered her mouth. Damn!

She hastily folded the clipping and placed it back inside the drawer, her eyes scanning the room to make sure everything was in place. Then she grabbed the papers she had copied and darted out the door, making sure to close it firmly and quietly behind her. There was no time to make it up the stairs; she could hear his footsteps coming down. She scooted into the fitness room and shoved the stack of papers beneath the small love seat across from the treadmill. Then she took a dust cloth from a shelf in the closet and began to wipe off the treadmill as she tried to slow down her breathing. Had she remembered to lock his door? She racked her brain trying to recall. She could clearly remember shutting the door but locking it she wasn't so sure. *Crap!*

Marcus stood in the doorway and stared at her, a puzzled expression on his face. Had he been to his office? Had he noticed something amiss?

"Why did you turn the chime on?" he asked.

"Oh," she said with relief. In all the rushing about, she'd forgotten about that. "I thought I heard a strange noise after I got out of the shower this morning. It spooked me, so I set the alarm."

His eyes narrowed. "You've never done that before in the middle of the day."

She shrugged, trying to act nonchalant. Could he hear her heart thumping? "First time for everything." She moved to dust the exercise bike. "You're home early. Only four o'clock. How was work?"

"Fine. The usual," he said. "I'll be going back out in about an hour. Meeting a client for dinner."

She nodded as he headed for his office, then closed her eyes, hoping that he would find everything intact. That all the file drawers were closed, the papers on his desk replaced just as he had left them, the copier clear. And most of all, that she had locked the damn door.

Ten minutes later, all was still calm. She breathed a sigh of relief and peeked out. The door to his office was closed, just how he usually left it when he was working inside. She retrieved the papers from beneath the couch, tiptoed past his door, and ran up the two flights of stairs to the spare bedroom she used as an office. She tucked the files in the back of a cabinet, then sank down into the chair at her desk, finally able to exhale. It looked like she had carried that off without getting her ass caught, but she was a nervous wreck.

She hadn't found anything related to Claudia, but she was still reeling from everything else she'd just uncovered, especially the files for the condo in DC. Though she wanted to know more about them, asking Marcus would mean admitting she'd been snooping in his office, something she wasn't ready to do. She had an uneasy feeling that Claudia was somehow involved. If she and Marcus were having an affair, no way Alexis would allow him to be in on the decision about their child. She needed to come up with a way to get to the bottom of exactly what was going on with those two. With a mere three days left to do it.

She also wanted to look into the clippings about Charlene that she hadn't had time to read. She noticed that many were from the *Baltimore Sun* and dated about ten to fifteen years back, around the time Charlene disappeared. Even if the newspaper didn't go back that far online, there was always the local library.

29

The rushed trip to the Central Branch of the Howard County Library System the following afternoon had Alexis's head whirling like a feather in a tornado as she drove home. One article after the other was filled with gripping details and speculation surrounding the disappearance of Charlene Roberts fifteen years earlier. She parked in front of the townhouse, shut off the engine, and sat still for a moment, staring out the window as she settled her thoughts. In the passenger seat were two canvas bags stuffed with months' worth of clippings from the *Baltimore Sun*, *Baltimore Magazine*, and the *Baltimore Afro-American*.

When Charlene's parents had first reported her missing, it had been widely assumed that she'd run off, an assumption that Marcus encouraged. It was well known among their family and close friends that the Roberts marriage had been holding on by a thread. They'd been unhappy for years, and unhappy people skipped out more often than most realized. There was no evidence otherwise, so the police dragged their feet, much to the dismay of Charlene's birth family. The only reason her disappearance got so much news coverage in the early days was that Charlene was the wife of Marcus Roberts, a prominent local attorney with some very powerful clients.

After several weeks lapsed with no word from Charlene, and at the insistence of her parents and younger sister Doreen, the police began to take a closer look. When they questioned Marcus, what they got was a story that changed with each telling. Initially, when asked why he'd never reported his wife missing, he said it was because she had been having an affair with a man at work and had often threatened to leave. When no secret affair at the office emerged after several police interviews with employees, Marcus claimed she'd really run off with a woman she had met at a bar in Silver Spring, Maryland, and that he had been too embarrassed to admit it.

Now more suspicious, detectives searched the Roberts house near Annapolis from top to bottom. They found it odd that Charlene had left so much of her clothing and jewelry behind if she'd left voluntarily. They searched the yacht that Marcus kept at a marina on the Chesapeake Bay as well as the Bentley parked in the couple's garage. In the end, they came up with no real evidence, and Marcus was never charged.

The last feature that Alexis read was an interview with Doreen in a small Annapolis weekly nearly a year after the disappearance. According to the article, Doreen had insisted that Charlene would never have run off and left her young sons behind, then ages ten and twelve. Doreen's theory was that Marcus had represented several well-connected local clients at the time, including a judge who'd been charged with sexual assault and a state's attorney who had been accused of embezzlement. Many of the cases Marcus took on back then were all over the news, both local and national. He was dubbed "Mr. Fix It." If you were a big shot accused of something scandalous, and you could afford him, he was your guy. Guilty or not. Doreen had said she suspected Marcus's stellar client list had a lot to do with what she believed had been a weak investigation.

Alexis could understand why the family might blame Marcus in the midst of their enormous grief. The marriage had been a rocky one, and after all, he *was* controlling, manipulative, stubborn. He was also extremely secretive. But that didn't make him a murderer.

She picked up the shoulder bag and exited the car. As she made her way across the pavement, her thoughts turned to how much Marcus's client list had changed over the years. It was a lot less distinguished now and she wondered why. Stanley, an executive at a local tech firm, was the most successful client she was aware of. The others included a mid-level federal government employee, a physical education teacher, and a bookkeeper in a law office.

She had just fished her key from her purse when out of the corner of her eye she noticed something move in the yard next door. She glanced back to see Sylvie coming up the walkway from her car, her hands crammed with shopping bags from CVS and Michaels art supply and craft store. Alexis was still puzzled by the aloof reaction she'd been getting from her once-friendly neighbor. When Sylvie reached the top of her walkway, Alexis smiled and nodded. Sylvie frowned and quickly glanced away. Okay, Alexis thought. She was about to be snubbed once again. Why, she had no idea. She turned back toward her door until she heard Sylvie's voice.

"You don't know much, do you?"

Alexis looked back, key in midair. "Excuse me?"

"I doubt you'd be speaking and smiling at me if you did," Sylvie added. "But surely, you must have some idea."

Alexis stared, speechless. What an odd thing to say. Was Sylvie talking about Marcus?

"What he's doing to Stanley . . ." Sylvie twisted her lips. "Down-right disgraceful. How can you live with someone like that?"

Okay, so it was about Marcus. Still, it made no sense to Alexis. "Um, I have no idea what you mean."

"Then you need to open your fricking eyes," Sylvie said, glaring. "He's an awful, awful man."

Alexis was taken aback at the bitter tone in Sylvie's voice. An uneasy feeling gripped her stomach. She wasn't sure she wanted to stick around to hear more. She inserted the key into the lock.

"Stanley fired him."

Alexis froze, turned to face Sylvie. "Stanley fired . . . Marcus?"

Sylvie nodded rapidly. "Your husband is a damn crook. Him and that woman. She's a lying . . ."

Just then, Stanley came flying out the door of their house dressed in shorts, a t-shirt, and slippers. He raised his arms, gesticulating wildly as he bounded down the stairs and into the yard. Alexis noticed him waving something dark in his right hand. Shit! Did this man have a gun?

She jumped back and slipped, only catching herself at the last second. She didn't know what a bullet felt like but feared she was about to find out. Then Stanley lowered his arm, and she saw that the only thing he was holding was a TV remote control. Alexis put her hand to her heart.

"Syl, get back in the house." He snarled at Alexis and aimed the remote in her direction. "That bastard husband of yours and his lying whore will not get away with this crap. If they think I'm going to roll over and put up with their insane blackmailing scheme . . . I'll see them in court. Him and Claudia both."

Alexis gripped her bags tightly, shook her head. She was too shocked to get a word out.

"Stanley, honey," Sylvie said. "I think she's clueless about this."

"The hell she is," he said. "I don't believe that for a second." He tossed Alexis another hateful glance, then shooed his wife up the walkway and followed her into the house.

Alexis stared after them, her feet glued to the pavement. What the hell had just happened?

* * *

She felt as if she were in a trance as she hung her jacket in the hallway closet and made her way up the stairs. All the while she tried to convince herself that she hadn't heard what she'd just heard. That she hadn't witnessed what she'd just seen. Stanley and Sylvie accusing Marcus and Claudia of working together and blackmailing him. It was crazy. Cheating together, maybe. She hated the thought, but that she could believe. That she even suspected. But colluding and blackmailing? That was a whole new level of duplicity and viciousness. Not to mention it was against the law. Then again, why would Stanley and Sylvie say such a thing if it wasn't true?

She tucked the newspaper clippings in the cabinet in her office along with the papers and files from Marcus that she had stashed there earlier. She paced up and down the carpeted floor. This was too, too much. Marcus and Claudia in cahoots? Was it possible? She thought back to Paul's accusations about seeing Marcus with another woman in DC. At the time, she thought Paul had been trying to come between her and Marcus, and she'd accused him of lying.

As much as she loathed reaching out to Paul, she had to figure out what the hell was going on with Marcus and Claudia. And soon. She was down to two days and counting.

She stopped pacing, sat down, and dialed Paul's number. It had been so long since she'd called him, it actually felt strange.

Paul was surprised to hear her instead of seeing her pop up on FaceTime.

"You can hear me so well," he said.

"Thanks," she said, barely able to get the words past her lips. Hearing his voice brought back so many bad memories of their last days together. She took a deep breath and pushed them aside. "I finally got the cochlear implant."

"Oh, cool! You like it?"

"Love it."

"I'm happy for you," he said. "Even though I miss being able to see you on video when we talk. In fact, I've missed you, period."

She was not in the mood for chatting. She wanted to get this over quickly. "Um, I have something important I need to ask you."

"Okay."

"Remember when you told me you saw Marcus in DC? With another woman?"

"Sure. Like it was yesterday. I was leaving a basketball game near American U. The traffic was a nightmare."

"So, you were telling the truth? And you're sure it was him?"

"Damn straight."

She rubbed her forehead. She felt a wicked headache coming on. "Uh-huh. Do . . . do you remember the street where you saw them?" She was so anxious about hearing that particular detail.

"Connecticut Avenue. Not far from Military Road."

She shut her eyes tightly. That was it. The answer she dreaded. Connecticut Avenue was the name of the street where the condo was located. Paul really *had* seen Marcus and Claudia together after their marriage.

"Alexis? Alexis? Can you hear me?"

Her eyes popped open. "Yes, Paul. What was your question?"

"Why are you asking me about that after all this time?"

Because I know a lot more now, she thought. Because I have finally wisened up. Because I'm starting to see what an ass I married. "Um, I stumbled across some things and wanted to check."

"Is he having an affair?" Paul asked bluntly.

Maybe that and a lot more, she thought. "I'm not sure what's going on. I'm so confused right now."

"Sounds like you need someone to talk to," he said. "Have drinks with me. Or we can go for ice cream and a run like we used to. Remember?"

Jeez, was this creep ever going to let go and move on? "Uh, Paul. I . . . I really have to go. Thanks for your help."

"Alexis, wait . . ."

She hung up and stared at the phone. That was cold, but Paul was one of the last people she needed in her life now. She sat there feeling numb for several minutes, waiting for tears that never came, and finally figured she must be in a state of shock.

* * *

By the time Marcus returned from work that evening, Alexis was on Google Maps, combing every inch of the neighborhood where the condo was located, block by block. For some reason, she was obsessed with knowing details about the location. Marcus had fixed himself a plate of food and headed straight down to his home office, and it was just as well, she thought. She wasn't ready to say anything about any of this to him. Why bother? He would simply smooth talk his way around it with his manipulative top-notch lawyer skills.

As soon as he went back out, she grabbed her cell phone and dialed Natasha. It was after ten o'clock, but she needed the opinion of someone whose judgment she could trust, and time was a luxury she did not have. Natasha was one of the most savvy and worldly women she knew. And she was a new mom. Although they spoke every couple of weeks, the last time she'd seen Natasha had been at her baby shower six months earlier.

Her friend could barely get in a hello before Alexis blurted out everything—the baby Marcus didn't want, her deception about the abortion, the probable cheating, the condo, the files.

"Damn, girl. Congratulations on the baby, but how the heck are you dealing with all of this madness?" Natasha asked when Alexis paused to catch her breath.

"Barely."

"I don't doubt it. It's a lot. You're going to leave him, right?"

Alexis sighed deeply. "I know this looks bad, but just because Paul saw them together doesn't mean they're having an affair, right? Maybe they remained friends. We're going through a rough spot for sure, but this is my marriage. I still want it to work, crazy as that may sound."

"But how the hell do you explain a secret condo?" Natasha asked. "That's what gets me."

"Given the central location, he could be using it as an office for his DC clients. Nothing in the files indicates Claudia has anything to do with it from what I can see. It's in Marcus's name only." Alexis sat up. She suddenly had an unshakable urge to see the condo. "I should drive by. Does that sound odd?"

"Yeah, it does. What good would that do?"

"It might give me a better sense of whether he could be using it as an office."

"True. You might even spot one of them coming or going. That's a long shot, though."

"You're right," Alexis said, slowly losing hope. "And he might even see my car. Too risky."

"We could take mine. He's never seen it."

"Are you serious?" Alexis asked. "You would do that for me?"

"Absolutely! If it might help you make up your mind about him and the baby. It's a crappy choice. I hate that you're having to decide between your husband and your unborn child. But we should go tomorrow. You don't have much time to try and figure this out."

"I know. What about Eugenia?"

"I'll call her sitter, get her to come for a few hours in the morning. We'll do a stakeout."

"Now you sound like you've been reading my novel," Alexis said. "Which I've neglected woefully of late."

"You're forgiven considering all you've got going on. I'm actually excited about getting out of the house and hanging out with a grownup girlfriend during the daytime. It's been too long."

30

At 9:30 the following morning, they cruised slowly up Connecticut Avenue in Natasha's silver metallic Audi SUV—too slowly for all the traffic piled up behind them. It was a busy street and cars began to swerve around and honk loudly. Natasha sped up, quickly turned onto a side street, made a U-turn, and parked on a corner with a clear view of the condo. They had decided that Alexis should sit with her back toward the building, facing Natasha, in case Marcus should come out and look in their direction. Alexis scanned the area looking for his BMW. Although she didn't see it along the sidewalks, that didn't mean he wasn't around as the building had a garage.

"So, it's in a busy area," Alexis said, noting several small restaurants and boutiques. "I could see him using this location as an in-town office."

"Maybe," Natasha said, shutting off the engine. "Pretty exclusive, too. Saks is not that far. He must have paid an arm and a leg. But why wouldn't he tell you about it if he's using it for work?"

Yes, he had paid a fortune for it, Alexis thought, thinking back to the overdue notices she had seen on his desk. And yes, it was concerning that he hadn't mentioned it. Still, that didn't make him a cheater. Or a blackmailer.

"He's always been very guarded, private, even when he's not doing anything wrong," Alexis said.

Natasha looked at her doubtfully.

"You think I'm being too easy on him, don't you?"

"I admit I always thought Marcus was a bit, I don't know, suave. Even slick. But Derrick likes him. They go way back."

"I know. Friends since childhood. They grew up in the same neighborhood in DC."

"Derrick says Marcus had a rough upbringing with his father being an alcoholic and taking off when he was so young, and his mom being deaf."

Alexis blinked. *Alcoholic? Marcus's dad was an alcoholic?*

"You didn't know his dad drank?" Natasha asked, raising her brows at her friend's puzzled expression.

Alexis shook her head in silence. Yet another thing he had neglected to tell his wife. She shifted in her seat, starting to feel stupid.

"He may be embarrassed about it," Natasha said, sensing Alexis's uneasiness.

"That could be it." Still, she was hurt that he had not shared it with her. Had he never reached a point in their relationship where he felt safe enough to open up about things like that?

"That may also explain why he's always felt a need to over-compensate," Natasha said. "To look better than others."

"So, he has his flaws," Alexis said. "Don't we all?"

"I hear you."

They sat in silence for a moment, Natasha watching the entrance to the condo, Alexis thinking about this newest revelation and skimming the articles "Pregnancy Week by Week" on thebump.com and "What Black Motherhood Means to Me" on motherhoodmag.com. She felt thankful to have a little something to soothe her growing anxiety while they waited.

"There's this car parked behind us," Natasha said in a tone that made the hairs stand up on Alexis's neck. Natasha was studying something in her side-view mirror.

"What about it?" Alexis said, her eyes looking up from her cell phone.

"I noticed it when we were driving up Military Road, and then it turned behind us onto Connecticut Avenue. The driver parked but never got out. It's weird."

Alexis turned to look anxiously. "What kind of car is it?"

"A dark Toyota sedan. Two cars back. You think it could be Paul? I know you said he was stalking you at one time."

"It's the kind of thing he might do," Alexis said, thinking she probably should never have reached out to him. But she soon realized with relief that the guy behind them looked nothing like Paul.

"No, that's not him," she said, exhaling with relief.

Natasha nodded. "Probably just a coincidence. Living in other countries, you develop a keen awareness of your surroundings. Sorry to scare you."

"No problem. I'm just glad it isn't him."

"So, you're about three months along?" Natasha asked, smiling as she switched to a more pleasant topic.

Alexis nodded with enthusiasm.

"Any morning sickness?"

"Only once so far, fortunately."

"Lucky. I had it for several weeks."

"Eugenia is about six months old, right? How do you like being a mom?"

Natasha's expression brightened. "She's the light of my life. She's perfect. I go back to work in a couple of weeks, and it's going to be so hard to tear myself away." She paused and smiled at Alexis. "You'll see what I mean soon enough. I just wish the circumstances were better for you."

"Honestly, the baby is the one bright spot in my life right now," Alexis said, patting her stomach tenderly. "Feels like everything else is falling apart."

"I'm so sorry."

Alexis smiled thinly. "I really appreciate you doing this for me, you know."

"That's what friends are for," Natasha said. She touched Alexis's arm gently. "Listen, I had a thought. Why not take the financial files you found to Jeffrey? He's a bookkeeper. He might be able to help you make sense of them."

Alexis nodded slowly. "That's something to think about." She wasn't thrilled about the notion of sharing that much personal information about her husband with a friend. It had been months since she'd talked to Jeffrey and nearly a year since she had seen him at her going-away party at AASNC. She wondered if he and Kim had gotten married yet.

Natasha suddenly jabbed Alexis on the arm, snapping her back to the present and filling her stomach with dread.

"You said this woman Claudia has long, dark brown hair?" Natasha said. "Very shapely? That might be her."

Alexis turned just fast enough to see a woman emerge from the building and walk down a short flight of stairs.

It was indeed Claudia.

It was easy enough to spot her. This was an area where Black people were scarce, especially coming out of such a hoity-toity building. Claudia was every bit as gorgeous as she had been the night they'd met on the balcony at the fundraiser. The weather was warm; her hoodie was opened enough to see the purple skin-tight workout clothing hugging her hourglass figure. She was alone and quickly slipped into a car waiting at the curb, probably an Uber taxi, with a familiarity that suggested to Alexis that she'd come out of that building and hopped into Ubers countless times before. The whole episode spoke volumes. Marcus might even be up there waiting for her return.

Alexis slumped back. She was crushed. Marcus was cheating on her and likely had been from the beginning. She had to finally admit at least that much. He was probably sneaking around on Claudia with her when they first met. He had even flirted with Michelle right under her nose. Her husband was a perpetual cheater. Why had she been so blind for so long? All the signs were there, but still she'd allowed him to woo her, to lure her in. To be taken in by the sexy smile and the oozing charm, the fancy law degree, and the perceived wealth. And the lifestyle it was all supposed to add up to.

"Was that her?" Natasha asked as the taxi pulled off into the traffic.

Alexis lowered her head. A tear rolled down her cheek.

"I'm so sorry," Natasha said, starting the engine.

They drove back in silence. It had been years since she'd felt this kind of confusion and sorrow about a man. And this wasn't just any man; this was her husband. Her marriage was a complete sham. Even though she had been suspicious for a while, it was something else entirely to have the truth rammed upside your face.

As Natasha drove closer to Columbia and the townhouse she had shared with Marcus for the past year and a half, a huge wave of anger began to build inside Alexis. "How dare he do this," she said, practically spitting out the words.

"I know," Natasha said, pulling up to the curb, "and I'm so sorry. Do you want me to go in with you?"

Alexis shook her head. "You've done more than enough. I've got this."

She stepped out and took in a deep breath of fresh afternoon air. She didn't know exactly what Marcus and Claudia were up to or how long it had been going on. What she did know was that her husband could not be trusted. At all. She would never allow Marcus to have a say in the fate of this child.

She was going to cancel her appointment at the family planning clinic first thing in the morning. She would keep the baby even if that meant raising it alone. Deaf, hearing, boy, girl; it didn't matter. Somehow, she would have to summon the strength and courage to do this on her own.

31

Marcus would kill her if he had any idea where she was now, Alexis thought as she rode up the elevator to Jeffrey's apartment in Columbia, a stone's throw from the mall, two days after her rendezvous in Chevy Chase with Natasha. It was in one of the newer mid-rise buildings, and this was Alexis's first visit.

They greeted each other warmly in the way friends who hadn't visited each other in ages often do. He had always been kind and protective of her and she'd missed him, she thought, noting the dimples framing his smile. But she had chosen to respect Marcus's wish for her not to spend time with Jeffrey. Until now.

She had slept little since uncovering the truth about Marcus and Claudia, tossing and turning each night into the wee hours of the morning. But love or no love—and her feelings were fading fast the more she thought about her husband's bad behavior—she was done. How could she possibly stay after all she had learned? How could she allow a man whose attention and affection lay elsewhere to decide what would happen with their baby? Of course, he didn't want a child restraining his lifestyle. He was only thinking of himself.

But she knew better than to just up and broach divorce with such a cunning and savvy man with no preparation. The more she knew before she made her move, the better off she would be.

Jeffrey's place looked like a typical bachelor pad, sparsely furnished with a few simple pieces here and there, but very neat. Everything seemed to have a place—family photos arranged carefully on a side table, a lone pillow perched just so on the love seat. It appeared that he was still very much unmarried. He took her jacket, hung it in the closet, and led her across the carpet to a small table with four chairs, one centered on each side.

"How's Kim?" she asked, as she placed two shopping bags filled with all the documents she had copied from Marcus's office on the table.

"She's fine. But we broke up."

Alexis paused and looked up at Jeffrey. "When? What happened?"

He shrugged. "A few months ago. We realized we weren't right for each other."

"I'm so sorry things didn't work out."

"Thanks, but it's all good. It was for the best."

She smiled warmly as they sat across from each other. "Let me know if I can be of help."

He nodded. "Good grief," he said, staring at the piles of documents as Alexis spread them across his table. "You've been busy."

"Unfortunately, yes."

"How have you been?" he asked as he picked up one of the folders and flipped through it.

She hesitated, trying to decide exactly how to respond to that question. Although she had told him little about her sinking relationship, Jeffrey obviously knew things weren't peachy keen. She was here with files she'd pilfered from her husband behind his back. She shrugged. "I've been better."

He eyed her with concern. "I was surprised when you called and said you wanted me to look at these financial documents. You always seemed more concerned about Paul than Marcus."

"Yep," she said, inhaling deeply at the memory of those days. "Things have definitely changed."

"He still bothering you?"

She shook her head. "Not really. I avoid him."

"Good." He picked up his eyeglasses from the table, then paused. "Oh, forgetting my manners. Can I get you something to drink? Water? Or a beer?" He chuckled as he stood. "That's all I have."

"Water would be nice."

He walked a short distance to the kitchen and filled a tall glass mug.

"And you?" she asked. "How have you been?"

"Still hanging out at AASNC," he said. "Michelle left not long after you did. Or did you know that?"

She shook her head. "I had no idea."

"She took a job in DC."

"Really?"

He grabbed a beer out of the refrigerator and sat back down. "I think she moved to DC, too."

"Interesting," she said. "I never pictured Michelle as a city dweller."

"I know, right? Okay, let's see what we have here."

Jeffrey picked up one of the thicker folders; she sat silently sipping her water while he pored over the files, taking brief notes on a pad. Her phone beeped with a text message from Natasha, asking how she was doing, and she explained that she was at Jeffrey's.

Cool, Natasha replied. I hope he helps you get to the bottom of some of this.

They were texting back and forth about the news that Michelle had left AASNC when Jeffrey removed his glasses and cleared his throat. **Got to go,** Alexis texted. **Catch you later.**

Jeffrey nodded thoughtfully, obviously still thinking about what he had seen. "There's a ton going on here," he said. "It's complicated. Way above my pay grade."

"I don't need a lot of detail, Jeffrey. Just a general picture. Does it all look aboveboard or . . . ?"

Jeffrey twisted his lips, cocked his head to the side. "Not really. First, he's got several personal bank accounts, and judging from the statements, he appears to be in debt. Deeply in debt."

Alexis nodded. That didn't totally surprise her. She had figured that might be the case based on glancing through the statements herself. "Can you tell about how much?"

He whistled. "I'd say easily hundreds of thousands of dollars. Could be more."

She took a deep breath, leaned back in her chair. Now that *did* surprise her.

"Unless he's got savings elsewhere, what I'm seeing here looks pretty dismal. Are there other savings accounts? Maybe some you don't have records for?"

"I have no idea," Alexis said. At this point, it wouldn't shock her at all if Marcus had money stashed away in the Cayman Islands or somewhere. "That's all I found."

"Okay. But you know what? Even if there are others, these statements and the bills show a pattern of extravagant and reckless spending. Looks like about the only thing he isn't behind on is the townhouse where you two live. He's starting to get behind on your other condo in DC."

Alexis did not admit that she had known absolutely nothing about the condo until recently. She was already embarrassed enough by her husband's rash and deceitful ways. What the heck was Marcus thinking?

"Now about the business papers," Jeffrey said, putting his glasses back on and pushing them up on his nose.

Alexis braced herself.

"It looks like he's keeping two sets of records." Jeffrey reopened a folder. "This appears to be for his legal work. Hours billed, payments received. What you would expect for an attorney." He reached across the table for another, thicker folder. "But this here seems to be something else entirely. Not sure what's going on, but these statements show random large deposits from several people over many years. For some reason, he's keeping these deposits separate from everything else, and there's far less recordkeeping."

She stared at Jeffrey, not sure what to make of it all. "So, what are you saying exactly?"

Jeffrey chuckled anxiously. "I'm thinking you probably need a lawyer, Alexis. To be honest. Maybe even a forensic accountant. Some of this looks questionable, at least to me. As his wife, I think you want to know exactly what's going on."

"You think it's that serious?"

He nodded rapidly, picked up a file. "Who is this Stanley Nelson?"

Alexis held her breath. "One of his clients. He recently told me that Marcus is blackmailing him."

Jeffrey arched his eyebrows. "Well, there may be something to that. Marcus has two sets of records for him, and they're recent. One shows billable hours going back about a year. Then there are these separate random deposits for thousands of dollars being made to another account almost weekly. They started to show up out of nowhere about four or five months ago."

Alexis was speechless. Stanley and Sylvie had been telling the truth? Marcus really was blackmailing them? It damn sure looked like it. This was turning out to be even worse than anything she had imagined. An honest to goodness shitshow.

* * *

Marcus was sitting at the kitchen table when she came in, eating a sandwich with his customary glass of red wine. He glanced up as she passed by, asked where she had been. "Shopping," was all she could manage. He asked another question, but Alexis barely heard it. He didn't deserve to know anything about where she'd been as far as she was concerned. He didn't even deserve a glance in his direction.

She climbed into bed and pulled the blanket up to her chin to ward off the chills rippling through her bones as her body shivered from head to toe. The person sitting down there in her kitchen was a complete stranger. Not Marcus, the man she had married. Or at least not the one she thought she had. The man down there behind the twinkling brown eyes had been deceiving her all this time, doing terrible things behind her back.

All she'd wanted when she married him was to be happy. To feel safe. To have a good life with a man she loved, who loved her in return. She had none of that. She was all alone. And scared. Who knew what the man downstairs was capable of if he ever found out she had just visited Jeffrey. Or that she had been sneaking around in his office behind his back. Or, heaven forbid, that she was still carrying his child. She shivered again at the thought, pulled the blanket tighter.

She would never understand how she had ever trusted him, how she had ever been so blindly in love. Was this what Charlene had come to feel? Was this why she'd left? Did she even leave him? For all Alexis knew, Charlene was buried somewhere six feet under.

She sprang up, rubbed her arms briskly up and down to warm them. No, no, she told herself. She was not going to go there.

She was not going to think that way. Marcus had done a lot of despicable things in his life. Cheating, lying, blackmailing. But murder? That was going too far.

Or was it?

She jumped out of bed, slipped into her bathrobe. Then she peeked out the door and down the hallway. She needed to get into her office, onto her laptop, but she did not want to run into Marcus. He was the last person on the planet she wanted to deal with. The door to the guest bedroom, where he slept now, was wide open. That meant he was not in there and likely all the way down in his basement office. With all his little secrets.

She tiptoed into her office, shut the door quietly, then fired up her laptop. She pulled up the guest list for the wedding invitations. Seeing the names of family and friends brought back memories of their wedding day, memories that now seemed a lifetime ago. Although Marcus had insisted his sons not be invited, she had gotten addresses and phone numbers for both of them out of him. She pulled up Owen, the eldest, who lived on Monroe Street in Northeast DC and stared at his number. He was the one who'd shown up at the wedding unexpectedly. She had no idea whether Owen would even talk to her. He hadn't exactly been cordial when they'd met. In fact, he had been downright rude. But she wanted desperately to learn more about his mother. Her heart thumped with nervous excitement as she punched the numbers on her phone.

The door swung open.

She looked up to see Marcus and immediately stopped dialing. Whatever happened to knocking? Or had she simply not heard with her heart pounding so loudly in her ears?

"You startled me," she said.

"Everything okay with you?" he asked, staring at her intently.

"Why wouldn't it be?"

"You were in such a rush when you came in."

I wanted to stay as far away from you as possible. "I had a headache, wanted to rest."

"You seem to be tired a lot lately. You're also putting on weight."

She almost fell out of her chair. Oh damn. He didn't just say that, did he? "Excuse me?"

"You're gaining weight," he said pointedly.

He seemed suspicious, and that would not do. She had to put him at ease. "Um, yeah. I probably am." She forced a tiny smile. "I've haven't been running lately."

He stood there in silence, his eyes fixed on her for what seemed an eternity. She shifted uneasily in her seat, unsure whether to keep talking or wait for his response. Did he somehow know?

Finally, he spoke. "That might explain it. Why did you stop?"

She breathed a tiny sigh of relief. "Just not feeling up to it. A lot on my mind." Surely that wouldn't seem odd to him, given that he thought she'd aborted their child less than a month earlier.

"You should get back to it soon. We don't want you getting too fat."

Bastard.

"I'm headed back to the office. I'll be late getting home."

The office or Connecticut Avenue? She was tempted to blurt out. Instead, she simply nodded as he backed out and shut the door. At least her response about her weight had seemed to put him at ease. For now. She rubbed her tummy and took deep breaths to calm herself. Then she locked the door, picked up her phone, and got back to placing the call.

32

She heard the dog barking first, even before she knocked. Whatever breed was behind that door, it sounded big enough, Alexis thought as she climbed the stairs to the front porch. She hesitated, now even less certain she wanted to go through with this. And not just because of the dog. She was on edge about meeting Owen, period, especially asking him about his mom. He'd been cool, detached, and hard to read when they spoke on the phone, saying the bare minimum. But at least he had agreed to meet with her.

She didn't have time to change her mind about knocking. The door swung open, and Owen stood there gripping the collar of a German shepherd straining eagerly to get loose. Fortunately, it appeared to be a puppy or perhaps an adolescent. Still, it was a German shepherd. The only thing between her and the dog was the screen door. Alexis normally loved dogs. But maybe not this one. She backed up.

"He's not as dangerous as he sounds," Owen said, raising his voice to be heard over the relentless barking. "He just gets excited when someone comes to the door. Some people excite him more than others."

"Oh, great," Alexis said. "I'm one of the lucky ones that really get him going."

He smiled, reminding Alexis of his father. At least Owen had smiled, she thought.

"Give me a minute to put him away." As he opened the screen door, he held the dog back. She stepped in gingerly, creating as much distance as possible until Owen and the dog disappeared around the corner. She relaxed a bit and looked around the living room, decorated in neutral tones with dark wood furniture and lots of artwork—paintings, sculptures, photographs. The earthy scent of incense burning reminded her of her youth. A large black-and-white print of an African woman and child caught her attention; she took a few steps to admire it close-up just as a petite young woman emerged from around the corner where Owen had departed. She appeared to be about Owen's age, with thick waist-length locks, and was dressed in ripped jeans.

She smiled at Alexis and gestured toward the couch, filled with very inviting stuffed pillows and throws. "Owen will be back out in a minute. I'm Olivia. His wife."

"Oh, hi. I'm Alexis." She started to add that she was his father's wife but decided not to. No telling how that would be received around here. They shook hands, and Alexis sat on the edge of the couch as Owen reappeared. His wife seemed friendly enough, Alexis thought. Hopefully Owen was the same.

"Sorry about Prince," he said. "He's still in training."

Alexis noticed the barking had stopped. "No problem. I didn't realize you were married."

He nodded. "It just happened."

"Last summer," Olivia added. "In Jamaica."

"Congratulations. I'll bet that was gorgeous." Alexis wondered if Marcus even knew his eldest son had recently tied the knot. She doubted it.

"Nice meeting you, Alexis," Olivia said as she grabbed a shoulder bag and set of keys off a small table near the front door.

Alexis nodded. "It was nice meeting you, too."

Olivia and Owen kissed goodbye briefly. As soon as Olivia left, he walked to a wooden bookshelf, and Alexis waited in silence as he scanned the titles, her anxiety ticking up a notch with each passing minute. She couldn't help but feel that he was ignoring her now that they were alone. Finally, he reached for a book and flipped through the pages, then brought it to the couch and handed it to her. She took the thick photo album as he sat next to her.

"I was reluctant to meet with you at first," he said. "But my wife pointed out that my beef isn't with you. Or it shouldn't be. It's with my father. You haven't done anything wrong."

A huge feeling of relief washed over her. She touched her heart with an open palm. "Thank you for saying that." He nodded and she opened the album to see pictures of Charlene. It was a face she had come to know well through the many articles she'd read about her disappearance. Marcus once had a lone photo of her on a side table in his living room, in which she was sitting with their sons in front of a house when the boys were around six or seven years old. It had disappeared shortly after their marriage.

Alexis slowly turned the pages, filled with dozens of images of the boys from the time they were tiny babies in their mother's arms up to the period just before her disappearance, when they were ages ten and twelve. They were smiling in front of a lit Christmas tree, playing in the yard with a baseball and bat, laughing on the swings at a park. Then suddenly, the photographs stopped, a stark reminder of the loving relationship between a mother and sons brought to an abrupt end by tragedy.

"What was she like?" Alexis asked as she turned a page to see Owen and Aaron flanking their mother, the trio sitting on a railing at the zoo, her arms wrapped around each of them.

"Sweet," he said. "Funny and a little bit quirky. She would read us stories at bedtime every night and put these weird twists on them that had me and Aaron cracking up. I remember her smothering us in kisses before she turned the lights off. We were her world."

He looked directly at Alexis. "What brings you here now? Why the sudden interest?"

She hesitated. How much should she reveal to him? She had no idea exactly what he thought about his mother's disappearance— only what Marcus had told her, and she could not rely on that. But if she wanted to know more about this woman and the state of her marriage to Marcus, she should be upfront with Owen. "I'll be honest. Your father and I are having some problems, and I wondered how things were between him and your mom. What it was like for her being married to him? I realize you were just a child, but do you have any memories at all of their relationship? Marcus doesn't talk much about that time."

Owen scoffed. "That doesn't surprise me one bit. They argued all the time, almost every night as we got older. There was a lot of shouting and cursing, especially on my father's part."

"What were they arguing about? If you don't mind me asking."

He shrugged. "In the beginning, you know, him never being around. He was always working and traveling for work. Or him being too tough on us. We were always getting punished for something, even just looking at him in a way he didn't like. She was protective of us."

Alexis nodded.

"Later on, it was mostly about money," he continued. "The bills kept piling up, and she didn't like that. Even though he didn't spend much time with us, he was always buying us stuff. New laptops and cell phones. The latest PlayStation. Three-wheelers.

Jewelry and clothes for my mother. You name it. Mama used to call him a shopaholic. She thought it was too much. I saw her cut up his credit cards once."

"Really? Do you remember a yacht? Fancy cars?"

He nodded. "We only went out on the boat with him once or twice, but yeah. I also remember them arguing about some land he invested in and lost a lot of money on."

Alexis remembered something about land in his files. None of this was surprising. In fact, it explained a lot. Marcus was terrible with money and a compulsive shopper. She had once read that they were often driven by a need to appear perfect, and that certainly fit Marcus. He had run up a lot of debt trying to live a lavish lifestyle, and now he was making feeble attempts to pay it off while still living way above his means. It was one of the oldest stories in the book. "What was it like when she left?"

His expression darkened, and he leaned back. Even all these years later, she could see pain on his face as he thought back to that time. "I remember my father sitting us down one night and telling us she left us and wouldn't be coming back. We believed that for years. We couldn't understand why she would do that to us, but we were just kids. And why would our father lie?" He lowered his head and shook it. "Now when I think about it, it's hard for me to imagine she could have been alive all this time and never once reached out to me or Aaron. Not once."

Alexis nodded with understanding. After seeing the photos and the loving relationship Charlene had with her boys, that was definitely more than baffling. Her baby hadn't even been born, yet she could never image abandoning her child for any reason.

He exhaled. "I hope she is, you know, still alive. But I don't see how."

"I get it," Alexis said. The agony in his voice was heartbreaking.

She wanted to reach out and comfort him but had no idea how he would react. They sat in silence for a moment.

"You should talk to my aunt Doreen, my mom's sister. They were really close. They talked all the time."

"I'd love to talk to her. Do you think she would agree to meet with me?"

"I don't see why not. I'll call her for you now."

* * *

Fifteen minutes later, Alexis was driving up Route 29 on her way to Olney, Maryland. Doreen lived in a semi-rural area, with lots of open space between houses. Alexis pulled onto a long driveway leading to a big country house with a large wraparound porch sitting on about an acre of land. She parked in front and walked around back as she had been instructed. In the distance, she saw a woman kneeling in a huge garden, surrounded by rows of seedlings and late-spring vegetables. She was dressed in tattered blue jeans and a cotton shirt. A wide-brimmed straw hat partially shielded her face against the sun. Alexis wasn't much of a gardener, but she recognized collards and kale as she made her way across the lawn toward Doreen, the earthy scent of fertilizer filling her nostrils.

"You must be Alexis," Doreen said, standing easily despite her plump size.

Alexis nodded. "And you're Doreen?"

"That's me. I'd shake but . . ." Doreen waved a gloved hand covered with soil in the air.

Alexis smiled. "Thank you for agreeing to see me on such short notice."

"You're in a heap of danger," Doreen blurted, picking a rake up off the ground and sifting a mound of dirt. "I hope you're aware of that."

Alexis stood alongside the garden and stared at her, speech-less.

Doreen paused. "No, you're not, are you? I can see that."

"I . . . I." Alexis shut her mouth. This felt like a time to keep quiet and listen.

Doreen stuck the rake in the ground, removed her gloves, and looked Alexis squarely in the eyes. "Your husband is a beast—a vicious, cruel excuse for a man."

Alexis's eyes widened.

"Oh, I know," Doreen continued. "I sound harsh. Well, I've never been one to mince words, I'll tell you that. I'm sure you've seen the sweet side. The charm. The elegance. We all have. He had our entire family fooled, too, for the longest time. We welcomed him with open arms. Me, my mother, my father. Huge mistake. The minute you cross him . . ." She shook her head.

"You . . . you obviously think he had something to do with Charlene's disappearance."

"I don't think it, I know it. She and I were less than two years apart and extremely close. We talked every single day, some-times multiple times a day. Charlene would never have left those boys. Not ever. She wouldn't have left my father either, especially so soon after my mother's death."

Alexis frowned. "When did your mother pass?"

"A couple of months before Charlene went missing. Cancer. My father was scheduled for triple bypass surgery, but he put it off to help care for my mother when she got sick. Then she died within six weeks of being diagnosed. My father had his surgery about a month later. So you see? There's no way on God's green earth that Charlene would have run off with some man then. Not with everything the family was going through."

"I see what you mean. And your father? How is he doing?"

"He died of a stroke less than a year after Charlene 'disappeared,'"

Doreen said, making quotation marks in the air. "They said it was a stroke. If you ask me, he died of a broken heart, and I blame that asshole for that, too."

Alexis exhaled. "I'm sorry to hear about your parents. Really. But why are you so sure Marcus murdered Charlene? Could it have been that all the tragedy was too much for her?"

Doreen stared at Alexis with astonishment. "No. No way. That bastard killed her. Charlene warned me that he might do something to her. He had his problems, but I never thought he would harm her."

"Charlene said he was going to hurt her? What made her think that?"

"It was so long ago I can't remember all the details, but she found out that two of his personal injury clients were accusing him of stealing from them. They had won a major settlement of some kind for several hundred thousand dollars, and they claimed that Marcus had kept a big chunk of the money. Way more than he was entitled to as their attorney."

Alexis sighed. She shouldn't be surprised about that. Still, it hurt to hear yet more about Marcus's dirty deeds when it came to his clients.

"Things had been going downhill between them for a while," Doreen said. "He cheated on her multiple times, and their finances were a complete mess."

That too sounded familiar, Alexis thought.

"But Charlene was terrified of leaving him. He was this big-shot lawyer with a lot of powerful contacts back then, and she didn't want to risk losing the boys. Then she found evidence in their bank accounts that he really was stealing from his clients and thought she could use that as ammunition. She told him she was leaving and taking the boys with her and threatened to go to the authorities with what she knew if he tried to stop her. I think that sent Marcus over the edge."

All of this began to sink in, and Alexis's head started spinning. She felt weak, faint. "Is there someplace I can sit for a minute? I don't feel very good."

Doreen looked her over, her eyes filled with concern. "Of course." She led Alexis to a lounge chair on the patio. "Can I get you some water?"

"Yes, thanks," Alexis said. She leaned back as Doreen entered the house through patio doors. The warm sun felt soothing on her face and she started to relax. She never wanted to get up. She dreaded the thought of returning home to Marcus.

Doreen soon returned and placed a pitcher of ice water and two tall glasses on an end table. She removed her straw hat and sat in the chair next to Alexis.

"You must have sensed something was wrong," Doreen said as she poured a glass and handed it to Alexis. "That's why you're here asking about her."

Alexis nodded reluctantly.

"Take a look at this," Doreen said. "This should convince you." She held out a gold ring with a wide band studded with diamonds.

"It's beautiful," Alexis said, turning it over in her hand.

"A few months after Charlene went missing, I managed to convince Marcus to allow me to go through her things and pick out a few keepsakes. Even though I was suspicious from the beginning, I was still giving him the benefit of the doubt. We were still cordial. But when I came across that ring in the drawer of a chest in their bedroom, I knew without a doubt that he had killed her. I haven't spoken to him since."

Alexis looked at Doreen, obviously puzzled.

"It was left to Charlene by our favorite aunt," Doreen continued. "She married this rich guy, or at least we all thought he was, and we always assumed the ring was worth thousands of dollars. Charlene wore that ring on her right ring finger every damn day for years. He knew how important it was to her and how valuable she believed it was. Just before she went missing, she had it appraised, thinking that if she left Marcus, she might need to sell it as much as she wouldn't want to. Well, damn."

Doreen paused and shook her head wryly. "Turns out it wasn't nearly as valuable as we all thought. It's gold plated and the diamonds are fake, cubic zirconia. But I doubt she would have mentioned that to Marcus since they were on the outs by then. She continued to wear it for sentimental reasons right up until the last time I saw her about a week before she went missing. I remember because we joked about it being pretty much worthless."

"So how did a ring she never took off end up in their bedroom, right?" Alexis said though she had a very good idea what Doreen thought.

"Exactly. Only one way it could have gotten there. He removed it before he killed her. He thought it was worth something. The valuable pieces of jewelry that he had given her were missing from her jewelry box. He probably sold them."

Or maybe she took them when she left, Alexis thought, and decided to leave the worthless piece behind. But she kept those thoughts to herself. "Owen said you tried to get the police to look into it. Did you tell them about the ring?"

Doreen nodded. "A detective I spoke to agreed that Marcus looked suspicious, but with no hard evidence, there was nothing they could do."

"I agree it all seems questionable," Alexis said. "But murder?" She shook her head, still not wanting to believe that Marcus would go that far.

"Yes murder," Doreen said firmly. "My advice is to leave, get out. My sister was disabled, but she was a strong woman. If she could get up the nerve to try and leave him, you can, too. But do it now, before it's too late."

"Wait. Your sister was disabled?"

"She was in a car accident as a teenager, and after surgery, one leg was a little shorter than the other. She walked with a slight limp most of her life."

Alexis's mouth fell open. She shut her eyes tightly. Was a pattern emerging here where her husband preyed on what he believed to be vulnerable women? She opened her eyes. "I have a hearing loss."

Doreen stared hard at Alexis as the words sank in. "Oh my God. The man is pure evil. He thinks you'll be easier to control. But the minute you show some strength and go against him . . ."

Doreen didn't finish her thought. She didn't need to. Alexis knew precisely where she was going. She drained the last of her water.

33

"I agree with Doreen a hundred percent," Natasha said through the phone, her voice high with anxiety after hearing the latest revelations about Marcus and Charlene. "You need to get out. The sooner, the better. Plus, you're pregnant. Some studies show that pregnant women are more likely to be killed than other women. It's not safe for you to stay there."

"Really?" Alexis said, frowning. She never knew that. "Why is that?"

"More domestic violence, especially around that time. I don't know exactly why. I just know you just need to take this seriously."

"You're right. I am so ready to leave Marcus. But I can't jump up and run. I need to find a place to live. And a job."

"Come stay with us until you get on your feet."

"That's very generous of you, Natasha, but I'll be fine. He's a crook, no doubt, but I have a hard time believing he harmed Charlene despite what his family thinks."

Natasha sighed. "Then at least go to the police. Tell them what you know about his finances and blackmailing his clients.

Hopefully, they'll question him and put him on alert that they're watching."

"I don't know about that. Jeffrey said there are gaps in what I have. And Marcus is cunning. He could probably twist things around in his favor. Besides, if he had anything to do with Charlene's disappearance, her threat to go to the police may have been the reason."

Natasha gasped. "You're right. Please, please be careful."

"All this time I thought Paul was the dangerous one," Alexis said. "Or maybe Stanley. I never imagined that the biggest threat could be sleeping in bed beside me." She laughed nervously at the irony.

"Not funny," Natasha said. "I'm worried."

* * *

In quiet moments alone, Alexis had to admit to herself that she was more concerned than she had let on. But she really did want to plan things out before making her move. She had more than enough to use in any divorce proceedings, with the affair and the paperwork she had copied from his office. But she had no job, very little in the bank. And she was with child. She could kick her own rear end for allowing herself to end up in this position, relying almost completely on Marcus for her well-being. Shame on her. Such foolishness would never happen again. But there was no point dwelling on it. For now, she had to figure out how to survive and support a child on her own.

Her savings from her part-time job were meager—a few hundred dollars, not even enough for a security deposit and one month's rent. And no one was going to rent to her until she found a job. So that was priority number one. And she needed to land one pronto. Marcus had already noted that she was gaining weight, and she was only going to put on more pounds as the weeks went by. She wouldn't be able to get away with disguising her pregnancy beneath bulky tops much longer. And then what would he do? She didn't even want to think about the possibilities.

To try and avoid suspicion and hopefully thaw the chill that had developed in their relationship until she could make her move, over the following weeks she did more cooking and cleaning around the house than ever before. She spent mornings secretly job hunting, then came home, tidied up, and fixed a big meal for dinner. She avoided getting into disagreements with him. That wasn't too difficult. He rarely came in earlier than ten or eleven at night anyway. No doubt he was with Claudia, probably at the condo in DC. She'd even overheard him on the phone out on the patio one Saturday afternoon making dinner plans with her. She had quickly ducked into the kitchen when he entered the house and never said a word. He was obviously having a full-blown affair and wasn't even trying that hard to be discreet about it.

At times, she worried that he suspected she was still pregnant and was planning to leave her. Or that he had somehow discovered she had been in his office going through his things. That was why, in addition to job and apartment hunting, to be on the safe side, she felt compelled to sign up for swimming lessons, something she had put off long enough. Living with a thirteen-foot-deep lake practically in her backyard had always made her uncomfortable. Now that her husband, the man living under the same roof with her, felt like a total stranger, the lake frightened the crap out of her.

34

Alexis heard him before she saw him. She was standing in her dressing room, her cotton blouse pulled up high over her head as she removed it, when Marcus's voice sent shock waves rippling through her body. Not just because of the tone—gruff and accusatory—but also because she had believed she was home alone. It was only six p.m. on a Friday evening, a time when Marcus was rarely home. She had just come in from a job interview and her third swimming lesson in a week and planned to take a nice, warm bath to relax and get the chlorine off her body.

She slipped her top all the way off and saw him glaring at her, his eyes fixed on the bare four-and-a-half-month baby bump peeking out over her black underwear. The bump she had so carefully kept hidden until now. She didn't want to believe what was happening at this moment, that Marcus was staring over every inch of her naked tummy.

"You're still pregnant, aren't you?" he repeated, taking a step in her direction.

There was no mistaking his words the second time he spoke.

She quickly grabbed a black sweater off a hanger, the closest item within reach, and began to button it. "No, of course not."

He yanked the sweater open. The buttons popped loose and scattered across the carpeted floor. "You lying bitch."

She shuddered, took a step back. She felt trapped in this closet, the only way out behind him. "I've gained some weight but . . ."

He grabbed her by the arm, something he'd never done. She yanked herself free. "Stop it, Marcus. Do *not* touch me."

He jabbed a finger in her face. "Give me the name of the doctor."

She frowned. "What?"

"The doctor who gave you the abortion pill. His name and number."

"Marcus, they will never talk to you. The law doesn't allow . . ."

"I damn sure don't need you citing the law to me, now do I?" His face was contorted, his lips twisted into a scowl. "Who the hell do you think you are? Give me that fucking number now."

"Okay, okay," she said, trying to stay calm. "I need to look it up."

"Do it," he said somewhat more softly. "Now."

She went into the bedroom and rummaged through her bag for her cell phone, reasoning she had little choice but to play along. He wasn't going to take no for an answer. She turned to find him standing right behind her. He snatched the phone out of her hand and copied the information into his own cell phone. Then he lifted his head and looked at her with a venom that made Alexis's heart flutter.

"You've been snooping around in my files, too. Don't think you're fooling anyone."

She gasped. "I . . . I don't know what you're talking about."

He smirked. "You're such a liar. My bank statements, the newspaper clippings. You think you're so damn clever, don't you?"

She stood there in silence. There was no point trying to deny it. She obviously hadn't been as careful about replacing his things as she'd thought. "I have a right to know about our finances, Marcus. I'm not a child. You don't tell me anything."

He ignored her. "And Doreen. You went to see her about a month ago. I'm sure she filled your head with a bunch of crap."

Damn! Alexis frowned, bit her bottom lip. How the hell did he know that? A light bulb went off, sending chills up her spine. "You're having me followed, aren't you? Really, Marcus. It's come to that?" She was starting to despise this man.

He tossed her phone onto the bed and took a menacing step toward her. "I will not have you or anyone else going behind my back and fucking double-crossing me. Don't let me find out you're still pregnant."

He strode out with not another word. Her entire body shook, partly out of anger, partly from fear. That bastard. He knew everything. *Everything.* Shit! This was a man whose wife had disappeared after daring to go against him. Staying in this house was riskier than she'd realized. She and her baby were not safe here. It was utterly foolish to delay her departure. She would take up Natasha on her offer or charge a hotel room somewhere.

She jumped up, pulled a suitcase down from a shelf in her closet, and tossed her things in. She would call Natasha tonight and take off first thing in the morning, right after Marcus left for work.

That night she slept with the bedroom door locked and her cochlear implant in place for the first time since they'd gotten married.

35

"Your husband just pulled up, Mrs. Roberts," Officer Sands said. Alexis peered up from the couch, hair and nightgown still damp from the lake, arms still wrapped in a towel. She wasn't sure how to feel about Marcus's arrival home after what had just happened, though she'd certainly anticipated it. She stood slowly and prepared to greet him even though she dreaded it. She could barely tolerate the sight of the man.

Her legs were wobbly; the officer reached out to steady her. "Are you alright, Mrs. Roberts?"

Alexis nodded and straightened herself as Marcus strode into the living room. He appeared to be in shock as he looked around at all the commotion and rushed to Alexis's side. "I left the office as soon as I heard," he said, looking from Alexis to Officer Sands and back to his wife. "You're all banged up. Do you want to go to the hospital?"

"No," Alexis said. "It's only a few bruises, some minor cuts. Probably looks worse than it is."

"You're sure?" he asked, putting his arm around her.

She recoiled, almost reflexively. She didn't want him touching her. The caring, dutiful husband act disgusted her. Fake asshole. "Yes," she said curtly.

"Tell me exactly what happened," he said, looking at Alexis. "All they told me outside is that someone broke in and attacked you. Didn't you turn on the alarm? How . . . ?"

"Mr. Roberts," Officer Sands said, interrupting. "We'd like to ask you a few questions before you talk to your wife. Do you mind?"

Marcus blinked, mouth partly open. "I . . . I guess not. If you think it will help catch whoever did this to her." He looked from the officer back to Alexis. "You'll be okay?"

Alexis nodded and sat back down on the couch, her eyes following the two of them walking toward the dining room. Her husband looked utterly baffled and confused, and it served him right. She believed it was the only true emotional reaction she'd seen from him in months. While she was getting cut up with glass and falling into the lake—courtesy of herself—he was down in DC screwing around with his side piece. Lying, conniving bastard.

She had come so close to walking away this morning, to taking her packed bags and calling Natasha after he left for the office. To running with the baby and hoping for the best, that he would leave them be and she would be able to go on and live her life in peace. But who knew what Marcus was capable of now that he was aware she had defied him repeatedly. That she had kept the baby and started to unearth all his dirty secrets about his shady finances and blackmailing his clients. Not to mention that she was talking to his family about Charlene. She was onto him now, and he knew it. That had raised the stakes and put her in serious danger.

But then she had thought, why? Why am *I* running like the guilty party? She had done absolutely nothing wrong. He was the one who should leave. He had accused her of double-crossing him. What a joke. He was the biggest crook alive.

She had been toying with this idea for weeks. But it was risky and also hazardous. She could accidentally drown or badly injure herself. It could easily backfire, and *she* would be the one who ended up behind bars. She wasn't ready to risk that. So, she'd decided to stick to finding a job and leaving once she got everything together.

Until that final argument last night when she had discovered he had been having her followed. She'd stayed awake all night perfecting a plan she hoped would finally bring Marcus to justice for the way he had treated her and many others for so long. And then she sprang into action.

First thing in the morning, she went to the Columbia Gym and practiced swimming. On the way home, she stopped at the drug store and picked up a bottle of Aleve. Later that evening, home alone, she tossed a few things around on her dresser, then threw the lamp in the sitting room onto the floor. She went down to the basement storeroom, got a hammer from the toolbox, and smashed the glass pane in the sitting room door, making sure to swing from outside, so the glass would shatter inward. Then came the hardest part, the part that almost made her back out. She took three Aleves, stuffed a facecloth between her teeth, held her breath, and smashed her elbow down on one of Marcus's weights in the fitness room. As hard as she could.

The pain had been agonizing. She'd shrieked and hopped around the room, cradling her elbow for what seemed an eternity. For a while, she thought she had overdone it; she doubled over and gasped for air. But it eventually subsided into a dull throbbing ache, and she continued on. After changing into a nightgown, she skipped across the broken glass in the sitting room and down to the lake, screaming loudly enough for the neighbors to hear. She felt relieved to see lights go on in a few of the other townhouses as she hid in the bushes. When she heard the sirens several minutes later, she slipped over the edge of the pier and into the lake. The swimming lessons had been more about building her confidence in the water than anything. She was able to dog paddle to stay afloat and hold on to the edge of the pier until a police officer heard her screams and finally rescued her.

It had been the most emotionally and physically draining day of her life. Now it was nearly midnight, and she was so exhausted there were moments as she was being questioned when she thought she'd pass out. She still didn't know whether all her efforts would pay off and be worth it in the end. She could only hope that Marcus would soon get his due. That he would end up in prison for all the people he had defrauded, at the very least. That he would be investigated more closely for Charlene's disappearance. She wasn't sure Marcus had harmed Charlene, but she'd heard enough to believe that the police needed to investigate him more thoroughly.

She wasn't expecting anything dramatic tonight. If she knew Marcus at all, he would most likely tell them he had been at his office in Baltimore while this was happening. Hopefully they would check up on his alibi and learn that he had lied, that he had really been in DC with Claudia. And that it would open a whole new can of worms once the police started to look into the two of them.

Marcus and the detective walked back into the living room and Alexis stood up. "Mrs. Roberts, can I get contact information for . . ." Officer Sands glanced at her notebook. "A Paul Jackson. Your ex-boyfriend."

Alexis blinked.

"Yes, honey," Marcus said. "I told them how jealous and obsessed he is with you. That he was lurking outside our window that night when you were here alone."

Her knees almost buckled. She racked her brain trying to

think how he could possibly have known about Paul. Then she remembered. He'd had detectives following and investigating her for longer than she'd realized. He may have even had someone dig into Paul.

"Um, he was at one time," she said. "I haven't seen or heard from him much at all recently." She did not want them looking into Paul. Or anyone besides Marcus and his mistress.

"Still, I'd like to get contact information for him," the officer said. "We need to talk to him."

"Yes, you never know about these dudes," Marcus said.

Alexis nodded weakly and gave Paul's number to Officer Sands.

As soon as the officers all left, Marcus's demeanor changed back into its usual cold, aloof self.

"I'm going to take a look at that door, then I'm going to bed," he said without glancing at her. "Hopefully they catch whoever did this quickly. Anything you need? Something for that elbow?"

She shook her head. She really wanted to leave, to get the hell out and be done with him once and for all. But she worried that doing so now would throw suspicion on her, and she had to avoid that. Fortunately, she was not as afraid of him as before. Marcus was reckless, even dangerous, but first and foremost, he looked out for himself. He would be foolish to hurt her now that the police were looking for the person who had attacked her. He had to know that as her husband he was a primary suspect and under intense scrutiny. She would stick around but keep on her toes; as soon as the time felt right, she was out of there.

"How long have you been having me followed?"

He smirked. "Ever since I realized I couldn't always trust you. A year off and on."

"You can't trust *me*?" She scoffed with irony. "You're a real piece of work." She shook her head, and they turned in opposite directions. He walked toward the sitting room. She went up to the master bathroom and rubbed her sore elbow with ointment as the tub filled with warm sudsy water. She slipped in and carefully bathed her sore feet. Then she leaned back and stared at the ceiling.

So, Marcus had had someone tailing her for a year. She thought back to the man on the walking path that rainy morning when she had suspected Paul was following her. And to the car parked behind her and Natasha in front of the condo in DC. And who knew where else? What a complete asshole he was. How she had ever fallen for such slime she would never be able to figure out. At least she was clearheaded now and saw him for exactly who he was. She could hardly wait to get away from him.

She thought about the files full of incriminating information on Marcus tucked away in her closet. He knew she had been in his office but didn't seem to be aware of the fact that she had made copies of much of the paperwork she'd found. She should take them to the police. Make sure they had every shred of evidence possible. But she couldn't be sure how valuable they would turn out to be. And what if she did and Marcus was able to worm his way above suspicion? He knew the law inside and out. He knew how the police worked. If she exposed him that way and he realized it was her, he might come after her.

She decided against it. It was safer to wait patiently and hope for the best as the police continued their investigation.

* * *

Three days later, the police called Marcus in for questioning a second time. He was baffled and a little pissed at them for taking

up his precious time. But Alexis's heart soared with encouragement. It was all she could do to keep from jumping for joy. Yes!
she thought to herself when he relayed the news.

"Really?" she said aloud to him, her face the perfect picture of
concern. "What do you think they want to talk to you about?"

"I have no idea why they're wasting their time on me instead
of looking for the real culprit who attacked you," he said as he
picked up his briefcase.

"Good point," she said innocently, then skipped up to her
home office to check out baby websites after he left. She included
a search of cochlear implants for babies. If her child were hearing
impaired, she wanted to be prepared.

She was even more encouraged when Doreen called while
Marcus was at the station and said the police had come by her
house the previous day and asked all sorts of questions about
Charlene and their relationship.

"I didn't mince any words," Doreen said. "Told them it was
unfortunate it took an attack on his second wife to wake their
asses up. Guilty, guilty, guilty."

Finally, the police were onto him, Alexis thought. Maybe they
would even arrest him on the spot.

She was sitting on the balcony with a tall glass of iced tea,
scrolling through a website about newborns on her cell phone
and imagining Marcus being led away in handcuffs when he
walked in a few hours later. He stepped outside, his expression
one of utter confidence and self-satisfaction, deflating her hope-
fulness like a popped balloon.

"What did they want?" she asked, slipping her cell phone onto
her lap beneath the patio table.

"They asked a lot of stupid questions about where I was the
night of the attack. I told them instead of wasting their time on
me, they need to look into your ex and Stanley next door."

"Stanley? Why Stanley?"

"He's a known sexual predator. I think they're going to check him out."

Fuck. Was Marcus going to get away with everything? Again. "Did Claudia come up?" she asked, her patience getting the better of her.

He glared at her. "Why do you bring her up?"

"I just wondered since she has accused Stanley of sexual harassment."

"True," he said.

"And you and I both know you spend a lot of time with her," Alexis said. "And about the condo in DC."

He stared at her silently for a moment, the wheels turning in his head. *Yes, I know your spy followed us to DC that day,* she thought, eyeing him with defiance.

Finally, he spoke. "You think I had something to do with what happened to you?"

She knew better than that, of course. She shook her head. "No, I know you didn't." He had no idea how true that was.

His eyes narrowed. "When you were snooping around in my office, did you make copies of anything?"

The hairs on her scalp tingled. She knew what he was thinking: she might have evidence that could paint him in a bad light. Why couldn't she have kept her big mouth shut? She gripped her phone and nervously replied, "No," not sure she sounded convincing.

He walked up to the patio table and leaned down until his face was within inches of hers, the sour smell of red wine all over his breath. "For your sake, you'd better not be lying to me. Yes, they asked about Claudia. And about Charlene. Charlene, Charlene, Charlene." He made his ex-wife's name sound like it was profanity. "But I'm not worried. You know why?"

She waited in silence.

He continued calmly, his voice barely above a whisper. She had to strain to hear him. "Because they'll never find enough evidence to pin a damn thing about her on me. It's too easy to make a body disappear when you have a boat." He paused, then added, pronouncing each word slowly: "Don't make me buy another fucking boat."

She stared in stricken silence as he stood erect, a twisted smile at the corners of his lips, a twinkle in his light brown eyes. "Don't even *think* of opening your mouth about our little chat," he continued. "You'll live to regret it. And remember, it'll be your word against mine." He turned his back and strolled into the house.

Now she was scared. It was time to get out. She lay wide awake all night, trying to keep her panic in check, thinking about breaking free from this monster and being a mom. When at last he left for work in the morning, she called Doreen and Natasha and the three of them devised a plan for her to take all the evidence she had gathered to the detective who had looked into Charlene's disappearance. And for her to get out of the house.

She packed the files carefully into cardboard boxes, then took them to Doreen's, where they made another set of copies to store in the attic. Doreen then followed Alexis to the police station in Annapolis and introduced her to Detective Harrison. She turned over the boxes of files and told him everything she knew about Claudia, Stanley, and the others. Finally, she played the most damning piece of evidence of all, the recording she had secretly made on her cell phone when Marcus boasted about how easy it was to make a body disappear with a boat.

She spent the following weeks at Natasha and Derrick's house, waiting and hoping. She was worried, of course. Marcus had warned that he might kill her if she ever exposed him. Which was exactly what she'd done. But how could she have gone on living under constant threat without doing everything in her power to see him put away?

She didn't have to wait long. The files, the brutal attack on her, and the recording had been sufficient to convince the police to reopen the investigation into Charlene's disappearance and a new investigation into Marcus's questionable business practices.

Epilogue

Right after Marcus was arrested and Claudia taken in for questioning, Alexis decided to get far, far away from Maryland. Directly following his release on bail, she had her lawyer call his and insist they sell the townhouse and split the proceeds as soon as possible. She needed the money to move on and start a new life; he needed funds to pay an attorney for his defense, not to mention the child he was legally obligated to help her support. He stubbornly refused at first, said he hated the idea of her getting a single penny of the money he had put into the house. But he clearly realized it was the best recourse and eventually came around.

A week after closing—at seven-and-a-half-months pregnant—she hopped on a plane and signed a lease on an apartment in Santa Fe, a place she had visited that had always brought her joy. The city was artsy, with so much culture. Not to mention sunny, wide-open spaces and a big blue sky that never seemed to quit. The people were friendly, laid-back, and welcoming. It was the perfect place to finally get back to writing her novel.

But most important of all, Santa Fe was the home of the New Mexico School for the Deaf, where she quickly landed a job in the athletics department. She was beyond excited to bring her daughter Joy into the world in her new town. Her mom would join her two weeks before her due date to help her finalize the baby's room. Then after the birth, her father would arrive, and both would stay until Joy was six weeks old.

Jeffrey called often to check up on her, even invited himself out to visit. Said he'd always wanted to see the Southwest. He was incredibly sweet. And after the over-the-top passion of Paul and cunning charm of Marcus, Jeffrey's quiet nerdiness was starting to grow on her. It felt refreshing. But she was a long way from dating or getting close to another man. Her entire focus now and for the foreseeable future would be on getting herself and Joy settled. She was all too aware that it would not be easy to raise a daughter alone, especially if she were hearing impaired. But after surviving everything she had been through over the past several months, Alexis was more than ready to face any challenges that lie ahead.

She told absolutely no one the truth about that night at the townhouse. Some things were better left unsaid.

Acknowledgments

This will be short and sweet since I keep things close to the vest when writing (don't want to jinx things and all that). Thank you so much to those who helped me get my very first suspense novel out into the world. In particular, thank you to Victoria Sanders, my extraordinary agent, who has been with me from the beginning nearly three decades ago, for inspiring me and always believing in my work. Thank you to my editors Benee Knauer and Patrik Henry Bass for their sharp insight and guidance while I navigated this exciting new direction. Thank you to the best family on earth, particularly my sister, Patty, for all her support and encouragement over the years. And to Leroy and Alyce, the best parents anyone could ever hope for, resting up there in heaven, for instilling in me a love of reading, the will to pursue my dreams, and unending curiosity.

About the Author

Connie Briscoe is an author of romantic and historical fiction and has been a full-time published author for nearly three decades. Her novels have hit the bestseller lists of the *New York Times*, *Chicago Tribune*, *Washington Post*, *Boston Globe*, *Boston Herald*, *USA Today*, and *Publishers Weekly*, and Briscoe has been featured in numerous publications and television programs, including *Good Morning America*. She was born with a mild hearing loss that progressed over the years but has never let that stop her from pursuing her writing dreams. In 2003 she had a cochlear implant, which restored much of her hearing. She lives in Maryland.